# WHO HUNTS THE WHALE

Laura Kate Dale     Jane Aerith Magnet

unbound

First published in 2023

Unbound
Level 1, Devonshire House, One Mayfair Place, London W1J 8AJ
www.unbound.com

This is a work of fiction. Names, characters, organisations and products
are the creation of the authors' imaginations, and any resemblance to
actual organisations or products, or to persons, living or dead, is entirely
coincidental.

Text design by PDQ Digital Media Solutions Ltd

A CIP record for this book is available from the British Library

ISBN 978-1-78965-160-7 (paperback)
ISBN 978-1-78965-159-1 (ebook)

Printed in Great Britain by Clays Ltd, Elcograf S.p.A.

1 3 5 7 9 8 6 4 2

To Phoenix, I love you, and look forward to one day getting that pizza.

*Jane Aerith Magnet*


Steph and Conrad, thank you for helping me feel like I'm not alone in seeing the horrors of the video-game industry. This book would not exist if I didn't have you both helping me to fight that good fight every week.

*Laura Kate Dale*

# CHAPTER 1

# New Start

**3 JANUARY**

New Year, new me, new journal. I fully expect this to be the one
I'm digging out to remind myself of all the amazing things that
I got to be there for during this time. This is the one to tell my
niblings about. 'Tell us another story about how you helped shape
the industry, Auntie,' they'll say.

And I'll smile back at them, sip my tea and regale them with
tales of the magic of video games.

Plus, this is a smart way to practise writing good, fast notes
in meetings. Thoughts down, no filter. What do you mean, lied
on my résumé? I merely added a little seasoning to the truth,
everyone does it, shut up.

I should clarify the résumé thing.

A few days ago I was just another millennial statistic, living
my most mediocre life post-college. As employable as I had been
four years previously, but now with a certificate, added debt, and a
taste for discount ramen. That is until my destiny finally got a fire
under its ass and let me know, via auto-generated email, that I'd
gotten an interview at Supremacy Software.

Yes, *the* Supremacy Software (formally Cupboard Software).

Ever since my aunt handed me my first hand-me-down console – along with copies of arcade shooter *Medal of Embers* and the greatest role-playing game ever written to a ROM chip: *Prophecy of Zebdo: Better Dink Again* – at age six, I've been obsessed with video games. Supremacy was one of those names that splashed across my TV screen at the start-up of game after game. That oh-so-familiar jingle bringing a smile to my little face.

I got side-tracked again.

My parents were at work, so I took my laptop into the living room, pointed the camera at the most boring wall I could find, and made myself waist-up presentable for my interview with Head of HR (Head no less) Hannah Lomad. My first challenge; convince her that I was the best person to do... whatever it was I'd applied for.

I'll be honest, I've been applying for so many jobs of late that I'm barely paying attention. I think I just saw the company name and decided to shoot for the moon.

At this point, I just want my little brother to stop stealing my degree from my bedroom wall and re-hanging it above the TP in the bathroom, with a sticky note saying 'in case of emergency, break glass'.

At nine on the dot, Hannah's call came in. Joke's on her, I'd been too frozen by anxiety to move from my prepared interview nest for ninety minutes. I have to wonder if she noticed this as before she'd even greeted me, she was scribbling a note.

'So... *Ms* Paige, why is it that you think you should become a member of the Supremacy Software family?' Her interview technique was as sharp as her features, her suit jacket and her bob cut.

'Well, um, I put a lot of work into getting a good mark in my degree, which I think covers a wide range of... disciplines, and I feel like I could be a helpful asset. I'm a very organised person.

I'm very skilled at managing multiple people's schedules, as demonstrated by the fact I was able to run a regular seven-person tabletop RPG campaign during my final exam year,' I sputtered, barely getting my metaphorical legs back under me at the sudden assault.

My career adviser had told me I should always bring up relevant examples, even if it's not work experience. Transferable skills and all that.

She made a short motion with her pen, not a full note, but more likely a tick than a cross... maybe. Please?

'I can see you worked *very* hard for your...' She glanced down and seemed to be mentally chewing the next words with a disdain I've come to recognise in certain more adulty adults. 'Liberal arts degree.'

'Well, I strongly believe a liberal arts education will have me fit right in there. I am experienced at handling large amounts of writing, I have an understanding of the basics of business, and I have spent enough time in arts education to know how to work well alongside the creatives making games.' *Oh yes, prepared response, I've practised enough to make it sound natural. Boom, what have you got now?*

'Your predecessor was a valuable part of this company, working alongside the executive team for a great many years. Where do you see yourself in five years' time?'

'I'll be right here, part of the Supremacy Software family.'

*How about some mirroring language for you there, Ms Grumpy?*

'A valuable tool for the team, seamlessly filling the gap and doing whatever is needed to help the executives be their best.'

Another short note was made, but there wasn't a single flicker of emotion.

NOTE TO SELF – never play poker with this woman.

'I have everything I need for now; my office will be in touch.' And with that, the call was cut.

Well, I must have done something right, because a couple of days later I was sitting in my bank manager's office with my mom, arranging a loan to cover my rent deposit and a minivan to get my stuff across the country to Supremacy Software's offices in New York, New York.

Wyoming, more like goodbyeoming! This plucky young hero was off to save the world. True, my sword may be made from cosplay-safe foam, and part of the hand guard snapped off when I dropped it that one time, but from such simple beginnings, many a hero has arisen.

Despite not taking much, I still struggled to squeeze all of it into my shoebox apartment. However, as long as I never let my clean clothes box get too empty, the impending avalanche of closet junk will remain sealed. As a safety precaution I drew the Sigil of Seven from *Ex Diabolica* on the side of the box, sealing away the darkness for another generation!

There's not enough room to swing a short sword in here, I can hear my neighbour's TV pretty loudly, and all the floorboards creak and the water pressure sucks, and my only cooking facility is a microwave, but at least I have my dream job. Plus, when they start paying me, I'll be able to upgrade all my gear.

That brings us up to today.

I woke to the sounds of gridlocked traffic and far too much light bleeding through the badly stained sheet of what I assume is paper, but my landlord assured me is a roller blind.

After a quick wash and checking in on the latest gaming news, I headed out into the wall of noise and frigid air. Luckily I'm only a couple of blocks from the office, and there's a TinySave on the way, so I grabbed a can of Crimson Method Bubblegum Brain Tsunami for the walk.

Finally I stood before the steel and glass monolith which reached up to stab the grey, forbidding sky. Five levels below ground, sixty-four above, and there at the very top my destiny.

The vast lobby area was bustling with besuited business drones, but somehow the sharp lines of Hannah stood out among them as she strode with a seemingly predatory purpose that made some primal, mammalian part of my brain want to flee under the nearest rock (a huge granite boulder which was placed 'artistically' off to one side of the vast, marble-floored area). They say the sign of good character design is one you can recognise from a silhouette, and that's certainly true for Hannah.

'This way,' she announced, turning on her heel and leading me towards the security desk. I say security, I've seen less armed and armoured military parades.

'New intake, Paige Avery, PA to executives, full access,' she announced to the ballistic vest behind the counter, who looked me up and down like he was performing a threat assessment and found nothing of concern.

'Stand on the white line, look here, don't smile.' He tapped a leather-gloved finger against a small camera mounted above his computer screen.

I'd barely stepped into place when he informed me 'all done' and reached beneath the desk to produce a white plastic card, my security ID pass, which he shoved at me.

'No chance of a do-over, I suppose?' I queried, glancing down at the abysmal photograph he'd taken.

'I've printed it now.' He shrugged.

Hannah handed me a company lanyard and ushered me towards the elevators, before I could say another word.

'Every day you will wear your pass, with your photograph clearly on display. Otherwise Security can get rather… excited.'

She tapped her own pass against a reader by the elevator and the doors slid open before us. Once inside she jabbed the button for 61 with a nail so sharp, it looked like she could have clawed right through the metal plate.

'You will ride to the sixty-first floor, to check in with our own reception. Failure to do so will result in disciplinary action.' This piece said, she didn't speak to me again until we arrived at our destination. Inside, I continued to fight the urge to flee.

The doors opened and Hannah took a sharp left and used her ID to tap through a small frosted-glass turnstile. I copied her, and was granted access. *I'm inside! I'm not hyperventilating, I don't know what you mean.*

Beyond the turnstile were two more elevators which took us up the final three floors to the executive level. Boss showdown ahead.

Things were very nice up here. Wide corridors with black marble floors shone like a dark lake, framed business awards hung along the route from the elevators, and here and there were lush green plants, adding a touch of life to the otherwise cold, hard decor.

As we drew near the boardroom, a tinted window looked into an office filled with row upon row of matching pinstriped suits, side partings and spectacles. They busied away on their computers in silence. Not one could be seen taking a moment to catch up about the weekend, or getting a round of coffees. The whole spectacle was uncanny, like a stock asset of an office.

'Legal,' announced Hannah.

At that precise moment, I could have sworn that several of them looked up and directly into me. Like inside of me. It was a deeply uncomfortable sensation and I was very pleased to turn another corner, putting them out of sight.

We strode by the executives' offices, the boardroom, a small kitchen and, finally, down a narrow corridor, largely dominated by a copy machine, to a door marked only by a small metal plate, upon which was etched the word 'assistant'. My very own top-floor office.

Inside was a bare, windowless room, lit by a single, rapidly flickering fluorescent tube light, which seemed distractingly loud. The walls were pockmarked and stained, in that way which suggests that at some point there had been shelving installed.

There was barely enough room to fit both of us, the desk and a single chair. My inner comedian wanted to joke that she'd need to breathe in so I could breathe out. Still, it was all mine.

Hannah picked up and handed me the half-sized ring binder which had been sitting neatly on the desk.

'This will be your office. Here's the job bible, read it. Don't mess up. Don't ask questions. You have forty-five minutes before the morning meeting.' Pep-talk concluded, she quick-turned and strode away.

'Thank you,' I called after her, as the door slammed shut. 'I'll see you later... I guess.'

I took a moment to be quietly very excited that it was actually happening. Up to that moment, it all felt a bit unreal. Like someone could jump out from behind a potted plant and tell me I'd been pranked.

Being the nerdy gamer girl at school, people always loved to pick on me like that, and honestly, even now I can feel the scars it left. I lost count of the number of times I was asked out by boys as a joke, or invited to parties only to be laughed out of the building by the popular kids. In the end, it just drove me deeper into video games.

Games let me enter another world. To be a nobody from nowhere, relying only on courage, determination and a long-forgotten weapon. To stand alone against the mightiest evils of all time, and emerge victorious. Not for riches or renown, but because that's what heroes do.

I've taken several shots at making my own games, but I'm not an artist, a particularly good fiction writer, and I'm definitely not a coder. Even some of those programs which do most of the technical stuff for you are beyond my skill. So I figured, maybe, I get a degree in something which is a benefit behind the scenes.

Those who can do, those who can't... take notes and bring drinks to those who can, I guess.

The job bible was thankfully a nice, easy read. Very clear, with marked chapters and even a troubleshooting section at the end. Although I was a little concerned to see the part about how to remove bodily fluids from the boardroom carpet. I definitely don't want to know what happened to earn it a laminated guideline in this folder.

Time to meet the top brass.

## Meeting minutes – 3 January

Drinks orders for the board:

Edwin – green power juice

Rick – four-shot latte

Chad – three-shot latte

I've heard about Edwin; he's been here for a long time, came in from an old electronics company that made home computer kits you had to solder yourself back in the 8os. Apparently his father just dropped the keys to Supremacy Software in his hands as he was retiring, and Edwin basically sat on the board here until everyone else left or died. Talk about the last man standing. He's in his mid-eighties, and years of fancy beach holidays and countless days spent out on the golf course have made the guy look like wealthy jerky in a suit that cost more than my university tuition. His green power juice smells disgusting, and I genuinely can't imagine trying to put that stuff in my mouth, but the single-use metal and plastic canister each portion comes in implies that it's super-expensive. Probably some weird rich people thing that will turn out to be useless at best and actively harmful at worst.

Rick and Chad could be twins, apart from the hair. I had to google company images to check which was which. I just need to remember Rick has brown hair, and Chad is the blonde. The similarity is uncanny though. Two thirty-something gamer boys who made it to the top of the heap, to the seat of power. When they talk they almost blend together, a whirlwind of high-powered enthusiasm, go-getting confidence and talking each other up. Like Edwin, they also wear expensive suits, but paired with a t-shirt and sneakers. I love that look. It says 'I'm professional, but my profession is way more fun than whatever you stiffs on Wall Street are doing, with your oppressive button-down collars and ties.'

I took a deep breath and reminded myself: *I'm supposed to be here* as I made my way around the huge glass and mahogany table which stretched down the middle of the room.

'A three-shot latte for you, sir.'

'Who are you?'

'Oh, hi, I'm the new assistant. My name's—'

'Doesn't matter. Get our drinks and sit down.'

As I announced Rick's order, and went to take my seat, Chad visibly bristled and in an almost childish tone called, 'Hey, you. I get a five shot from now on, write that down.'

NOTE TO SELF – update the drinks order chart.

Edwin sat almost unmoving at the head of the table. Looking for all the world like he was about ready to nap right there, even as Rick and Chad started to go through their folders full of very dry charts and graphs. That said, I could have sworn I saw a hint of a smile and the faintest twinkle in his eyes when those huge dollar figures were being read out. Beyond that though, he remained, for the most part, as impassive as the figurehead on the bow of this corporate vessel.

When you've been in the industry for forty-plus years, one successful year-end financial breakdown is much like any other.

'So, the numbers are in,' Rick began, 'and you'll be glad to hear they are way up. Ten billion USD for the full year, with 6.9 billion—'

'NICE!'

'Ha. Six point nine coming from the final financial quarter alone.'

'Gotta love that Primary Gifting Period. The cornerstone of every year.'

I couldn't really tell what all the paperwork meant, but there were a lot of graphs showing massive growth and huge dollar numbers, each more immense than the last. I've not seen two boys act like that around a pile of paper since that time my cousins and I found the remains of a dirty magazine in the woods while we were riding our bikes. Chuckling and cheering and looking so darned pleased with themselves.

Next they moved on to the topic of bonuses.

'So, someone's gotta throw out the first number. I think you did last year so I'll shoot first. How about...' Chad paused for a moment 'Three million each?'

'Four?'

'We did five last year, and this year's numbers did go up, so it's only fair we go at least a little higher.'

'TEN MILLION.'

'Ohhhh how I *love* to see those double digits.'

'Do I hear eleven?' Edwin, suddenly more animated than he's been all meeting, chimed in.

Something about the way he said it had me imagining him sitting there, waving a small wooden gavel like an auctioneer.

'You know, I might suggest eleven if we'd released a game last year that saw near universal critical acclaim. Oh yeah, we did.'

'Eleven to the blonde. Do I hear—'

'TWELVE. People talk about "turning it up to eleven", but I say that is small thinking; we take it up to twelve.'

'See, I was going to suggest thirteen, but I hear that's an unlucky number.'

'And we can't do fourteen, that has a four in it, and I hear that's Chinese for death.'

'And you know how much I hate superstition.'

'So, fifteen?'

'SOLD, to the handsome executives in this very room!' Edwin shouted, banging his gavel.

'Executive bonuses suggest company health.'

'And strong leadership.'

Fifteen million dollars.

Fifteen. Million. Dollars.

Each.

If that's what they were looking at at the top, who knows what I'll be in line for next year. Heck, even 1 per cent of that would be life-changing for me. I could pay off my student loans. Maybe even get financially stable and look at doing a saving plan (just one, I'm not greedy). I could get ahead on my rent, have a bit of a safety net, or put down a deposit on my own apartment. I could donate to crowdfunding campaigns, put something by for retirement. I could have my own gaming room, get mint in-box, graded copies of all my favourite video games, and not have to deal with emulators.

NOTE TO SELF – ask the dev team how much they got paid last year. It's got to be pretty staggering since they did all the hard work.

Next item – Chad raised the question about what should be worked on this year.

This was the good bit, the bit I'd been waiting for. I was going to know what's happening before any other human on the planet. Aaaaaaaaah! Not even the jerks on the forums know before me. No 'my uncle works at Supremacy Software and he says...' I'd know first and, more importantly, I'd know accurately. In your face, xXStabbyCat42069Xx; your snide gatekeeping has no more power over me.

Edwin said that as the numbers are still up, this year's focus will be another first-person shooter – which he called 'the shooty bang-bang games.'

Honestly, you'd think that after working here for most of his adult life he'd have picked up *some* of the terminology. It feels like you'd have to be actively disinterested to fail at picking up the most basic terms.

'So, if we're doing another FPS, what should this year's *Call of Shooty* focus on?' asked Rick.

'What about making this one a Vietnam shooter? They made a whole bunch of movies about Nam back in the day; those always seemed real popular. By now that war's got to have moved into nostalgia territory. What better time for some high-action gunplay?'

I sat in quiet excitement. A Vietnam shooter, ditching the modern aspects of the series for something more calculated and meticulously paced. That sure would be a gameplay shakeup, and something that I could really see working.

'While I'd usually be the first one to take a real world conflict and turn it into fiction so we can ride the emotional impact of real world deaths in a way that makes it seem like we're really deep, I have to ask, did you see the train wreck over at Adagio Interactive?'

'The *One Week in Kuwait* guys? I thought that got cancelled for being "insensitive to the families impacted",' Chad air-quoted.

'Yeah, I dunno anything about the war itself, something about guns. Anyway, they decided out of nowhere to take another shot at it. Next thing they know, some group started a ruckus about it, the press went with some high and mighty angle, called it "an atrocity too raw to be trivialised in a video game".'

'So much for games as art, huh?'

This raised a short, derisory chuckle from all three. I was less impressed. That *One Week in Kuwait* game was incredibly tasteless in its execution, and I would really hope that as another game dev studio in a similar space, the executives here would have taken some time to learn the specifics of what went so wrong there. At the very least, learning some mistakes to avoid would seem wise.

'Okay, scrap Vietnam. We need a fictional war. Let's say it's set in a place we never name, but our players will assume is the Middle East, because there's sand, and we – the media – have conditioned them to make that assumption for us.'

'What if it's very much *like* a war for oil. We don't ever have to *say* oil, just make sure there's always those iconic nodding pumpjacks on the horizon; they'll work it out.'

'What if we filled it with comically evil bad guys, like as evil as possible, who just happen to dress in a manner appropriate to desert life in this fictional region we made up, which is fictional?'

'Yeah, and the heroes will wear combat fatigues, so they could be from anywhere, probably not America, who can say? And then we show a cutscene of the main soldier saving a puppy from a falling building or something like that. That way it's impossible to criticise.'

'You can't criticise anyone who'd save a dog, that's just science.'

'And the dog can grow up and go on missions with the team. Give him a little hat, they love that shit, and everyone knows if you have a dog, you're the heroes.'

The fact they think they're being clever by faintly obfuscating the intended nationalities of either side of this conflict is frankly baffling. 'They're probably not American, because we said so' doesn't play as well as they seem to think, especially since they were only seconds away from having the 'heroes' flown in on a bald eagle carrying a colour-changed version of our flag. Definitely not our flag though, 'because we changed the colours, see?'

That flurry of creative passion passed, Rick floated the idea of a single-player campaign.

Here we go, this is my jam. Because as much as I love gaming, Gamers™ aren't always the best people to play with. I can only hear so many times about an angry, caffeinated twelve-year-old's claimed exploits with my mother in voice chat. C'mon, story-rich experience.

'We have data on that,' announced Chad, rifling through his stack of papers and finally pulling out some uninspiring pie charts. 'The focus groups reported that the average gamer, if you leave their phone next to them while they play, will check their social media every seven minutes. And, like, I don't know if the short game modes make them check that regularly, or that's just their natural rhythms, but numbers don't lie, and we need to design around the numbers we have. If the *numbers* say "every seven minutes they need to take a break to look at their social posts", we gotta work with that.'

'Right, okay, so they've got seven minutes of focus. To me, that says we have to do a six-minute-long campaign. It's optimised.'

'Polished.'

'"The most highly polished, single-player experience this series has ever seen."'

'They whined about repetition when we gave them 150-hour long campaigns, they'll love this.'

'"A campaign for your modern lifestyle". The copy writes itself.'

'Absolutely. While we're there, multiplayer should stick to the same length.' Here Chad clicked his fingers to emphasise each word. 'Keep the ole dopamine factory firing on that victory screen.'

To say I was disappointed was an understatement. I knew the last few years Supremacy Software had shifted ever more towards multiplayer-focused titles, but I always assumed it was some kind of complicated decision based on player feedback. To see them basically dismiss the idea of a proper campaign, based entirely on a small focus group of social media addicts was a massive let-down.

I'm not completely naive, I recognise that a company's ultimate goal is to turn a profit, but the fact that none of them seemed in the least bit concerned with what would make the best product from a player perspective was a bit of a wake-up call.

The rest of the meeting was somewhat of a blur. Chad ran a presentation on the huge monitor that takes up most of the wall across from Edwin's seat at the head of the table. Lots of stock animations and clipart thrown in among yet more charts and graphs. To be honest that was just the level of wow I needed in order to not fall into an utterly disinterested coma. For nearly an hour he rattled on and on about player retention, user-spending conversion and things of that nature. Riveting stuff which completely flew over my head. He seemed very pleased with himself though.

End of meeting. Minutes to be typed, printed and filed (the amount of hard copy in this office is frankly surprising for a company which is outwardly so incredibly modern).

Chad has requested I head down to HR and sit in on some of the interviews for new development staff this afternoon. Apparently he's off for a game of squash after lunch, but wants someone from the top keeping an eye on things: 'keep them on their toes'.

It wasn't until I was back in my little office that I realised that not one person asked me my name or, even for the most part, acknowledged my existence. Still, they're very busy. Lots of figures to consider and big decisions to make. As the job bible says, I'm 'there to help, not get involved'.

I felt like my first meeting with the executives hadn't gone amazingly, but, to be honest, I wasn't too worried. I'd basically had to sit and listen to these men look at the games I love through the lens of finance, and they didn't seem to want me to take up even a little space in the meeting, but it was probably just a new year routine. I was sure, at the very least, walking through the development hall would get me back on track and energised.

These were the people actually making games. If anyone here was going to be passionate about game development, it was going to be them.

## LUNCH

I went to the cafeteria, down on the first floor, and boy that place is fancy. Sure, it looks like an oversized low-budget deli/cafe/pasta bar, but a single slice of organic banana bread with chia seeds cost me my entire lunch budget for the week. I guess it's sandwiches from home until I start getting those bonuses.

I've noticed that a lot of the other businesses which share the building are in the finance industry, which no doubt means that they barely consider the price when they're eating here.

## P.M. – INTERVIEWS

I had to walk through the development floor to get to HR and the place was deserted, like the whole floor had been abandoned. Less than half the lights were on, and in the dark it was hard to make out exactly what the ocean of mysterious shapes were. The ambience was made ever more unusual by the fact I could hear the sounds of crickets chirping... and then a freaking wolf howled.

I must have let out a yelp of some kind because the next thing I heard was a chuckle from behind and a friendly voice asking, 'You lost, new blood?'

I turned to face the silhouetted figure behind me. In the dim light I could just about make out a broad smile from the man, who appeared to be folding a sheet.

'Yeah, I'm... trying to get to HR. I was told it was through the dev floor.'

He pointed to the far side of the vast, open room, where I could just make out a lit corridor entrance. 'Head right across this floor. See that tiny light in the distance? That's the corridor to the HR department.'

'Thanks. Hey, I was expecting this place to be full of developers, but there's literally no one.'

'Literally no one? Gee, thanks.'

'Gods, I'm so sorry, I didn't mean it like that. I used to work as a cleaner, I know how people can be. I swear I'm not like that,' I blurted.

He chuckled again and raised his hands in a reassuring gesture. 'It's okay, I was just playing with you. I'm Clark, by the way. As you correctly surmised, I'm the cleaner.'

'Hi, I'm—' I was cut off by what I'm pretty sure was an owl's screech which caused me to cower once again. 'What's with the wildlife?'

Clark's smile broadened and his eyes twinkled in a mischievous manner, somewhat reminiscent of a kindly uncle character in a made-for-TV holiday movie. 'I enjoy the sounds of nature while I work, and I don't tend to bother with headphones during the off-season.'

'Huh.' I shrugged. 'I can appreciate that. I'm Avery, by the way. So, where is everyone else?'

'The development staff don't tend to stick around.'

'How come?'

'One year's enough for most folk. As for long term, there's the executives on high, of course; they're largely kept out of trouble by Legal, who you must have passed a few times already—'

'Legal are so sinister.'

'That they are. Best avoided, if you know what's good. Anyway, then there's middle management, they're scattered all over the place; HR we've mentioned; our in-house mobile development team – Candace and Jenette – well, their office is one floor up; it's the unlabelled door nearest the fire exit. You should call in once you're settled.'

'Thanks, I'll do that.'

Clark resumed folding the large dust sheet as the crickets sang on. 'There's me too, I've had my eye on this place a decade last fall.'

'So you've seen everything, huh?'

He fixed me with a stare that was more difficult than usual to meet and said, 'You have no idea.'

'It's been a treat to meet you, I'd better run though,' I said, suddenly remembering what I'd been on my way to.

'Never wise to keep Hannah waiting. See you around.'

I gave a wave and hurried away, suddenly concerned that I might displease Hannah, thus activating her haircut and unleashing maximum Karen.

As I got closer to the corridor light, I realised the reason for the room's strange topography was the sheets covering every desk and chair. To my left, at intervals of about thirty feet, stood dark and silent monoliths of un-powered vending machines. No doubt these would be fuelling waves of intense creativity once things come back to life down here.

Rounding the corner I arrived, blinking into some kind of waiting area packed full of mostly nervous-looking, cleanly dressed people. Several held portfolios and I spotted a lot of what were clearly video game-assets, most within the folders, a few tattooed upon their owners. Several of the interviewees looked hopefully up at me, but seemed to lose interest when I didn't immediately start calling names.

Picking my way carefully through the throng, I finally came to Hannah's office. There, in her own private domain, she cut an even more impressive figure. Maybe it was just the layout of the room, maybe it was how she dressed, maybe it was a combination of these elements, but I was getting major evil villain vibes from the whole scene before me.

One side of the room was a floor-to-ceiling smart window. Whereas the boardroom's had been set to a slight tint, likely for security, Hannah's was in the frosted mode. Letting in the bright stony grey of winter, something about the quality of that light seemed to suck all the colour out of the room and its owner.

Mounted to the wall behind the desk, in an acrylic case, was a highly polished wooden club, its handle wound with purple-and-white tape.

'Nice... club?' I attempted.

'It's a field hockey stick. I was captain of my college team. GO, ROYALS!!!!!' she bellowed.

Her outburst was startling and aggressive in equal measures. In an instant her controlled and precise demeanour had dropped away, and I was instead picturing her covered in bruises, scrapes and the blood of her vanquished foes, pumped up on post-match adrenaline. It made her usual quiet control all the more intimidating, knowing that at any moment that façade could evaporate.

'Go, Royals?' I responded, trying to sound supportive.

'Oh, we were the best. I made sure we won *every* game. Defeat was *not* an option.'

Apart from the stick, there was not a single sign of personalisation in that room. It's really hard to tell much about such a person beyond 'I will break your ankles with a wooden club if you come between my team and victory' in those circumstances. Best to stay on her team, I think.

I'd definitely pegged her as the type to own a cactus. Perhaps a touch too colourful though.

We headed outside, down a corridor, and entered a small interview room. The walls were the kind of boring off-white that landlords love. As I took my seat at the white plastic-topped table next to Hannah, I noted the way the fluorescent tube lights were diffused through a sheet of semi-opaque plastic in the ceiling which had the uncanny effect that almost nothing cast a proper shadow.

With one of her glossy, sanguine-painted two-inch talons, my colleague jabbed at the featureless black plastic disc which sat on the table by her side.

'Next!'

For a few moments there was only the sound of the lights and our quiet breathing. Then, with only the hint of a fumble, the door opened and the first candidate entered, carefully guiding their portfolio in ahead of them. The automatic closing arm of the door seemed to want to make this task as difficult as possible.

'Résumé?'

The interviewee, clearly a little off balance from the door and Hannah's emotionless tone, fumbled with the unwieldy portfolio before handing it over. Beads of sweat were already starting to form on his brow.

'You may sit.'

While the words were clearly an offer, her delivery was all command. As if speaking to a puppy in training.

'Th-thank you.'

As she scanned the document before her, Hannah clicked her tongue, the sound reverberating painfully around the small room.

Without looking up from the paper in her hand, Hannah instructed him: 'You've brought your portfolio, so you may *quickly* talk us through what you have to show.'

He seemed to be pulling himself together at last. Clearly the presentation was something he'd been able to practise.

'Well, here are some examples of 3D-modelling I did for a week-long Game Jam my team took part in in my second year of university. Here is a prototype game I spent last summer working on. It's about a ball that can build momentum with each bounce, and these are final render images of a volumetric lighting system I implemented for ray tracing in a PC port of a retro game based on its source code getting released online.'

'Why do you want this job?'

'Well, I've always dreamed of working in game development, and—'

'And why should *WE*... hire *YOU*?' The venom with which she spat out the words 'we' and 'you' brought a flashback of the time I met a professional dominatrix at a house party in college. Probably best not to ask a senior colleague about outside hobbies of that nature though.

'Well, I know all of the basics of all of the major 3D game-development engines, with a specialisation in the Inten-finity engine, which I know you've used for most of your big-budget titles over the last few years. I am very well versed both in your existing library of games, as well as the wider industry, and the mechanics and ideas that would be well suited to incorporate into your existing series.'

'What's the worst decision you've ever made?'

The interviewee and I both froze in terror and it took me a few seconds to process that I was not the one who was going to have to answer. It's the kind of interview question that should be banned under some kind of international convention. It's cruel and unusual.

He blinked a few times, then opened and closed his mouth like a fish, while Hannah impassively drank in his fear. Eventually, she released his gaze and began scribbling furious notes in what I recognised from my Gram Gram as shorthand. What took me longer to realise was that it was gibberish. This was all designed to provoke a reaction. Was this all in the name of weeding out those who might think the industry is all fun and, well, games?

He was still gasping like a trout when Hannah finally let him off the hook.

'Thank you for your time, please head along to the next room to your right, for the final stage of the interview.'

He gathered himself in a hurry and looked about ready to bolt, nervously swallowing every few seconds – probably hoping to find his vocal cords somewhere in there. When that didn't work I think his brain short-circuited and he bowed to each of us before leaving.

For Hannah it seemed like business as usual. A process to be followed. The forms for each new face just seemed to be a series of tick boxes, and pretty much anyone who had the relevant experience was passed on to the next room for a practical skills test.

The afternoon wore on; very highly skilled people showed off incredible work histories (or as much as they could get through in a strictly regimented five-minute slot). There were indie games, game jam prototypes, design sheets, concept art, stunning backgrounds, sprite sheets for pixel art games.

Coders came through, talking about how they'd turned down corporate web development jobs with much higher pay cheques to follow the dream of doing something they really loved as a career. Incredible 3D artists spoke of walking away from movie studios for their shot with Supremacy Software. A few showed off tattoos I recognised from some of the company's biggest titles of yesteryear. It was a parade of youngsters eager to be a part of the magic. Part of the family.

These kids reminded me how I had felt just this morning: optimistic about getting to be a part of making things they love. Desperate for their break into the industry, and ready to commit themselves wholeheartedly to making the best video games they could.

Late in the day, there was a sudden shock to the status quo.

As the afternoon wound on, and the parade of hopefuls seemed never-ending, I could tell Hannah was getting bored with the whole process. Her tone softened from venomous to plain disinterested. In many ways, these later interviewees were getting a much easier ride.

And then *she* walked in, her face set with determination rather than excitement. The young woman strode in with a powerful confidence. She even navigated the aggressive door like it was nothing.

For the most part her head was closely shaved, but at the front was a small purple tuft, gelled to a sharp point. Through her septum she wore a piercing which looked like it weighed more than the average house cat.

She had no unwieldy portfolio, just the kind of heavy-duty laptop they use on building sites, which was covered in stickers for various punk bands, anime shows and indie games.

Before Hannah had had a chance to ask, the young woman had handed over and started to explain her résumé. Years of experience across multiple studios, and a track record of solid results. I caught the name Matilda at the top of the first page, which seemed oddly familiar for some reason.

'As you can see, I took part in twelve game jams during my final year of university, focusing mostly on forty-eight-hour game jams. I specifically signed up for jams which included a panel of industry professionals, so that I could get considered feedback on the work myself and my team put in. My team and I were shortlisted finalists at eleven of those events, and we took home top spots at eight of them.'

As she scrolled through her digital portfolio, I spotted something which caught my eye. One of the game jam titles I had definitely seen before.

'Wait, is that *To The Stars*?! I've played that. It got a mention on the WGN "Best indie games you NEED to play" list last year. I picked it up in that big charity bundle in August. You're VolTilda, right? I really loved how—' My gushing was cut short by a look from Hannah which could have curdled milk. I embarrassedly nodded and gestured for Matilda to continue.

And continue she did.

'I know your starting salary is below industry standards. Here's what you should be paying a new starter, much less someone with my experience in the industry.' Bold.

Hannah responded, 'That's not what we pay here. Don't you want to be a part of making the greatest games in the world?'

'Not if you don't plan to pay me properly.' She leaned in, eyes full of fire.

'If you really loved games, you'd be willing to work based on your own passion, we don't want anyone who's just here for a pay cheque.' Hannah matched her posture and they stared each other down, mere inches apart.

'Tell that to the CEOs. I bet they're not working for minimum wage, for the love of the games.' Honestly, I was feeling massive respect for this woman. She knows what she's worth and she was going to demand it.

Our head of HR, however, was clearly not as awed as I, responding simply: 'We aren't hiring for CEOs. Excitable kids are always banging down our doors for a chance to be part of our family.'

That certainly seemed to be the case, if today was anything to go by.

Realising that there was no way Hannah was going to give an inch, Matilda thanked us, stood up, and left, head held high. I think that woman's my new hero. I've never seen such confidence in the face of a decent pay cheque.

After that, very few others even mentioned money. They were mostly just excited to be in the building. One especially so; he had no qualifications, nothing in his portfolio, just a clean shirt and a tie which bore the Sigil of Seven pattern I'd so recently used to protect my closet.

He kept saying how he'd be happy with any role, as long as he could be part of the team making his favourite titles. I recognised a lot of myself in his desire to just be here, but that eagerness without mentioning salary felt a little less idealistic now I'd seen someone actually demand decent treatment.

I certainly found his enthusiasm contagious. Not Hannah though, she sat as impassive as always, reading out the set questions in her most monotonous tone yet, marked his score (a solid o), and thanked him for his time. No practical test for that guy.

Today I saw a lot of excited faces. Lots of young people eager to live the dream, to be part of the family. I really hope to see them on the development floor soon. This place could do with that level of enthusiasm about the games rather than just the bonuses. That's what I thought I was signing up for when I took the job, but today has left me a little less confident it's going to be my reality.

## CHAPTER 2

# Full House

It's nearly a month now since I began here, and things are just about starting to fall into a proper routine.

Every morning I come into the office, open any post for the board, forward on anything they actually have time for, and either pass the rest on to another department, or file it in the cylindrical metal cabinet by the door. Then I check on the executive email inbox, once again passing on anything valid, and delegating or deleting anything else. Press enquiries of any sort get sent to PR, while job applications attempting to bypass HR and go straight to the top get deleted along with just about everything else.

After that I distribute drinks to the company heads and go downstairs to join the middle-management meeting on sixty-three, where I act as the eyes and ears of Edwin, Rick and Chad while they get on with the really tough jobs of running the wider company.

While on paper answering emails and writing up meeting minutes should be my entire job, it seems like I'm being used to fill in a lot of unexpected odd jobs that come up in the day-to-day running of the studio. You say dogsbody, I say: 'I'm the mystical force holding this company together'.

Today, for example, I've been organising a crew from the warehouse (yes, we have a whole warehouse in one of the basements) to reload the vending machines. Somehow the dev team managed to chew down every single can of Crimson Method Energy Gel between the hours of 1 a.m., when the night crew topped them up and 9 a.m., when the morning shift started.

Not one drink in those machines has less than 30mg of caffeine per 100ml and any time you walk through that floor, the constant, staccato sound of cans being dispensed is like a giant robot very slowly falling over.

My face lit by the radioactive, acid-green glow of the vending machine, I placed the last can inside and swung the heavy door shut. Almost immediately, I was shoved out of the way and nearly trampled by the baying mob of cold-turkey coders who'd been gathering behind me as I worked. I swear I've fed cats less keen to stick their heads in the bowl while trying to supply them with the nourishment they desire. This lot can be animals.

Thankfully, moments before I was crushed, I heard the familiar clink of surgical steel and rough Brooklyn accent of Fidget beating a path towards me. Above me, the crowd parted and she and Ezmeralda pulled me up with an elbow under each arm. One glare from Ez, who's had the whites of her eyes tattooed black, is enough to send most of these men scurrying.

'You wanna be careful there, Top Floor, those guys get pretty savage if they don't get their fix,' joked Fidget, leading me away from the baying mob.

I'd first met Ez and Fidget a few weeks back. Given the prohibitive cost of eating in the on-site facilities, and how lonely and far from anything my little office is, I'd taken to spending my lunch breaks, where possible, down on the dev floor, in a corner, out of everyone's way. I don't really understand on a technical level the specifics of what's being worked on right now, but it's been nice to soak in the ambience, and feel like I'm a part of the creative side of things.

There *is* a bit of a boys' club mentality around here. Most of the new hires were men – unsurprisingly – and some of that 'gamer culture' does rumble around the floor. As such, outside of meetings, I try to stay as inconspicuous as possible.

One afternoon, the two most tattooed and pierced people in the building spied me eating a homemade sandwich at my makeshift cardboard box dining table, partially concealed by a potted ficus, and invited me to sit with them. Since then we've really hit it off, I think, and we see each other for lunch most days.

Fidget is loud, brash and has a contagious energy that screams 'I'm taking up space and if you don't like it, you can just fuck the fuck off'. She has a wardrobe full of red flannel and ripped jeans and her whole vibe makes me think of running away to join the kind of noisecore punk band where no one can actually play an instrument, but they've got a lot of feelings they need to express as loudly as possible.

Apparently her siblings gave her the nickname Fidget at a very young age, because she couldn't keep still. It was only a few years later that she was formally diagnosed with ADHD and after that there was no shaking the name.

Ez, on the other hand, is like the poster child for modern goth workwear. She wears a lot of pinstriped corsets and dresses, with what I'd generally consider highly impractical boots, if I hadn't once seen her sprint across the dev floor like some kind of demonic, monochrome, Victorian gazelle. Her hair has a splash of colour, being the same neon-green shade as a fresh can of Meth.

'Fidg ordered pizza, should be here any minute. Care to join, Top Floor?'

'I'd love to, and thanks for the rescue back there.'

'They don't mess with our spy,' joked Fidget.

As I mentioned, I had been trying to be inconspicuous and out of the way when I came down at lunchtime, and since they found me under a small tree, they've taken to joking that I'm a covert spy for the executives. I've been called way worse than Top Floor, and in far more malicious ways, so I'm fine with it.

As we each pulled up a swivel chair and huddled around Ez's desk, she cracked open a can of Crimson Method Psynaptic Frenzy, downed it in one go and threw the empty can into the trash on the other side of the room with perfect precision.

'Three points!' she shouted in celebration, a break from her usual teasingly austere vampire façade which only happens in close company.

'Before we had cause to rescue you, Fidg and I were discussing our favourite games of all time. Care to add your thoughts, Top Floor?'

'*Prophecy of Zebdo – Flute of the Future.* No question about it, no competition. It was the first 3D game in the series, the first one I paid for with my own money, and I've replayed it every summer since it came out. I love that game, I love that series, and just like Dink, I'm going to save the world one day.'

'Alright then, as a connoisseur of the series, where do you stand on the subject of our hero and speech? Is he a silent protagonist or does he never shut up?'

'Trick question; Dink talks plenty, but the dialogue is always written as people responding to him, and they almost never show what he's actually saying.'

'Oh, see, I always thought of him as non-verbal, but that he has other ways of making himself understood. Sometimes we all need representation headcanons, because gods know no one in AAA space is bothering to include positive examples of neurodiversity,' Ez responded.

'Woke pandering!' chimed in Kyle from a nearby desk.

At this, Ezmeralda spun in her chair and with a dangerous smirk retorted, 'No one cares for your opinions in meatspace, little boy. Why don't you fuck off back behind a keyboard, where people can just block you.' And then, in a move which deeply impressed me, she snarled like a wolf. It rumbled up her throat and through her nose in a genuinely animalistic way.

'You've been practising that,' said Fidget, as Ez rotated back into the conversation and gave a little bow.

'Now, where were we?'

'We were talking about—' Fidget stopped dead, her brain seemingly having encountered a fatal exception error and frozen. Luckily she was quickly shaken free of the brain lockout when her phone started buzzing to let her know that our lunch was down in reception. 'I'll be right back.'

As she scurried off towards the stairs, Ez and I got into the matter of her favourite game, *Housegueist II*.

'It's a shame they've never bested the second entry. You'd have thought after twenty-plus years, fourteen additional mainline releases, a comic run and a mildly disturbing whack-a-mole game for the arcades, they'd have managed to capture some of the true psychological horror of the first two, but no. I'm honestly not even excited for this new one they're supposed to be working on.'

'It's hard to love a series which used to be all about the care and attention to detail, real deep-diving into the lore behind every character and every enemy, but now they'll offer the franchise out to any team willing to agree to a big enough percentage profit split. Not one of whom seems capable of understanding the most basic principles that led to the first five titles becoming the beloved classics they are today.'

'Absolutely. It's gone from a tense, lore-rich series of stand-alone stories set in the same universe to "let's just throw thousands of zombies, and that one boss we've completely stripped of purpose, at you to shoot. Here, have almost unlimited ammo because gods forbid you should get any sense of tension from having to conserve your supplies".'

'It's been endless waves of moaning undead for fifteen years now.'

'That's no way to talk about my polycule!' laughed Fidget as she emerged from behind a group of passing interns.

We worked our way through delicious cheesy slices, occasionally back and forthing about the state of horror games before I became aware that I could hear Hannah's voice in the distance. Looking around, I could see her chewing out one of the younger developers, in full view of the rest of the team.

'There she goes again. Like, I get the need to discipline people on occasion, but to scream at a grown adult, in front of the whole team, is super unprofessional,' said Fidget, with a sour look.

'She's making an example of him. Harrison is pretty popular, so by dressing him down in front of his bros she's putting them all in line. I don't agree with it, but I absolutely see what her thinking is,' Ez added.

'Does this happen a lot, then?' I asked.

'It's been happening less and less, but I suspect that's only because she's starting to break some of them. While they do need to learn that, despite the lack of dress code, they're not in college anymore, that's no excuse to scream at them like they're misbehaving kids at the shopping mall.'

Eventually Hannah ran out of steam, and disappeared back

towards her office. Soon after, the regular background level of friendly chatter returned to the floor. Enthusiastic, talented people putting their skills to the test for something special. Much more the contagious vibe I've come to expect from the team.

As we finished our lunch, I took a good long look around the dev floor. Hannah seemingly chose well, as everyone here is obviously very excited to be here. It's catching too, as I always feel invigorated after a trip down there. Contagious energy, or possibly caffeine osmosis.

## Meeting minutes – 27 January

Drinks orders for the board:
Edwin – blue power juice (apparently it's got seaweed in it, and still smells like misery)
Rick – four-shot latte
Chad – five-shot latte

I made the mistake of announcing everyone's drinks as I passed them out again. Rick, not one to ever be in last place, immediately upped his four-shot latte to six. Seems that there's some kind of pissing contest going on between the two of them so I think I'll be keeping everyone's order on the down low from now on, or risk having to constantly update and laminate new sheets for the manual.

NOTE TO SELF – update the drinks order chart, again.

Rick kicks off the meeting by jumping straight into how things are progressing on *Call of Shooty* (they've seemingly run out of weird subtitles to tack on at this point and are soft-rebooting the series so they can use the same title we first saw back in the late nineties. This would be fine, if it wasn't the third time they've done it in as many decades). Now that the new hires have had a few weeks to get to grips with the design documents and get head-first into full development, Chad wanted to take some time to consider our next steps.

The target for completion of the project is eight months' time, at the latest. That's so that they can hit 'the primary gifting period' (Thanksgiving and the winter holidays).

'We're seeing a pretty decent amount of voluntary overtime, which is a good sign. All the newbies are really excited to pour all of their free hours into this. We have yet to need to mandate, or even suggest, overtime so seeing these additional unpaid hours put in means we should crush that deadline.'

'Got to love that dedication to the family. Nobody wants to be the first one going home, leaving more work for everyone else. The system works,' replied Rick, nodding.

'Right? If we need to do a bunch of overtime near launch day, that's going to be easy to implement.' Something about Chad's tone seemed to imply this would be less of a question and more of an inevitability.

'You've been down there pretty regularly. Everything seem okay...' Here Chad paused, fumbling for the rest of his question. 'Umm, you?'

I was a little startled to be asked my opinion on anything, as the three of them usually only acknowledge me directly when they want to complain about their drinks. So much so, that I barely even processed that he'd clearly forgotten my name again.

'Well, they're all getting on with their assigned tasks. As you said, there's no sign that anyone is clock-watching. Most of them are still there when I go home and already hard at work when I come in every morning.'

This seemed to be exactly what Chad was hoping to hear and as he turned back to face his peers, with a grand wave of one arm he flicked a note across the table which stopped neatly under my notebook with the other. The kind of classic misdirect, sleight of hand my younger brother would show off to impress our cousins during the holidays. I half expected to unfold a two of hearts with my signature on the front. However it just turned out to be a message informing me he'd upped his coffee order again.

'So, as they're so keen, I think this is the perfect time to pull a select team away, and get them working on some extra content for last year's entry,' he announced.

'Ah, some free downloadable content, huh?'

*Oh yes, free DLC. Call of Shooty: Prehistoric Warfare is such a good game, but I've played the current content to death. See, that's the kind of reward for the fans that makes this company great; just a little thank-you for their continued support.*

My eyes lit up and my pulse began to race. What could we be getting? New story, new maps, new weapons, a new game mode?

Then I noticed the looks they were shooting each other. Each held back an impish grin and barely concealed looks of glee, glancing back and forth between each of their colleagues. It was just a matter of who would break first. After a moment the dam broke and I was treated to nearly five solid minutes of derisive laughter, complete with table pounding and tears running down their faces at the very idea of free anything.

I took the opportunity to put away my misplaced and slightly battered optimism.

When they finally regained their composure, Rick declared, 'I always say, money today is better than money tomorrow, and with most of this year before the new game releases, we gotta get that interim cash flow moving. Paid DLC is a *must*. They've had plenty out of us for the sale price already.'

'We'll need a theme.'

There were a few moments of racking their brains for clues, and checking calendars on their phones, before they settled on something Valentine's Day themed.

What followed was half an hour of the most low-effort suggestions being batted around the table. 'Put hearts on everything', 'put them in something approaching lingerie', 'give them little kissy animations when you kill someone', 'a dating minigame'. Chad seriously suggested putting a T-Rex in a red G-string and heart-shaped nipple pasties and having it twerk against a tree in the background of the Dust Bowl level for the whole month. Gross.

'Kinda disappointing that this will have to be a single purchase expansion though. What with having already shown the Electronic Games Rating Commission that we didn't include randomised purchases. Still, it's the price we paid for getting rated suitable for ages seven and up', bemoaned Rick.

'Oh, don't worry about that. I had Legal look into it, and there's a loophole we can use to get right around that. The ratings board only actually rates the on-disc version of the game, the launch day build. Any changes added post-launch don't matter. As soon as the finished game was on store shelves, that rating was locked in. We can change whatever we want now.'

'Perfect, so we can keep selling it to little Timmy, but that T-Rex can gyrate around in a G-string all month?'

'Absolutely!'

They seemed so utterly pleased with themselves, but I couldn't help flashing back to release day when the reviews were full of praise for our ethical monetisation practices and the fact it was a game for all ages to enjoy. Meanwhile, here we come, slapping sparkly hearts on the side of an assault rifle and labelling it 'Epic Tier Loot' while a pole-dancing reptile jiggles suggestively for the duration.

As Edwin grew ever closer to falling asleep in his chair, the younger pair got on to discussing how they would encourage players to buy all the new content. Trailers would be the obvious thought, but that kind of thing takes time to make and they ideally wanted everything ready to go by the end of the week.

'Here's what I'm thinking,' Chad began. 'We fill up as many lobbies as we can with our guys, dressed head-to-toe in the latest gear. We quietly edit their player stats a bit so they seem more talented than they are, and then we force everyone without the new items into games with them, call it "inspiration".'

'Exactly. Give them something to aspire to. Plus, for extra motivation, I say we have our guys shouting into their headsets about what a bunch of default scrub losers they are until they pay up.'

'Oh yeah, that's how we get the whales in. We'll look up who's spent the most money in the past and keep them locked in with our guys until they've completed the set.'

'We can lower their accuracy across the board until they've made a big enough purchase, then we let them win one and, bam, we've Schrödinger-ed their ass.'

'Just to be sure they understand the urgency, we make it clear this stuff is only available for two weeks. Then we hammer it home with a countdown emailed to them twice daily for the last five days; that way we capitalise on that sweet, sweet FOMO.'

They were practically drooling in capitalistic rapture and while I usually keep quiet during meetings, as the job bible instructed, I felt I had to raise one small point.'

'I'm sorry to interrupt, but, I mean, this all sounds a tiny bit... malicious.' They turned and stared at me with looks of confusion, tinged with mild disgust. 'I know that everyone kind of does this with their microtransactions, but isn't there a way we could sell DLC without being quite so... predatory?'

Rick was the first to recover. 'This way earns the most money.

We're a business, and we're all about making money. You actually pay attention in these meetings, you listen to the professionals here...' He gestured to himself. '...and even your pretty little head might absorb a basic understanding of economics. Now, anything else or can the experienced professionals get back to our very intelligent brainstorming session?'

Assuming that would close the matter, they turned back to face one another.

'There was just... one other thing.'

They slowly turned back, eyes wide with incredulity at my daring to continue. In hindsight I should have got the hint, but social cues have never been my forte.

'It's just... is it really wise to take so many staff away from the new project. Would it not potentially... derail all that good progress.'

Chad snorted and waved me away. 'As you said, they're passionate about it. They'll make the time up later—'

'Like they always do,' Rick finished.

The rest of the meeting continued without incident. Edwin nearly passed out in his power juice. He was only stopped when his head dipped low enough to the glass that I assume the foul odour jarred him back to the waking world.

With a loud harrumph, he straightened in his chair and in one smooth movement sank the whole glass. It left him shuddering like the $6 budget bourbon my college roommate would bring back every week.

I sat there, feeling vicariously ill at the sight, as he triumphantly announced: 'Meeting adjourned.' The boys, who'd been loudly congratulating themselves on the extreme callousness of their marketing strategy, shrugged and started making their way out of the room, leaving me to tidy up their papers. As I did so I came across a note from Rick simply stating: 'Whatever his drink is, mine had better be two stronger.'

Children.

Back in my office, I typed up the morning's minutes and shot an email across to middle management outlining the board's plans re DLC and related marketing as well as the people who'd need to be brought over to handle the project.

## P.M.

I headed down to 'The Gamer Zone' – where the interns spend most of their time, to check on the stock levels in the vending machines. That area is in the middle of the building, so there's no actual windows, it's just a walled-off area roughly the size of an elementary school classroom (and short furniture to match) with an old promotional poster from 2015's *Retaliation Vargoa* on the wall. It's designed to look like you're gazing through a portal into the game's vast, fantastical world, so I guess it's kind of like a window.

The pseudo-window was probably the most pleasant part of that room. Despite the air conditioning, the atmosphere is thick and humid, full of the combined smell of unwashed gamers, cheap, greasy takeaway, Hatchet body spray and, of course, the chemical scent of strongly caffeinated soda.

Every one of the junior-sized desks was tightly packed with glowing monitors, which in turn were covered in sticky notes concerning bugs, glitches and – perhaps idealistically – suggestions for possible features to implement.

NOTE TO SELF – get Bubblegum Brain Tsunami restocked in The Gamer Zone before there's another stampede.

Typically at a game-development studio, QA Testers would be their own job role – not paid great money, but at least paid for their work. From what I can tell, Supremacy Software have essentially replaced the role with enthusiastic, unpaid interns. The kind of people excited to be able to tell everyone they meet that they play video games for a living, without having made sure the 'for a living' part is actually in place. It's like how you see enthusiast game critics reviewing video games for no money so they can play them before anyone else. Except here there are office hours being mandated.

Among the excited faces I spotted that guy who wore the Sigil of Seven tie to his interview. He definitely suits office casual wear more than a shirt and tie, and he certainly appeared more comfortable today.

As I was checking the vending machine, I heard the familiar tap-tap-tap of acrylic on acrylic. Hannah was drumming her lethal-looking nails on a bright-red clipboard. Since sitting in on the interviews, I've found out she has a nail technician visit her once a month to fit her with these frankly terrifying and glorious nails. This time she'd had bits taken out of the middles at each tip, in order to make them look like cat ears, they were then painted white with little face details on each. Absolutely adorable, but long and sharp enough to pluck someone's eyeballs out if the desire struck her.

She was already in full flow to the assembled interns about how happy she was with their bug reports. 'Totally nailed it', apparently. However, this was quickly followed up with a harsh scolding that 'we need to see vastly increased metrics from all of you'.

One intern piped up to ask what that actually meant, as, to be fair, 'metrics' is about as vague a term as you can get. 'Like, is that increased player engagement? Longer play sessions? More recurrent spending?' Higher accuracy of litter into the damn bins (please).

Our highly intimidating head of HR smiled coldly and scribbled a brief note on her clipboard. All the while clicking her tongue in a way that seemed like a sonic weapon in any small room.

'*The* metrics. Every one of them. If there's a metric we can monitor, I want to see it go up. Graphs that increase are the only graphs that matter.' I'd heard this exact speech a few times while visiting Fidget and Ez for lunch. She repeated it to them like a mantra, emphasising the extreme importance of making unspecified, nebulous numbers increase, without any explanation of what that meant in any kind of practical sense, or even how that might be achieved.

Ez has told me it's not uncommon – following one of Hannah's more aggressively assertive recitals – for interns to start pulling all-nighters in the office; desperate attempts to raise these clandestine statistics to whatever unspoken threshold they absolutely must reach.

Today she followed up in a less acerbic tone. 'I completely understand that you're *currently* unpaid. You're working for the love of the job, for the industry. Because you want to be part of something bigger, part of the Supremacy Software family. But that's a great privilege; many people work for years to get to the top of this industry and join us. You have to show us that you're worthy to stand among them. Not just some loser who "got a lucky break".'

She continued, 'You'll no doubt be excited to hear that there will be… a *few* paid positions opening up pretty soon and those of you who can show you've got the drive, the ambition, the need to be the very best… Those of you who can impress me… Well, you'll be first in line, when the time comes.'

The spokesintern raised his hand immediately. 'Do we have a timeline on those vacancies opening up?' A very reasonable question, I thought.

Hannah's eyes narrowed dangerously and, for a moment, I imagined her pouncing on him in front of everyone and peeling his skin off with her expertly designed, lethal nails, as a warning to the others.

After a moment though, she cracked a mirthless smile and hastily added another note, firing off high-powered clicks of her tongue that left my ears ringing.

Finally, in a tone I can only describe as menacing, she responded, 'Management are doing their utmost to ensure the available resources are properly distributed, before making their final decisions on actual figures. Suffice to say, any day now, *some* of you, those of you who prove you truly belong, will be heading up that corporate ladder of progress. Meritocracy and all that.'

I heard a quiet chuckle by my shoulder and turned to see Clark shaking his head as he dusted the top of the vending machine.

Behind me I heard Hannah, striding out of The Gamer Zone. When the door clicked shut behind her, there was an audible release of breath from the interns as they collectively relaxed.

'Every year the same,' he said quietly, as if sharing a thought with the drinks machine.

'Huh?'

'They do this every year,' he continued, never turning to look at me, his tone quiet, but clear. It was like we were meeting at opposite ends of a park bench and he was passing government secrets to his informant while pretending to read a newspaper.

'Do what?'

'There's always one or two who'll stand up for themselves, start speaking for their co-workers. Just like that, the carrot comes on down. "Hey, kids, you fall in line, like she says, and you'll be rewarded." Just like that, well, they're fighting over who's gonna get picked.'

'And that works?'

'Not only does it work, those caught up in that spell, they'll be trying to silence the rabble rousers themselves. As they see it, it's the ones making all the fuss who are holding everyone else back. And if that's not enough, well, those freethinkers suddenly find themselves with a lot more free time for thinking.'

'Surely they can't keep working here for nothing. This city isn't cheap.'

'Those who can't afford it just have to give it up. Hannah, she'll pass a few of them off as the chosen ones, now too senior to hang around, or gone to work in another office.'

'And, I guess, anyone who *can* keep coming to a job that isn't paying them probably isn't struggling for necessities anyway.'

'Exactly, they have all the time in the world; what better way to spend it than getting the inside scoop on this place. Maybe bragging about it with the boys at the bar on a Friday night.'

It was all making horrible sense and I stood there, staring through the wall in front of me as my brain took a moment to process this lore-dump.

'This industry is *full* of fresh faces who'll happily take a few scoldings from the likes of Hannah if it means they can point to their name in the credits of the latest thing.'

I could feel the call to action, my quest log getting updated. Do not power off your console when you see this icon. There's evil to fight and a world to save.

'We should tell them. The cycle has to end. They can't keep doing this to people.' I could feel my heart pounding in my chest. Clark finally turned and fixed me with a hard look.

'Won't do any good, new blood. Anyone causing trouble, riling up the others, rocking the van, well, they just don't come back. You make a move that big and you'll be gone. Probably anyone they think was listening to you too. They'll have replaced every last one of you before the week is out, and nothing will have changed. Hell, by the end of the month, no one inside will even remember it happened.'

Of course, I'm a fool, that's the main quest. I'm going to have to do a few dungeon runs, gain some experience and pick up some new weapons before I can defeat the final boss. Okay, I can do that. Just one thing...

'Sorry, did you mean "rocking the boat", or is that a New York thing?'

'Oh, just an inside joke with some friends. Rocking the boat, if you prefer. Please excuse me, I must be getting on.' He gave me a look that might have been sympathetic and headed out.

I've really wanted to believe in the magic of this industry, but actually seeing it makes that harder and harder by the day. There's wonderful creative work being done here, but it's all covered in the lingering stain of manipulative management. I have to do something to make this better; I just need to work out what and how.

Walking out onto the dev floor, I took a deep breath, trying to calm down enough to not just start uselessly screaming at anyone who'd listen about the injustice of it all. As usual, a quiet moment and a deep breath down here was enough to invigorate me.

Looking out over the screen-lit faces of smiling, engaged developers, typing away or chatting together, I knew that, in time, I had to find a way to make things right for them. They're good people, mostly, and they deserve better than to be casually exploited for lazy cash grabs.

# CHAPTER 3

# Schmooze Fest

6 MARCH

Early March means that a few of us get to stretch out and see a bit more of the world than just the office. Right now I'm working from a laptop, in a conference room, in the back of a huge convention centre on the West coast of the US. A constant cacophony of voices manages to be audible despite us being about as far away from the actual conference attendees as possible.

We've spent the last few days at the Grand Gamer Forum (GGF). It's the largest conference of game developers in the world. Those smart cookies who have the bright ideas for interesting mechanics, as well as those who can overcome the tricky parts of actually making those ideas come to life, are here to give talks on the how and why of the industry. There's a lot of veterans here, the old guard who made the games that first got me into playing. I'll be honest, a lot of the technical bits fly over my head, but it's fascinating nonetheless.

I've got a few minutes now to catch up on emails while Rick and Chad are schmoozing at the bar with a couple of other young execs from SkeeviSoft – another massive company with a history not dissimilar to ours. They've been trading tales of conquest at the top of the gaming industry and slowly drinking the private bar dry.

The executives have been on a good few 'business' trips this year, but given that they usually return with suntans and astronomical 'entertainment' expenses, I'm not convinced they've been the most work-heavy trips. This, however, is very definitely a work trip and I suspect the only reason I've been brought along is to do anything more strenuous than share war stories with rival executives over staggeringly expensive cocktails and fancy finger food.

I currently find myself hunched over my laptop on a makeshift desk of plastic-wrapped water bottles in a large, open all-purpose events room, away from the main conference. All around me are journalists and other PAs hard at work for their own executives. There's an odd stillness here. No one wishes to disturb anyone; just focusing on their own thing. It's like some stark future library where all the books are digital and the promised neon lights revealed to have been a lie sold to us by Hollywood to make us think dystopias would have the decency to look cool.

Since arriving at the conference, I've been mostly free to do my own thing. I managed to catch some indies discussing low CPU demand rendering techniques, a presentation about the timelessness of certain art styles in our medium, a really cool talk about trans representation in the indie scene, and even one about the ways big-budget development house work can teach people the skills needed to eventually start their own small studios.

My main quest for the event has been keeping an eye out for journalists and steering them away from the execs. Luckily Rick and Chad can walk at a reasonable pace and I don't auto-fail if they happen to get too far away.

Officially, they're not to be disturbed due to 'confidentiality concerns'. I've done my best to keep them safely away from the press, palming journos off with business cards and inviting them to email me directly with any questions. Hence the currently bulging nature of my inbox. Thankfully, I can get away with passing much of it straight on to the PR team, so it's a lot of bulk forwarding things on.

There is one member of the press who's been far more persistent than the others. I first encountered him the evening we arrived. It was almost like he was waiting in the lobby just to catch us. Helpfully, he was already wearing his bright-purple GGF press pass and I was able to immediately spring into action.

He strode towards the executives like a purposeful giant (he's nearly seven feet tall) and I slid right in there for the interception. 'Can I help you at all?' I enquired.

He paused, looked down at me and was kind enough to take a half step back, so as not to just fully loom over me. 'Gareth Lane, *World Gaming News*. I was wondering if I might have a few words with your employers?'

I'd been mentally practising for this on the flight over. 'I'm afraid the executives are on a very tight schedule during their time here. However, if you'd like to contact me directly...' Here I presented him with a freshly printed business card. 'I'll make sure that any enquiries are passed on accordingly.'

He peered past and over my head. 'I just have a few quick questions regarding the working conditions at your company. I'm sure it wouldn't take up too much time.'

'I'm afraid they're fully booked for the duration of the week's events, with many important meetings, as well as conversations which will delve into NDA-covered topics, and as such will not be available for unplanned, impromptu conversations. Of course, should you require a more immediate response, you could always contact our PR department. It's "PR@ the same domain as myself".'

'Ah, of course. I do have these details, but thus far they have proved either unwilling or unable to respond to my enquiries, so you see I've been left with very little choice.'

His wavy bright-orange hair stretched nearly down to the middle of his back. This, combined with a luxurious, well-kept beard, and the way he was currently being lit from behind made me feel like I was holding a conversation with a very polite and well-spoken bipedal lion. If nothing else, he'd be easy to pick out in a crowd, should he try to approach the execs again.

'As I've said, if you contact me directly, I'll see that you receive a timely response.'

He smiled kindly, graciously accepted defeat and departed. As he did so, I noticed him reach into his jacket pocket and pull out a small digital Dictaphone, which he then shut off. Of course, he'd been wearing a wire, how exciting.

After catching up with the boys in one of the VIP bar areas, I took a moment to look into the legality of Lane's recording of our conversation. Lucky for him, this is a 'one party consent state' so only one person taking part needs to be aware it's being recorded. Out of curiosity, I looked up New York and found the same rules apply. Maybe I could live up to Fidget's theory and actually turn spy.

I've since bumped into Lane on a few more occasions, and there's no malice there. Just an almost cartoonish 'foiled again' expression when he notices me moving to intercept him, before leaving without an argument. I've appreciated that. Plenty of men I've encountered would have absolutely used the size advantage to threaten or intimidate me. Lane is always quick to put a few feet between us, away from the execs, if I've managed to catch him in close proximity.

I kind of admire his tenacity too. He's onto some kind of lead and pursuing it doggedly. Most of the others who've said they want a focused interview have tried to be a little pushy at first, but quickly agreed to take a card, whereupon I've not seen them again.

Earlier today Rick and Chad took to the stage to give their own talk. It wasn't about game design, mechanics, narrative concepts, or how to make games more fun to play. No, theirs was on 'Monetisation and Player Base Retention'. Big surprise. Still, I guess it was on their minds after the success of the big Valentine's day event, which went so well for them.

'Hi, I'm Chad, from the executive team at Supremacy Software, and I'm here today to talk about how to hunt a whale.

'We all know about whales; recurrent spenders who outpace their game playing contemporaries in impulsivity of purchases, amount spent and compulsive spending to complete time-limited or artificially rarefied sets of collectables in real money DLC stores.

'Now, we could waste time talking about the morality of hunting for whales, but let's put that aside for the time being and we can circle back later if anyone would like to hear more.'

To my complete lack of surprise, they did not circle back.

'The reality is that there are players who will spend huge amounts of money, seemingly without much thought, given the correct push. Today we'd like to talk about how best to ensure the health of our respective studios, by providing players like these with the kind of content they *have* to spend money on. We're going to show you actual numerical data confirming exactly what gets them to spend, and spend big.

'Don't think of today's talk as instructions on how to get money out of players, simply an education on behavioural psychology, so that *you* can better understand your most financially invested players, and how they behave.

'Every game you've ever seen at the top of the charts in terms of earnings will make sure that it is possible – though not *required* – to spend $2,500 on in-app purchases within the twelve-month period following a product launch. I'm not saying you need to create an amount of content that justifies that kind of spend, so long as your rarity stats are set low enough that, if someone does become invested in these randomised rewards, they're not likely to reach an upper limit on spending too soon, where they have spent enough money to have statistically completed their collections.

'The last thing you want is to get a whale on the hook, but suddenly find you lack the spending opportunities to reel in their true financial potential. If possible, set that minimum spend to earn everything far higher than that. If you can conceive of a high-end player spending it, make sure things are rare enough they end up reaching that top end of cost.'

I was taking notes throughout, but I can barely remember anything of what they were saying, now I think back on it. It was mostly the same spiel they gave in the board meeting last month, just dressed up with more plausibly deniable language. Less gloating about huge payouts for themselves, more discussions of 'ensuring the financial health of the studio', but at its core it was very clear they were just selling other lightly inebriated execs on how best to pressure money out of people who didn't necessarily want to spend it, and thereby improve executive bonuses.

The most depressing part? The other big AAA studios in attendance ate it all up. They cheered at the idea of manipulating 'whales' into obsessive spending, then making that spending a habit to be fed. The way they talked about it, those 'whales' didn't represent real people, just an exploitable revenue stream.

'Remember that not all whales exist for the same reason. Some want cosmetic collectables, some want to complete the game faster, some want to win more often, and others want new novel experiences. Ideally, all of these groups should be catered to. Let players pay to play better. Let them pay to look cooler. Let them pay to skip any grind you were smart enough to include, and let them pay to see new things, even if they are just the smallest remixes of things they have already experienced.

'Get them hooked in with some kind of great value first microtransaction, to break the ice. Make the first hit too good and too affordable to pass them by. Then, when you've shown them, "Hey, this isn't so bad. Just a fun little extra," when they've taken the first step towards your warm, welcoming, waiting arms, that's when you take a step away from them while setting the hook. Then you make spending a habit, make it something they do regularly. Maybe they don't even think about it. You make it so easy to spend just a little more. They haven't played today; email them a deal. They're getting close to completing a set, you tell them time is running out. Make them scared to miss the full collection, and if time does run out, pat them on the backs: "There, there, champ. You were real close. Sure you'll do it next time."

'Make them into a capital "g" Gamer. It's not just a distraction or a hobby. It's a way of life. It's their world. A Gamer who invests their whole personality into their love of your game will direct most of their disposable income right into your wallet. And not only that, they'll make sure everyone they know has to get on board too. That's when they'll be working *for* you.'

As they concluded their disgusting spectacle, the room erupted in rapturous applause. I half expected the crowd of adoring, would-be exploiters to sweep forward and carry them above their heads to the nearest VIP bar.

Oleaginous, gammon-faced business leaders slimed forwards, tripping over each other, hands outstretched to congratulate Rick and Chad for their masterful understanding of psychological manipulation techniques aimed at exploiting anyone with a console and a connected bank account.

'Amazing talk,' declared the first to get a hand on Rick. 'I loved some of the ideas you put forward there.' I could tell by the way he suddenly winced that my boss had taken the opportunity to crush the other man's hand in a needlessly destructive shake.

'Sure. Look, nothing I said there was totally original, but if you truly believe in the economic systems you are selling, then minds smart enough to comprehend what you're saying will know that it's achievable. People want to hear about how to make the big bucks from those who are proven to have those big bucks.'

I couldn't tell if he was trying to deliberately confuse the sycophant, or had just gotten into a flow and was enjoying the smell of his own bullshit.

He continued, 'Now, I hear some people after my talks, they'll say, "Hey, you didn't talk about how to make games in your games talk," but that's not what games are about, at least not here. You go next door if you wanna listen to some developer nerd go on about teraflops, or whatever. Any fool can make a video game: you just pay someone to make it for you. Making a game that makes you money – that's the bit it'll pay you to learn.' The adoring horde smiled greasily and nodded along with enthusiasm as their new lords continued to pontificate.

I saw Mr Lane moving forward in the crowd, and started towards him before checking myself. What if, just this once, I just let him slip by and ask his questions this time? Even if he doesn't get an answer, I know there's every chance he could make them just a little uncomfortable. They've certainly earned some discomfort here.

We're still on the road and exhaustion is hitting me pretty hard. With GGF out of the way, we flew right across the country for the Amusement Arcade Expo South-South-East in Florida (AAX SSE – colloquially pronounced 'Excessy' for ease).

While our trip to the GGF was mostly about letting Rick and Chad flex their egos in front of their industry peers, these days AAX SSE is a largely consumer-facing convention. It's much more focused on showing off our games, and checking out what the competition is up to. Rick and Chad call it 'market research', but the way they were discussing it on the flight was considerably more targeted.

When we arrived at the convention centre yesterday (which seems big enough to house the entire homeless population of two continents, let alone this circus of interactive electronic wonder), my employers rushed off to some unexplained meeting, and left me with instructions for the first day: Walk the show floor and make detailed notes on what all of our competition has on display. Which developers have brought games? What are the plots? Which games have new mechanics we've not seen elsewhere? Which games have the longest lines? Which games do the majority of journalists seem to be booking appointments to check out?

Luckily, like the journalists, I got to schedule hands-on time at each display thanks to my industry pass. This made my job infinitely more manageable, as I wouldn't have gotten very much done if I'd had to spend upwards of three hours in line for a single game, like the poor members of the public.

I spent the day running from booth to booth, wandering crowded halls, taking notes along the way and pictures where permitted. I went in with a tablet and a spare power brick, but by lunch-time I had a canvas bag full of lanyards, badges, posters, t-shirts and business cards. That is to say nothing of the twisted ankle I got from nearly falling over an elaborately attired anime character who was sitting with her legs outstretched into the busy aisles. They'd been queueing to see some new fighting game due out next year.

There were plenty of other cosplay kids and adults alike of course. On top of that, every booth had a mix of professionals in highly detailed costumes and sugary PR representatives handing out equally sugary drinks, in cans which were custom-printed with their branding. Lest anyone forget which game loved them most, so the attendees could show those games some love in return.

I've spread out on the bed, my head still swimming as I try to recall every brightly lit booth, booming with excitement and upbeat music. Meanwhile pizza is on the way up and I have a towel full of ice wrapped around my throbbing ankle.

Today was amazing. Everyone seems to be making games that have such interesting new ideas. By comparison, *Call of Shooty* feels bland, generic and somewhat dated.

## Meeting minutes – 12 March
Drinks orders for the board:
Rick – nine-shot latte
Chad – seven-shot latte

In a bit of a change, I was told to kick off the meeting by presenting my notes from yesterday, highlighting what's new and interesting on the show floor.

'This year's *Doctrines of Death* title features time travel and teleportation mechanics, so you can use past versions of yourself as a distraction, while future you hops out of a nearby dumpster and shanks their target in the kidneys with a razor-sharp graphics card shard.'

'And, how did the players respond to the levels of violence? Did the blood get a rise out of them?'

'I mean, yeah, they seemed to be having fun.'

'More violence equals more fun. Perfect!'

As I enthused about my favourite featured games, Rick and Chad nodded along, occasionally taking notes or grilling me about how long the queues had been, or if I'd struggled to book an appointment to return and try something out. I filled them in on what was generating the most interest, including a rundown on what the morning games press had been highlighting.

'*Wheels of Warfare 6* has a new mechanic whereby players can run around on the ceiling, and perform stealth takedowns with an energy chainsaw, as the start of a combo into regular gameplay.'

'And how was the queue? We talking thirty minutes? An hour? A day?'

'Well, any time a game has brand-new mechanics that people haven't had a chance to try yet, the lines get pretty long. They had four-hour queues last I checked.'

'Perfect. Next?'

'The new *Critter County* has a friendship meter, where spending time with different people living on your peninsula will cause them to develop deeper friendships with the player character, eventually leading to you settling down to a domestic life in the countryside.'

'And what was the demographic spread like?'

'Pretty broad. Age ranges from birth to death, all across the gender spectrum. Some notable overlap with players of more violent game franchises too. It's good for everyone.'

'Cool, so everyone will play our violent game if it has friendship meters. Good info,' he praised, having latched onto quite unexpected aspects of my report.

'There's a new *Prophecy of Zebdo*.' Still no sign of a playable Zebdo in this iteration, come on, devs, sort it out. 'This one allows players to interact with the world through a series of physics-based puzzle mechanics, all of which work in consistent ways, allowing for highly creative world exploration outside the bounds of developer-intended progression.'

'So I'm hearing bigger world, more ways to break intended progression, creative use of mechanics. Got it, next.'

'*Dance Dance Keep on Dancing – Don't You Ever Stop Dancing 20XX* edition features a style meter, where you create your own unique motion-controlled dance move to perform during quiet moments and increase your Stylin'-O-Meter rating.'

'Don't gamers hate moving?' queried Chad.

'Sure they do,' Rick responded, 'but if we can get them to move enough to hold back a serious health condition, while they're still of working age, they can keep buying our products for longer.'

Chad smiled and nodded approvingly. 'Right, perfect, that's everything we need to know'

'Fire an email back to the dev team. *Call of Shooty* update. It's now a first-person shooter—'

'With time travel and teleportation mechanics.'

'Stealth kills, friendship meters for deep and complex relationships, physics-based platforming mechanics...'

'Those need to work in highly unpredictable ways.'

'And it needs a style meter for motion-controlled emote actions which can add humiliation points when you kill opponents.'

If either of them noticed the look of utter horror I was sure had fallen over my face, neither commented on it. They bounced back and forth adding more and more amputated limbs to this Frankenstein game they were pitching.

I couldn't quite believe what I was hearing. Half of those mechanics make no sense for a gritty first-person shooter and plenty more seem like they're going to be massively complicated to implement, especially since they weren't in the design process from the beginning. At the same time, that physics system is going to be a nightmare to QA test with such a short development cycle. That's to say nothing of the fact that every one of those ideas was stolen from another developer.

It was like watching a live version of that trope where someone has to come up with an idea on the spot and they just start naming everything they can see.

Choosing my words as carefully as possible, I asked, 'Can we do that? Legally speaking?'

'You can't patent an idea of a gameplay mechanic, kid. I mean... you can. We did do that with the SmartEnemy system from that *Horde of the Things* series a few years back.'

'As long as we frame it as "taking inspiration" rather than stealing, there's basically no one bigger than us, and there's nothing they can do that we can't just wait out in court.'

'At enormous expense to them.'

Indeed, as the great Lobachevsky said, 'Call it, please, research.'

They see themselves as untouchable, and since CoS is due out in October, there's every chance that we'd actually be first to market with most of these ideas. By the time the original creators get their games out, the features will be old news at best, or considered to be copied from us at worst.

Once again, my former excitement of being in the room when the big decisions are made had been thrown in my face. I may know first, I may know accurately, but that knowing never seems to be for anything good. The monkey's paw curls a finger, just to flip me off.

This year's *Call of Shooty* is going to be a cluttered mess, and I'm not even sure it's possible to finish it all in the time they're allowing.

The rest of the meeting passed without incident. They patted themselves on the back for *their* amazing new gameplay concepts. I sat and took notes of every little thing they waffled on about. Eventually they headed off to some roof-top party for the industry elites and I was sent back into the convention hall in search of anything which had arrived fresh today.

The hall was full of PR teams whose key selling points I'd just scooped up and handed over to the behemoth of Supremacy Software. More than usual, I struggled to meet anyone's eye.

### 14 MARCH

A week and a half of air travel, as well as the miles I trekked around that small, temporary city of video gaming, have taken their toll. It'll be a good long while before I get fully over the jet lag, but at least I get to sleep in my own bed again.

This morning I met with the senior dev team and middle management. As expected, those who actually understood the changes were at least mildly horrified by the executive decision to upend the entire toy chest into their lovely, detailed, battle-terrain diorama, even if middle management were, as usual, as positive and upbeat as the recruitment team for a sex cult.

'So... we, er, we did manage to get a new design document ready, but we were wondering if, maybe, if the board had really considered how all these features might work together?' a distressed-looking senior developer queried.

'I'm afraid I did raise that point to them, but they're absolutely adamant that this is what they want the game to be going forward.'

'Of-of course, yes. And, er. I don't suppose they might see

their way to allowing us some extra resources in order to help implement them?'

'That's something you'd need to discuss with Hannah's team as she's the one who would have to approve the budget on any extra staff.'

His face fell at the mention of Hannah.

'I'm sorry, I realise this is a lot,' I concluded.

Fear spread across his features and his next words came out in a panicked hurry. 'No, not at all. We're ready for the challenge, we appreciate the opportunity. The family will pull together.'

'Absolutely,' chimed in Roger, one of the middle managers. 'The team is itching to get going and I'll be personally standing behind every desk, getting hands on where needed, keeping a close eye on things for the board. Making sure every team member is up to the task. You can count on me.' He smiled like a used-car salesman about to sell me a decaying three-wheeled shopping cart for the price of a brand-new, top-of-the-line sports car. Meanwhile, further down the table, the senior developers visibly sagged in defeat.

I couldn't help but feel personally responsible. If I'd known better before giving my report, I could have avoided the worst of it. I was a fool for not seeing it coming.

As they filed out of the meeting room, I noticed a few were already on their phones, calling loved ones to let them know some late nights would be coming up. Depressing as all that was, once we were out on the main floor, surrounded by the bustle of creativity and keen faces, I did feel my funk start to lift.

What I could see on screens was looking way more readable as actual game assets than it had when I was last here. I just hoped they could pull all those disparate ideas together into something fun and playable.

Since the rest of my day was looking fairly quiet (thanks to having gotten on top of my emails while I was still at AAX SSE), I finally had time to visit the mobile team and introduce myself. Just as Clark had directed, there was a small, unmarked door at the end of a corridor whose only other door was an emergency exit, leading to a fire escape.

I knocked, unsure how big the office would be, hoping it wasn't so big that no one would hear me and leave me standing anxiously out there alone.

There seemed to be a flurry of activity and the sound of someone urgently hammering a keyboard. Finally a voice whispered, 'Clear, go!'

With that, the door popped open releasing a comforting waft of air scented with soothing lavender and baked goods. A bespectacled older woman peeked out and looked me up and down briefly, before throwing the door as wide as it would go, and smiling broadly.

'Ah, here at last. Welcome, sweetie, Clark mentioned you'd come by eventually.' She reached out for a closer look at my security ID, her many bangles and bracelets jingling like bar chimes as she moved. 'Oh dear, you must have caught them on a really bad day to get one like that.'

'He said he'd already printed it, so wouldn't let me take another one,' I replied sheepishly.

'Sounds about right,' came a voice from within. 'Compassion isn't their strong suit.'

'Aesthetics even less so,' my greeter concluded. 'Candace, by the way, pleased to meet you. You a hugger?'

I'll be honest, I'm not usually one for being touched by strangers at all, but she had such kind auntie energy that I took her up on the offer.

'Get in, before anyone upstairs realises we're here,' urged the voice from within.

Inside of the tiny room, which was barely larger than my own office, was a sharp juxtaposition to the rest of Supremacy's offices. The walls were painted a deep crimson and covered in magazine clippings of half-naked handsome and beautiful people, held in place with thumbtacks which had also been used to hold up a set of warm white string lights. Somehow, despite a motion sensor clearly triggering on the ceiling, there was no automatic blast of fluorescent lighting to assault the senses.

'Where's the box?' Candace asked the woman I took to be Jenette.

'If you've lived forty-seven years and can't yet find your box, you're well beyond my help,' she replied drily, before adding, 'It's tucked down by the fridge... because you needed to cool off.'

Candace tittered and fumbled around to retrieve a firm but comfortable cube of fabric, which felt like it had been upcycled from old sofa cushions, upon which she directed me to sit. She proceeded to offer to make tea, which I gratefully accepted.

I had expected her to head down the hall to one of the kitchens, but instead she reached across her desk and filled an electric kettle.

'Are you British, then?' I asked.

'No, dear, but it really is the only way to make proper tea.'

'Proper tea is theft,' responded Jenette, and they both chuckled.

I complimented them on how cosy they'd made the space as I was handed a warm, steamy mug.

'Well, thank you, sweetie. We did our best with it. Clark helped, of course.'

'And we had to bring the armchairs in during the weekend, so no one would see. It helps that very few people even remember that we're an in-house team. We keep making our games, bringing in regular income, and they've kindly forgotten to interfere for over nine years now.' Jenette finally turned to look at me. 'Are you down here to change that?'

'Oh no, no, no. I just... Clark, he said you... I should speak to you,' I stammered, spilling hot tea over my knees.

'Clark is an excellent judge of people,' affirmed Candace, shooting a chastising look at her colleague and passing me some paper towel.

Over the remains of my tea, they told me all about the types of games they make. Mostly match-three or hidden object affairs, all tied together with steamy romance stories. For which the attractive magazine clippings were to be used as reference.

'Yes, "reference",' Jenette air-quoted, with a wink.

Their current project, Amy at Evening Classes, was about a thirty-something woman who moves to a small town and takes evening classes in the hope of meeting new people; romance and intrigue ensue.

Their sales strategy is simple, and largely unused by modern standards. Rather than filling their games with aggressive microtransactions, they show a single, skippable advert between each puzzle attempt, but for a one-off fee of a couple of bucks, they can be removed entirely. At that price point, they sell a huge number of upgrades, but no one is ever locked out of playing.

I've since had a look into company records and those two have been pulling in massive funds for years. Not only that, but they never seem to stop cranking out new titles. There were four new games last year alone. Each one entirely coded and scored by Candace, while Jenette did all the art assets and writing. Keeping themselves surprisingly restrained, they've kept everything PG-13 enough that the app stores can't kick them off for obscenity.

I have to admire their consistency too, not one of their titles has a less than 4.8/5 star rating. Those two are virtually pioneers in the industry. Hell, they practically *are* that industry.

As I started to say my goodbyes, Candace went to offer me a home-cooked hazelnut brownie, but then caught herself, checked the clock (it was about two-thirty) and said, 'Probably a little early for that. Some other time.'

I didn't query further, having at least a sneaking suspicion as to the reason, but I can't deny I was a little sad to miss out, because they smelled amazing.

I thanked them for their hospitality, and, before I could reach for the door handle, Jenette spun around and slowly rose from her armchair. Taking a moment to stretch out a little, she stole forward, opened the door, peeked up and down the hallway outside, closed the door again and leaned in conspiratorially. 'Before you go, I don't know if you've met anyone around the office named Roger. Late forties, about five feet five, oily-looking and acts like he's in charge of things he isn't.'

'I think I was in a meeting with him earlier. He seemed to think he'd have a hand in overseeing some major changes being implemented.'

She pulled a sour face. 'A genuinely sinister choice of words. Listen, nobody can prove anything, this isn't something HR can action due to lack of evidence, but he's got a reputation for being a bit... "handsy". Especially with younger women.'

'Eww, gross.'

'Exactly. I'd advise you to try and avoid being alone with him, and keeping your wits about you in a crowd he might be a part of.'

I thanked her for the warning.

'And if you could *quietly* get the message out to the new starters, I think that might be for the best.'

'I've got a couple of discreet friends down there, I'll make sure the warning gets passed around.'

Jenette gave me a curiously appraising look and said, 'You're alright,' before opening the door and leading me outside.

'One last thing, dearie.' She held up her cell. 'I'm terrible with faces, if you don't mind, a quick picture?'

I agreed, and she was kind enough to ask if I was happy with the result before saving it.

Candace poked her head out. 'You come back and visit our little nook any time, sweetie.'

Jenette turned to her and teased, 'Doesn't your nook get enough action already?' which set them both off giggling.

Back in my little office, I checked my email, expecting to find it full of yet more enquiries better suited for the PR department than the executives. I'm not sure what they think going to the top of the company will achieve, but it's got real 'I want to speak to the manager' vibes.

Moving on to my own inbox, I found an urgent email from Fidget.

*Hey Top Floor,*

*Sorry to bother you, but I am really struggling, and need some help and support. As you know, I started working here in January, after the release of* Call of Shooty: Prehistoric Warfare. *However, a whole bunch of the player base has got it in their heads that I'm responsible for basically every design decision in that game they don't like.*

*It all kicked off when I posted a selfie online saying how excited I was that I get to work here, and before I know it, I'm getting a torrent of sexist and homophobic abuse. I deleted the picture, but after some investigation I've found screenshots of it on one of those anonymous forums. They've posted my home address, my emails, my parents' address, everything. I've been fully doxxed.*

*I know I should probably go to Hannah for something like this, but she scares the crap out of me and I'd rather talk to you anyway.*

*Fidget*


Of course the Gamers™ are immediately blaming all the ills of their tiny worlds on a visibly queer woman who dares to work in *their* industry. Funny how it's always women who are somehow at fault for every real or perceived evil in the games industry.

Why let a little thing like the facts get in the way of an old-fashioned pile-on? Who cares that she wasn't even involved in last year's game? Heck, she wasn't even part of the sub-team who did the DLC last month.

I emailed Hannah to ask what could be done, before heading downstairs and locating Fidget in the bathroom by the stairs.

'I'm so sorry about all this. Is there anything I can get you or do? I've already contacted Hannah on your behalf.'

Her face was streaked with tears and smudged mascara, her breathing rapid. I recognised the signs of an anxiety attack.

'I'M NOT OKAY!' she suddenly cried out, eyes darting back and forth.

'I understand. I'm here to help,' I replied, keeping my tone soft and even.

For a few more minutes she twitched and panted, but the way she was rubbing the back of her hand with the pointer and middle fingers of her other hand told me she was using some kind of self-soothing technique. Eventually, she sagged and sat down on the lid of the toilet.

'I thought all this was in the past. I can't go through it all again,' she said, her voice a weak and defeated monotone.

'Again?'

'Yeah... I did some freelance work as a story consultant. I was a known, publicly queer writer who worked for cheap. I got hired for a big franchise RPG. Said they wanted to avoid another ham-fisted and community-panned character in the series' next entry. Decided to make a big PR splash about how they were listening to feedback and that I'd be giving some input. Next thing I know, I'm getting death threats along with packages of white powder delivered to my apartment. Some first-name-bunch-of-numbers account posted and tagged me in a photograph where I was asleep on my couch the night before. Topped that off with an invite to anyone else who was "sick of these degenerates infesting our games" to drop by along with my full address.'

'Gods, that's... I can't even imagine.'

'I stopped writing, moved, twice. They found the first place within a month. Officially changed my name. Stopped going outside for a long time. That's when I taught myself 3D modelling and animation.' She sighed heavily. 'Here we are again though. How dare a woman, eh?'

I was hoping – Supremacy being a bigger company and, as repeatedly stated, 'a family' – that we could make sure Fidget wouldn't be left to deal with all this on her own.

Not long thereafter, I was disabused of that notion when I received a response from Hannah.

*While we recognise that one of the dev team is experiencing distress, these factors are outside the company's control. It is not corporate policy to provide workplace resources for the handling of external matters.*

*However, since this may reflect poorly on the company, I can authorise enactment of the standard procedure (outlined fully in your job bible) using keywords 'harassment', 'female staff', 'no discernible reason', 'single period' only.*

*Ensure that this does not interfere with the execution of your regular duties.*

*Regards,*

*Hannah Lomad*

'I've had an email back from Hannah. She says there's a procedure for all this, I just need to look it up in my job bible. Will you be okay while I go and organise this for you? I can go grab Ez, if you'd like.'

'She's busy, I don't want to bother anyone. I'll be here.' Her face was smooshed against the cubicle wall, eyes focused on some midpoint between me and the sink, and she was rocking back and forth ever so slightly.

'I'll be back as quickly as I can.'

Upstairs, the manual quickly directed me to a very simple form on the company intranet and how to use it. I just clicked on a dropdown box, selected the authorised keyword, clicked the plus icon to add any additional words, and then selected 'generate'. Next thing I know there was an automatically generated email window, with Maria (the community manager)'s address prefilled. Attached was a file named 'solemn.jpg'.

Partly out of curiosity, and partly because I wanted to check my work, I opened it before hitting Send. The image was of white text on a black, lightly textured background, surrounded about an inch from the edge by a narrow white square frame.

*Dear Gamers,*

*We understand our fans are passionate about the properties we create, it's one of the things we love most about you.*

*We ask that you respect our staff in this troubled time. Delays regarding updates on our latest products are a concern, but rest assured that our team is working very hard to bring you the products you deserve.*

*We are terribly sorry you were put in a position where you felt the need to bring this behaviour to our attention and ask that you allow us to absolutely guarantee that we will make sure that those who are responsible are dealt with in a swift and appropriate manner.*

*Supremacy Software*

I was dumbfounded. It was worse than no response; addressing nothing and making it sound like Gamers™ were correct, if a little overzealous, in their actions.

Just to be sure I hadn't entered something incorrectly, I ran through the whole process again, but no, it was exactly the same as the first.

What. The. Fuck.

I felt my stomach turn. I'd left Fidget making it sound like I'd be back with the start of some solution, but this was worse than nothing. Guiltily, I hit Send and headed back to check on my friend.

She'd barely moved, save to be slightly more hunched forward and less impeded in her rocking.

'We need to get on lockdown,' I said. 'If you give me your phone, I can start privating all your socials and setting up two-factor authentication on the important stuff. Can I message one of your partners?'

She limply offered me her phone.

The vibration of new messages was almost constant and the notification bar looked like a swatch of every single alert icon to grace the app store.

It took nearly an hour, but I was able to block and mute enough accounts that the slew of incoming abuse slowed to only a couple of new messages every ten minutes. Every social platform and email which offered two-factor had been secured, and I'd had to start a fraud investigation with her online banking service, because some jerk had already infiltrated her online payment processor.

It wasn't even aimed at me, but some of the things I saw made me want to escape to the woods and live as a hermit, never having to hear from another human being as long as I lived.

No time for that right now, though. I could do my best, but she'd need someone longer term. I asked her who she'd like me to contact, and she muttered a name that sounded at a guess like Fred. I went looking through her contacts, but couldn't see a Fred in the Fs section.

'I'm not seeing a Fred.'

She wearily looked up at me. 'Bread. They/them.'

'Right, yes. Ringing now.'

Bread was lovely and they agreed to drive to her apartment and pick up some essentials, then come collect Fidg and take her back to their place.

Not long after, there was an incoming call from an unknown number. Thinking it might be one of her partners, I answered.

Someone clearly attempting to disguise their voice immediately launched into a disgusting, homophobic and misogynistic tirade.

End call.

Definitely not one of the partners, so I blocked the number.

Eventually, Bread called to say they were down at the pickup zone in basement one. I grabbed Fidget's bag and battle jacket, escorted her down in the lifts, and helped her into the back of their car. She buckled in, lay down and pulled a thick blanket over her, like a suspect leaving court, trying to avoid the press.

'You're Top Floor, right?'

'Oh, er, yes.'

'Thanks for looking out for her. Look, take my number, send me a message with your details and we can keep you updated.' They leaned close to my ear and whispered, 'There was a brick through her window, so we're keeping her away from there. Sarah's at the apartment now boarding it up, so it should be secure until things settle down.'

'I'm just glad she has people looking out for her and a place to stay.'

Once they were gone, I returned again to my little office, where I sat, staring into nothing, trying to understand how the hell anyone could think treating another person like that was a reasonable response to the imagined idea they'd included features in a game which you didn't like.

Parts of Rick and Chad's talk at AAX SSE floated into my mind. The nurturing of tribalistic behaviour, making sure that players make Supremacy's games their whole life. To that kind of person, deep in the cult, injury to the game is an injury to them.

As for the company response, while I wasn't expecting Hannah to start personally chastising furious Gamer bros, I couldn't believe there wasn't at least some kindness, a touch of human empathy. If this is a family, it's a neglectful one.

I can't rely on anyone in power here. They're bosses. Just like Dink in every *Prophecy of Zebdo* game, it's my job to defeat bosses, and save the kingdom. I will stand against the darkness and triumph over evil.

# CHAPTER 4

# Eggs, Eggs Everywhere

Fidget isn't coming back. HR barely acknowledged her resignation letter, outlining her reasons for leaving. Bread messaged to let me know they'd received nothing more than a simple acknowledgement of the resignation, along with a reminder that she'd need to return her ID and any other company property within ten business days. Meanwhile, online shit rained down on her like they'd filled the Hoover Dam with raw sewage and blown a hole in it right above her head.

Last weekend I took the bus over to visit her and her partners. It was very welcoming and homely, impressive what you can afford with seven people sharing the bills and responsibilities. We ran a tabletop RPG session which Sarah had designed. I played a penguin postal worker who was secretly passing intel to the bunny resistance. It was great; we got to overthrow a fascist poodle and Fidg acquired a magical talking sword that only spoke in limericks and had a hilarious 'Bri'ish' accent – 'cor blimey' and all that.

Afterwards, we sat quietly together and Fidg told me her plans.

'I love games, I'll probably still play them... but I never want to be involved in them again. I'm not going on forums or fan pages

71

and I'm definitely not reading the comments section on a review. Games are wonderful. Gamers™ are… inhuman.

'I've got something lined up with an animation studio. They need prop and furniture modelling for some super-detailed sci-fi movie. My home rig is powerful enough to run their software, so I don't even have to leave the house.' Her jaw tightened and she turned away from me, as if that small acknowledgement of her fear of what was out there had brought it all back.

Composure regained, she continued, 'My new boss was really understanding. I told him a little about Supremacy Software during the interview, when asked about why I left my last job, and he was very sympathetic. Immediately gave me details of the staff union, talked me through their policies regarding staff harassment, pointed me to examples of how they'd taken action in the past. Imagine that: a plan *and* a proven history of implementing it.'

'I'm really glad they could show you that up front. It's got to be comforting.'

'It really is. I think it's just what I need right now.' She smiled.

## Meeting minutes – 4 April
Drinks orders for the board:
Edwin – purple power juice
Rick – eleven-shot latte
Chad – twelve-shot latte

Now that we're back in the office, keeping Rick and Chad's drink orders a secret has become more complicated. Chad went to the effort of having a small video communication thing installed in the executive kitchen, so he could watch me prepare the coffees this morning. He wants to make absolutely sure that he's getting the greater amount of espresso in his cup.

I simultaneously almost crapped my pants and scalded myself when, as I was taking shots four and five off of the machine, his voice came suddenly out of the tinny speaker that formed part of the camera setup. No harm done, luckily, to clothing or skin.

Edwin's order this morning contained activated charcoal. It's become a popular ingredient in recent years, not just black ice cream at Halloween, but toothpastes and apparently health drinks now. The problem is, they also use it in medical settings for preventing drug absorption. I really hope he doesn't take any important medications, as this stuff could stop them working entirely. I did try to warn him, but he muttered something about 'bunch of snowflake kids these days', grabbed his beverage, and, staring me straight in the eye, drank it down in one go. After which, he added, 'You know what, I think I'll have another.' And slid the empty glass down the table towards me like I was the bartender in a Western.

That's the most he's spoken to me since I started work here, and I'm looking forward to resuming my usual status of being largely ignored.

Once Edwin was furnished with his second shot of charcoal and liquid vitamins, the meeting was permitted to begin.

'So, second quarter. Things have started to slow again. How about some, uh, some free DLC.' Chad's smile was already on his face as he looked to the others for approval and validation.

I'd seen this already. Yep. Next they all laugh like it's the first time they've heard it.

*cue laughter*

They'll need a theme, let's see, April. Of course.

'Who has suggestions for some Easter content?' Chad asked.

Eggs on everything.

'Gotta be eggs on everything.'

Am I stuck in a time loop? Is it just going to be reskinned versions of the same meeting every few months until the company bank balance becomes so massive that it collapses in on itself like a black hole and crushes the earth to the size of a grain of sand?

'What if the bomb was an egg?'

'Egg grenades!'

'Give the T-Rex bunny ears.'

'Can we get away with a T-posing Jesus on a cross in the hills level? T-pose is still a meme, right?'

Part of me knew that I should have been horrified, watching it all unfold, but four months in and I can already feel myself becoming numb to the predictable mundanity of corporate greed.

If it wasn't for the loan I took to get here, I'd be gone. I begged and pleaded with Mom to sign the guarantee, so I could get approved. Now I can't risk messing up or I screw her life up too. So much for my 'dream job'.

I can't even go to another big company for a similar job. From what I saw while we were travelling, it's the same everywhere.

Outside of the developer panels the GGF was full of self-congratulatory execs repeating their excuses time and time again. Perhaps hoping that with repetition even they would start to believe their own bullshit.

'Gamers need to be constantly dripfed a diet of limited-time, paid DLC.'

'A high workforce turnover is healthy and *necessary*, to keep things fresh.' Definitely nothing to do with people burning out, or worse. Certainly not.

While wandering the show floor at AAX SSE, I saw half a dozen companies peddling builds of games which looked too good to be true, while men in suits refused to answer the tough questions.

'Will your ambitious list of new features be ready in time for launch?'

'Has your annual release cycle forced you to crunch your developers considerably beyond their contracted hours?'

'Has the shift to DLC in recent years led to you holding features back from your main releases, so you have something in the bank that you can sell as a later add-on?'

'Following reports that your QA department were unhappy with their treatment at the company and that many were seeking to organise collective action, would you care to comment on the rumours that you've responded to this by engaging in union-busting tactics?'

Their PAs, much like myself, were being used as a shield for delicate sensibilities. Gods forbid an executive feel the discomfort of having to actually give an account of their callous actions.

That was the event where, while sitting in that backroom dystopia, a fellow PA from Game CommandPost invited me to join a private chat server for people in our position. Said it was a 'healthy void to scream into'.

I've checked it out; there's a lot of memes and shitposts, but also a whole channel dedicated to airing grievances about the latest shady nonsense our companies have been up to.

I'm too scared of anyone finding me out to dare risk breaching Supremacy's iron-tight non-disclosure agreement by posting anything myself, but it's been curious seeing what others on the inside have to share.

```
Me: *brings my boss their coffee the same way for
    two years*
Boss: *sips coffee*
spittake.jpg
```

```
Boss: wtf is wrong with you? I stopped taking
      sugar at the weekend.
Boss: *throws coffee on the floor for me to clean
      up*
Me *didn't pick the psychic perk*
sad_trombone.mp3
```

```
stuck in a board meeting today. 6 men spent 2 hours
bouncing ideas around for how best to make our main
character (cute female racoon) 'more explicitly
fuck-worthy'. I love being a woman in this industry.
I feel totally safe. hahahahah, save me
```

```
Was made to tell the dev team we're doubling
their workload from today. the reason? man up
top wants the art style changed from realistic
to saturday morning cartoon. shouldn't take too
long, right? not like animation is completely
dependent on the character's proportions or
anything #TellMyWifeILoveHer
```

This industry is rotten to the core.

Back to the meeting. They were still droning on and on. Spewing out low-effort, definitely offensive, religious iconography they could slap on the side of a gun or in a loot box. Eventually they tired themselves out and moved on to X3 – the eXtreme electronicX eXpo (a name so forced it should come in robes and carry a laser sword) which is coming up at the start of June.

'We need to wow that crowd. We gotta make it big, bigger than big. Huge. Let's give them a spectacle they won't soon forget,' Rick enthused.

'Yeah. We need multimedia. It's a Hollywood level-trailer, full CGI, a soundtrack that will make their ears bleed; we're in uniform to give the announcement.'

'Good, but more. Uh... It's not a booth, it's a set, it's an experience.'

'They need to run through the sand and dodge bullets, if they wanna go hands-on with this thing.'

'Well if they're going hands-on, you know what we have to do.'

There was a brief pause before Rick and Chad cried in unison, 'Vertical slice time.'

Leaving aside for a moment Chad's suggestion that we have people shooting at members of the public who just want some free merch and a chance to see the game – something which I'm sure will absolutely thrill the legal team – we're left with the fundamental dishonesty of a 'vertical slice demo.'

Do you have a game you're desperate to publicise? Is it nowhere near finished? Why not make a highly scripted and narrowly focused tech demo. Be sure to try such classic vertical slice features as: gameplay elements which will never be seen again, pre-rendered graphics which couldn't possibly exist in your real game engine, and on-rails sections designed to give the illusion that the player is in control. All this and more could be yours with a vertical slice demo.

Not only are they all smoke and mirrors, but more than once, they've completely backfired on the companies who used them. Not five years ago, Andrew Hopworth showed off a vertical slice demo of *Company Soldiers: Void Battle*. The games press went wild for it. It was right at the top of every outlet's 'most anticipated games of the year' list. And then it released.

The graphics looked nothing alike; no fancy lighting, no ray-traced shadows. No sign of the promised procedurally generated water effects. No evidence of the smart AI system which could allegedly form advanced tactics based on real world military strategy. Instead enemies would run into corners and pound their heads against the wall as if they'd been programmed with severe artificial depression.

In six months it went from being the most pre-ordered game in history, to a multi-million-dollar class-action lawsuit.

Mr Hopworth said he was 'very sorry to anyone who felt disappointed or misled' and that he'd 'learned a lot from this experience'.

Somehow he's still head of that company, though. Somehow he still earned a huge bonus that year.

No mention of whoever was running their socials or the number of death threats they received. Of course.

'This has to be perfect, so I say we put two thirds of the development team on the project,' insisted Rick.

I asked – just to be sure I understood the situation, 'Is taking so many people off the main game, again, definitely a good idea? It's just that they've not yet had a single calendar month in which the full team was working on the main game and, er, that release window is getting pretty close.'

Rick looked almost pityingly at me and replied, 'Nothing gets done by the timid, sweetheart. You wanna go far, you go hard, go big, and you make damn sure everyone's talking about you like you're bigger than gods. Then us here and every one of those nerds downstairs ride the hype train right to the top of the mountain.'

He really believes that's all the project requires: hype. Sure, who needs time and resources when you have the hype train (careening dangerously around a sharp corner at ridiculous speeds and looking ready to run out of track in, oh I don't know, about six months).

'Look, if the developers aren't willing to put in the needed work, we let them all go and hire new people: people with vision. Make a press release, tell them it's a whole new team taking over to make our game the best it can be – they'll eat it all up.'

Forget for a second the gross injustice of just disposing of people who don't prove themselves to be superhuman, there is no way a whole new team could just step in, understand what's already been done, and continue on with it at this late stage. These men are unbelievable: they don't have the first clue about the realities of what they're asking.

It seemed like we were ready to wrap up when Chad, chuckling mirthlessly down at his notes, said, 'I guess we should really talk about the Roger... thing.'

The previously jovial energy seemed to evaporate and Rick sighed loudly.

Finally, some good news. Hopefully they're doing something about that creep before some other junior or intern gets caught in a lift with him. After my warning from Candace and Jenette, I've stayed well clear, but the couple of interns I warned said they'd already experienced him 'first *hand*'. I didn't like the emphasis on 'hand'.

Still, news has reached the top floor that Roger has been having 'a bit of fun with some of the newbies' and apparently it was reported to HR. For a moment I'd hoped that Hannah would have torn him a new one and had him out on his ear. No such luck: he's being 'reallocated to another department'. Turns out this is about the fourth time that they've organised 'the ol' cushioned landing' for Mr Roger Meinder.

It's not good enough. Staff that are being treated like crap by the public are unsupported and left to deal with it on their own. Meanwhile, creeps like Roger are handled with kid gloves and gently moved around the company so as not to cause a fuss. As for his victims, they're supposed to just accept his 'reallocation' as sufficient punishment for the harm done. On top of that, Finance will actually be paying him better than his previous role, so technically this is a promotion. I feel physically sick just thinking about it, but I'm not going to let this break me. I've been taking notes, I'll copy emails, keep the receipts, and, when the time finally comes, all this will come out. Then they'll get what they deserve.

Considering how loose-lipped they are, I probably won't have to wait long for them to entirely incriminate themselves.

### LUNCH

I'm still on sandwiches from home, but that's the price of paying down my loan as fast as possible. I don't know about tightening my belt, it's basically a waist trainer at this point. I had intended on sharing lunch with Ez today, but she didn't show. Hopefully it wasn't anything too serious.

There was one pleasant surprise though. Just as I was getting ready to head downstairs, one of the guys from the post room dropped by with a chunky envelope. The 'Private and Confidential, To Be Opened By Addressee ONLY' stamp was worrying, as it was giving me debt-collector vibes. However, inside was a new security pass. A new pass, with a new photograph. The one Jenette took of me a couple of weeks back.

NOTE TO SELF – Send thank-you cake to Jenette.

### P.M.

I headed to the dev floor to break the news to the team leaders about the numbers needed for the Easter event and the vertical slice. The mood was pretty grim, but there was no argument this time, just resigned grunts before they shuffled out of the room and back to their teams. I really can't blame them: the shifting whims of the executive team are exhausting.

As I was heading back upstairs, I bumped into Ez, hurriedly shovelling a slice of pizza into her face while walking back to her desk.

'Oh hey, missed you at lunch today.'

'Gods, yeah, sorry. Completely lost track of time. They pulled us into a catch-up meeting with the team. Well, less of a catch-up and more of a "hey, we're splitting the team up again because upstairs wants more DLC" meeting. You're looking at the new face of pastel egg duty. I'm sure you can think of no one more colourful and fluffy than I to take on this role.' Despite dark circles around her eyes, she still managed to look somewhat upbeat.

'Yikes. That sounds like actual torture, to surround you with that much pastel, that many bunnies.'

'Didn't even get T-posing Jesus. I'd have loved that.'

'The stigmata will never be the same without you.'

'Right?!'

I saw a light flick on in her mind, followed by a quick scan of the area, before she grabbed my arm with surprising strength, pushing me close to the wall where she whispered, 'Thank you so much for the warning about Roger. That guy is a sex pest of the highest order.' She forced a smile and through gritted teeth continued, 'He's "got a thing for tattooed ladies" you know.'

'Freaking yikes.' I did my own quick survey of the area before leaning in and quietly adding, 'It sounds like they're moving him to another department, so hopefully you won't see him again.'

'Moving him? They need to fire him.'

'Tell me about it. Listen, if you do need to report anything to HR, probably best to do so in writing, so you have a paper trail. You can always BCC me in if you want an extra witness.'

'Smart. Oh, and I don't know if the grapevine runs all the way upstairs, word is there's some journalist sniffing around. Not just after Roger, but Hannah and the whole damn executive team. So... be careful, yeah?'

She seemed to go limp. Like she'd sputtered to a halt after running the last few miles on empty. 'I'd better get back. Those high-powered assault rifles won't just make themselves pretty and pink.'

I waved goodbye and watched her slouch towards her desk.

I didn't dare openly discuss that I'm also gathering information, but every scrap of evidence could be important when the time comes. If I can help make things better in the industry, even for just these few people, perhaps coming to work here wasn't quite so near the epic end of the fail scale as I've been beginning to fear. I might even get some justice for Fidget.

# CHAPTER 5

# Fresh Air and Sunlight

## 2ND MAY

X3 is now just a few short weeks away, and the deadline for the development team to finish working on the vertical slice is rapidly diminishing. While this polished chunk of game started strong, a month in and the team are majorly starting to flag. The executive team's demands for the demo are completely excessive, and as a result I have watched the dev floor go from a lively and energetic hub of creativity to a future dystopia shanty town populated by the animated corpses of the former dev team. (I shouldn't mention that too loudly, the execs will be stealing the idea for a game— Oh, wait. That's probably too new and untested to be considered marketable.)

Just as I was about to leave the office yesterday, I got a calendar invite from Hannah. Meeting: 9:00 a.m., no subject.

As you can imagine, I slept wonderfully last night and definitely didn't lie awake in the semi-dark making up an infinity of the worst possible scenarios for what she wanted. No, sir.

I forced a Nuclear Blue Raspberry Tornado flavour Meth down myself, in the hopes of not immediately passing out the moment I sat down across from her. She'd chosen to hold the meeting in the same interview room we'd occupied during the dev hiring process. Though I noted that someone, probably Clark, had adjusted the automatic close arm on the door to a more forgiving setting.

'It's been brought to my attention that you've taken it upon yourself to meddle with the executive drink orders lately.'

Oh, that. Really?

So, since purple power juice became Edwin's regular order, he's seemed a lot more alert, but also somewhat erratic. I've been genuinely concerned for his health, so I may have deliberately brought him blue instead of purple, because as far as I'm aware, spirulina doesn't have the drug interactions that charcoal does. He chewed me out at the time, but I thought that was the end of it. I guess not.

'I'd like it on record that I'm worried that his drink of choice might be damaging his physical and or mental health.'

'That's not your job. You don't get to make those decisions. If he asks for a twenty-five-gallon drum of water, drawn fresh from the Hudson that morning, you make damn sure it's there with a fucking cocktail umbrella by the time that meeting starts, or you will find yourself back in Wyoming mining coal with your fucking teeth. Do I make myself clear?'

I could feel myself freaking out. Between the ambient noise and brightness of the room, the way every syllable had reverberated off the wall in a disorienting cacophony, and the fact that a particle of her spit had landed in my eye during her rant, my head felt like it was full of angry bees.

I fumbled around the last few successfully firing synapses for a publicly acceptable repetitive motion and settled with rubbing the tips of my thumbs together and rocking slightly.

Shit – Hannah had asked me something, but I hadn't processed it.

Keep rubbing, try and focus. 'I—'

'Do. I. Make. Myself. Clear?'

'Y-y-y-yes,' I eventually forced out.

'Good.' She stood and headed for the door. 'Sort yourself out before you walk across the dev floor. No one wants to see that.' The door clicked shut behind her, leaving me to deal with the bees alone.

In unseen solitude I was able to calm down in my own way, without fear of how anyone else would react to it. In ten minutes I'd contained the worst of it, and figured I could make it safely upstairs.

As I walked back through the development floor, I was praying I wouldn't bump into Ez. I was up and moving like normal, but I was quite sure my voice would be out of service for a while yet.

Looking over the ocean of desks littered with trash, I noticed a few small structures had been built at some of the workstations. There were sleeping bags under tables, desktop microwaves stationed at the end of aisles, and at least a few staff taking wet-wipe showers while still at their keyboards.

I spotted Ez busily typing away and, a desk or two over, where Kyle usually sits, a small hut, consisting of takeaway boxes and what I was fairly certain was one of the cubicle doors from the bathroom.

NOTE TO SELF – Let Clark know about the missing door. Probably best to just get a new one rather than try to wrestle it back from Kyle, who appears to be going feral.

It's pretty clear to me that the whole team is on the brink of total burnout. They desperately need a break to recover before they all collapse. They're not getting much actual work done, despite the literal days some of them sit in front of their computers.

Once back in the familiar safety of my little office, I checked my inbox to find that the executives had called an emergency meeting for an hour's time. I should just about be able to brew the requisite amount of espresso by then.

## Meeting minutes – 5 May

Drinks orders for the board:

Edwin – a double purple power juice (just to show me – a snowflake kid – what's dangerous or not)

Rick – fifteen-shot latte

Chad – fourteen-shot latte

'So, what are we going to do about the fact our developers are broken? We're already at stage two exhaustion, and it's four per cent earlier than last time.'

'What about a few days of paid time off?'

Here it comes.

*cue laugther, etc.*

Except... it wasn't quite the same as usual. The boys were doing the standard routine, but Edwin was going louder and longer than the others. Almost aggressively so. It was like he'd taken up professional, competitive laughing at a tired joke and was determined to go for gold. His face went beet red and the veins in his forehead bulged and pulsated as he went on and on, until the others had fallen silent and he was absolutely sure he'd beaten them.

Something wasn't right, but Hannah had made it painfully clear that it was none of my concern.

Once he settled down, Rick proposed an overnight corporate team-building exercise. I was initially worried that this would mean weird group activities like building a bridge out of pasta while blindfolded and hopping, but apparently he was actually thinking of paintball. The idea being 'fresh air and exercise' would 'get their creative juices flowing again'.

I didn't bother asking what that meant for the remaining time on the vertical slice demo, as it's clear by now they don't even care about practicality. The universe must bend to their combined will.

Still, it's been said that a change is as good as a holiday; maybe it will help with morale.

## P.M.

The afternoon was spent booking tickets and arranging coaches to collect everyone first thing in the morning to head to Splat Zone.

It's about an hour out of the city with clear traffic, but Chad wants everyone 'up and at 'em by 5 a.m. so we don't waste the day'.

I made the announcement to management about it and there were a few strange looks around the table. I wasn't quite sure what it was about until I got back to my office and realised I'd been – most likely accidentally – tagged into a sweepstake among the seniors to bet on which of the dev team wouldn't be coming back.

Yikes, and, furthermore, ew.

## 6 MAY

Barely awake, I managed to get an OovooCar to the office in time to help round up everyone for the trip. The driver was perfect and happy to forgo chat. Initially, I thought he'd taken one look at me and realised I was barely awake at that time of the morning.

If the bags under my eyes didn't give it away, the strange feeling on my head as I climbed out made me realise I still had a towel wrapped around it. I managed to whip it off and into my bag as fast as lightning, but I know he saw. Well, that's something new to add to my list of personal failures that run screaming through my mind in the small hours of the morning when insomnia is kicking my ass.

I paid him more than my month's food budget in fares and topped it up with the most generous tip I could muster, in the hope that the extra green would offset any memory of Towel Woman, should someone later ask if he's had any oddballs in the back today. Anyway, I'm going to slip the receipt in with the executive expenses and hope that no one notices. I mean, it *was* a business expense that I had to be in at that unholy hour of the morning.

Up on the dev floor, there was some trouble getting Kyle out of his makeshift home away from home. At one point he tried to bite someone, but one of the security guards grabbed him by the back of the neck and carried the poor, confused guy off like a puppy.

Outside stood a line of ancient school buses which looked like they'd been decommissioned from use when my Gram Gram was still in school. Their paintwork was faded and flaked, some had moss growing on the wheel arches, and all of them looked like they'd been rotting in a yard somewhere until I'd called the hire place yesterday (as directed by the job bible, naturally).

Once everyone was loaded up, I took my place on board the lead vehicle, feeling like the teacher in charge of a school trip. Luckily, my charges were very well behaved, just a little confused by the outside world as a whole. Well, what little of the outside world could be seen through the lichen-tinted windows. As the sun finally rose, bathing the cabin in a sickly-looking light, I noticed Kyle, breathing in short, shallow breaths, muttering something about how he hadn't implemented that yet and someone must be messing with his code.

Most of the others had quickly passed out on the cheap, dusty bench seats as we made our way out of the city. Possibly the first good sleep many of them have had in weeks. Although that only lasted forty minutes or so. When we pulled off the main road around 06:30 and onto the muddy, potholed track towards the collection of log cabins, huts and tents that comprised the public entrance to Splat Zone itself, several of us were catapulted into the ceiling of the decrepit vehicles. Part of me worried that someone was going to end up with tetanus if they had managed to break through the rusty shell, but luckily we were able to avoid that particular peril.

Stepping off the bus, we were greeted by a shorter woman, dressed head to toe in black combat fatigues, with enough belts and pouches to look like she'd been lifted right out of *Penultimate Legacy XXVIII-α*. She marched smartly up to me and I introduced myself as the one in charge of getting us here. She shot back a sharp salute and barked, 'Rosario, Splat Sergeant Major and owner of the Zone.'

Her hair was very dark, cut military short, and her arms looked powerful enough to snap everyone who was currently stepping off those buses in half and use us like toothpicks. She went for a handshake and I momentarily feared that she'd crush me to dust. Since I'm writing this, you know that she managed to hold back, but only barely. Something definitely made a popping sound.

It was then that I noticed on her upper arm was a huge tattoo of a dagger through a skull with a snake wrapped around it. To be honest, if you'd described her to me and said, 'She has a tattoo – guess what it is', that's exactly what I would have predicted, but I'd have been too scared to laugh about that because she might somehow find out, track me down, kill me, and make it look like a wild animal attack.

The introductions done, she turned on her heel, strode past me and went immediately into full drill-sergeant mode. Bellowing safety instructions and ordering the barely conscious devs to get their 'worthless hides' into one of the huts to get kitted out in appropriate clothing. Then bellowing again to order them to another hut to pick up a weapon. The poor devs didn't even seem to know what day it was, and suddenly they were being treated like they were in boot camp.

I later caught one of the 3D artists trying to 'fix a shader issue' on a tree, so I felt like some of them might need time to adjust to the outside world.

They all looked somewhat dazed, standing around in their ill-fitting, muddy red shirts, oversized and torn camo trousers and grimy plastic goggles. Though that may just be the caffeine-withdrawal headaches setting in.

Two hours later, an all-black-and-chrome military-style vehicle rolled up, somehow completely untouched by any of the mud from the dirt track. Out stepped Rick and Chad in full camo outfits. Not your typical army-surplus gear, either. For a start it was fully tailored, for another thing I saw the label, and it's all from the Costose Stronzate wartime range. No way either of them was wearing less than $4,000 suits, even in the woods. I'm fairly certain their boots were Stephenie Dunn originals too. Gods, I could have put down a deposit on a shoebox apartment of my very own for the price of their outfits for the day.

It didn't end there, either. From the back of the vehicle, they pulled out matching leather cases. Each contained a very fancy-looking paintball gun in sleek matte black. Nothing at all like the dirty, sticky, paint-splattered guns that had clearly seen a lot of use by excitable children hopped up on sugar from The Quartermaster's Tent currently being toted by my coachmates. These looked as good as new and at least ten times the cost.

The boys stood spinning their weapons around, checking the

completely unnecessary laser sights and posing for about fifteen minutes before Hannah arrived to do their camo make-up. How she managed that with her three-inch tactical assault nails, I'll never quite understand, but she was able to pull it off without any accidental eye removal or transorbital lobotomies.

This was followed by a further ten minutes of selfies, posturing and self-congratulation. Finally Rick announced that the teams would be developers and interns on one side and myself, Legal, HR and the executives on the other. I was initially surprised that they'd pit such a small number against the combined might of nearly 200 sleep-deprived people who have every right to want to actually kill them for their actions. Especially since it was at this point someone announced that The Quartermaster's Tent stocked Crimson Method Tactical Fusion Matrix, and the opposition marched off to get their caffeine goo fix.

Rosario called out for those of us who didn't have guns to go and get equipped in the armoury hut. I noted that the guns we were being handed seemed in much better condition than those given to our opponents. While theirs had seemed like what might be pulled out for an eleventh birthday party, ours looked like those saved for capable adults and staff. Definitely less chance of chewing gum in the firing mechanism, to be sure.

In the other hut I was handed a full set of clean (and surprisingly fresh-smelling) camo, along with a full face mask – no basic plastic goggles for us, it seemed. It wasn't until I got my gear on  – a concerningly good fit – that I noticed the embroidered Supremacy Software logo on the pocket. I really don't want to think about how they got my measurements, but it was clear that everyone on my team had a kit that actually fit them and not the generic weekend warrior basic camo they usually hand out at these places.

Outside again, I took the opportunity to head to the test range to try out my gun. Nothing special, but it seemed to fire mostly straight with a reasonable drop off over distance. Unlike some of my colleagues, who I noted seemed to have weapons that would fire constantly to one side, just dribble out of the barrel and onto the floor, or occasionally jam entirely. Luckily the marshals on site were able to instruct them on how to clear jams, though it looked like a real hassle. Still, it was just to be a friendly day in the woods, no need to worry about a minute or two of downtime here and there.

Finally, at around 10 a.m., Rosario called us all to order and gave us the rundown on rules and how we could identify the outer boundaries of the play area that would be our home for the next twenty-four hours. Getting hit didn't mean that you were out, but it did force you to hold up your hand and walk back ten yards.

As we were the smaller team, we were granted a five-minute head start. And so, at the sound of a shrill whistle, we sprinted off into the woods with Rick and Chad in the lead. Initially it seemed odd that they and the legal team were of one mind concerning our best direction. However, after a short while, we came upon a fortified tower in the centre of the play area. This was the second red flag that something was up with this whole outing.

Inside the tower were beds, supplies, a microwave and fridge-freezer as well as wall sockets for charging phones. The fridge was filled with light beer and ice tea. The freezer, to my surprise, was packed to the brim with spare ammo. They'd taken the drawers and shelves out and filled the entire space with boxes and boxes of paintballs. Something that confused me as the temperature was pretty manageable, so unlikely that there was a risk of them just melting before we could use them.

The boys took up positions at the top of the tower and started making practice shots of their own. I noted that their ammo was doing less of a splash as it impacted on trees. More of a dull, hard thud.

Not long afterwards, the first squad of freshly caffeinated devs came screaming out of the trees and into the clearing around the fortress before fanning out, attempting to surround us. For a moment, I felt a smile forming. A little harmless revenge on those in charge should be pretty cathartic for the dev team, and surely their sheer numbers would be enough to see them receive that reward. I could imagine them overtaking this tower and kicking us out before the hour was up.

All around me was the 'putt-putt' sound of gas-propelled pellets, punctuated with yelps as people were hit. Though it seemed that all of those were coming from outside.

I huddled close to the edge of the window before me, peering carefully out before sliding around to take my shots. Despite having carefully avoided firing a real gun my whole life, it seemed that my time playing arcade shooters had prepared me sufficiently.

With a wet splat, bright-orange liquid erupted from the shoulder of my target, causing them to reel back with a yelp. They raised their hands and started to step back, as per the rules, but that didn't stop several more shots from either side of me thudding into the surrendering developer, who gave up on procedure, turned tail and fled beyond sight.

Sensing that their initial rush was having no effect, a few of the devs took shelter behind a fallen tree, while others retreated back into the dense cover at the edge of the clearing. From that range it was obvious that, even with some height correction, their shots were falling well short of reaching our location.

Not so from above though. Rick and Chad's shots met their marks with pinpoint accuracy and seemingly much greater force. When Ez popped up from the cover of a stump and began retreating while firing blindly behind, I watched as a shot whizzed out from above and caught her in the calf, sending her rolling in agony into the leaf litter, whereupon those around me drove the point home by peppering her with additional injury. She howled and swore and, barely able to get her feet under her, scrambled away to safety on all fours.

Watching my friend brutally kicked while she was down, I wiped the last notion that this was just some harmless fun from my mind, or that there was any chance this was a fair game that the devs might have a chance of winning. It was made all the worse as I could hear cruel laughter echoing from on high as they saw off the last of our opposition from the clearing. I just sat there, the barrel of my paintball gun balanced on the ledge, staring out at the scene before me. Unwilling to fire and feeling like the worst kind of traitor.

Shortly after, the boys called for beer, with which they toasted the successful repulsion of the initial assault.

I guess that the devs took some time to form a plan of attack, as things were quiet for nearly half an hour. Then, from the far side of the clearing, I heard a long war cry. There was a scramble all around as Legal took up positions to protect the rear. A small group of background artists, moving in tight formation, charged our position. Shots rained down on them, but since our team had broken the bond of trust that we wouldn't shoot those who had acknowledged being hit, they were no longer just surrendering and walking back.

They got within fifty feet before Alex, one of the younger guys who specialises in architectural features, stumbled on a tree root and tumbled to the floor. As he went down, I saw he'd been shielding a team of three within the approaching group. Each of them was dual-wielding guns, which they began to raise, thinking this was the moment to open fire upon us, only to trip over the lead man, sending the whole party down. The paint-bath which followed was barbaric.

'They're coming from both sides!' Rick cried from above.

There was a brief stampede as half of our team moved back to default positions. Sure enough, I saw Kyle's face leaning in at my window. He rapidly fired into the building, hitting several of those who were heading back in that direction, before scrambling up the outer wall, seemingly planning to get to the execs.

The next thing I knew, he fell past my line of sight and hit the ground with a loud thud. The sound of shots was overwhelmingly loud as swift revenge rained down upon him.

He wailed and cursed as he hopped the outer fence, ready to escape, but his belt got snagged on a bent nail and he found himself trapped. From that distance I could hear the repeated thud of gel pellets against barely protected skin, even above the sound of the constant gas release.

'Stop! I— Someone help me! Ah! Please. Fuck.' He sobbed and begged and fought with the buckle to try and get free, but there was no quarter, no help, just more cruel laughter and a seemingly endless onslaught of pain.

By the time he escaped from his tether on the fence, he looked like he'd been dropped in the slime tank on some Saturday-morning kids' show.

I must have started to dissociate, as the next thing I knew, I was being shouted at to bring more beer and ammo to the executives.

'That shot in the back was some awesome work!' Rick congratulated his colleague as I reached their vantage point.

'Oh yeah, and it's way more satisfying than when I did that big game hunt. I couldn't believe they tranquillised the lions for tourist hunters.'

I handed them their beers in silence, wanting nothing to do with either one, but as I collected up the empties from the ledge before Chad's window he asked, 'Liking the view from the top, sweetheart?'

I gave a fairly neutral noncommittal grunt in response and made my way back below.

'The view from the top.' It echoed around in my mind on repeat. By virtue of my position in the company, I had been given special perks. I was seen as one of them, no matter how much I consider myself more on the level of Ez and the devs. Suddenly 'Top Floor' felt less affectionate and more a sign of my being an outsider.

This is meant to be a team-building event, but up there, untouchable in the tower, with only Rick and Chad for company, I realised that this was no different to the way things are any other day, back at the office. Those far below will suffer and struggle, meanwhile I, by proximity to those in power, am protected from the worst of things.

There were a few more attacks during the day, but it seemed like a lot of the fight had gone out of the development team, and who could blame them. Even at close range, their weapons couldn't reach the lords in their tower.

Come nightfall, the attempts on our stronghold had dwindled yet further, but as the last light of the sun sank behind the treeline, I heard a familiar power-up noise coming from upstairs. This was followed by gas gunfire, and the now-familiar squelch of immediate bruising from outside.

I later found out that night-vision goggles don't actually make that noise, which means that the boys must have had theirs custom-made to sound like they do in the movies. To me, it comes across as pretty pathetic. Ego-stroking men just wanting to feel yet more powerful.

Not long after, Rosario turned up with a lit flare, pushing a wheelbarrow full of Chinese takeaway. We ate well.

Ez dropped me a text to let me know that the dev team had to go back to The Quartermaster's Tent and pay for their food. A little difficult for some as they'd been poured out of the office and onto the bus without much warning. I promised I'd do my best to text her updates regularly, so she could help others organise and avoid the worst of the damage. Any info I could feed down to reduce harm to the devs felt like the least I could do.

In the small hours an alarm went off on somebody's phone, and HR were sent on a sortie to find our opponents while they slept. I woke up when they returned several hours later, looking very pleased with themselves. According to Ez, shots were fired at near point blank range. Some of those shot are refusing to go back to sleep, and are now determined to stay awake until the bus back, to keep others safe.

At some point during the following morning, after a fresh delivery of frozen ammo to Rick, I watched a rock-hard paintball shatter Marta's safety goggles and smash into luminous-orange chunks on the floor. Luckily she wasn't hurt, and even the legal team had the decency to not keep firing while she was unprotected. Some shred of humanity left in them perhaps, or maybe just a lawsuit they didn't think even they could win.

Thankfully, a few hours after sunrise, a siren sounded to declare the event over. As we made our way back to base, someone shot Chad in the back of the head. I struggled to keep from laughing, as it was the closest either of them had come to liquid paint for the whole event. Chad looked absolutely furious though, and it didn't escape my notice that in the week or so that followed the six people in the party behind us vanished from the payroll and their desks.

The ride back to the office was awkward. Many of the devs were sporting huge, painful bruises; Marta's forehead was so swollen you couldn't see her eyes; some struggled to even sit down due to the pain of their many and various injuries; and several were curled into balls by the windows, sobbing silently. The rest certainly did look more alert, if a little twitchy. Anxiety mixing with Crimson Method and adrenaline. Nobody slept on the ride back, they seemed afraid to let their guard down. This is a workforce fuelled by fear.

Once I'd finished helping my injured colleagues off of the bus, I was summoned up to the boardroom for a debrief. The boys seemed to think that everything had gone swimmingly and that this would definitely lead to improved focus and speed in the development team's work.

While I thought it had all been considered and accounted for in advance, Chad informed me that we were now behind on working on the vertical slice demo. As such, he's ordering everyone except Jeremy over to work on the demo, to make sure it's perfect in time for X3.

While I'm told Jeremy is 'a real jack of all trades', I'm not sure how much he can really achieve, trying to solo a project this size, regardless of how multi-talented he may be.

### 19 MAY

About 11 a.m., I got an email from Rick, asking me to arrange a private ambulance to the office. No further explanation apart from that it had to be the discreet service and that the paramedics were to pull up into the executive car park and use their private elevator.

As usual, the manual provided all the details for this and, remarkably quickly, I was informed by security that they'd arrived.

I'd never been down there before, but it was no surprise that in a parking lot with at least ten spaces, somehow the three people permitted to park down there had managed to use every single one, thanks to their unique style of parking.

I was greeted by two gentlemen in white boiler suits and mirrored shades. They were tall and imposing, their faces emotionless, their clothes almost glowing in the fluorescent lighting. Between them, they pushed a crash trolley, loaded up with a large white bag which had many pockets, presumably bulging with supplies. Behind them stood a white recreational-style vehicle, with frosted side and rear windows. It was as unmarked as the people who'd driven it here.

Without a word, they flashed ID wallets at me like they were federal agents, and I led them to the elevator. On the ride up to the top floor, I felt deep discomfort. I couldn't hear any breathing but my own, and they made no sign of wanting to ask why they were here. After a painfully long time, which seemed to stretch on into eternity, the lift pinged to announce our arrival. As the doors slid open, we were greeted by Rick, who quickly ushered us into Edwin's office where, much to my shock and surprise, the old man lay splayed on the floor.

I left the ambulance crew to their work and waited outside for further instruction. The boys stood around the door, craning to see what was happening and furiously typing on their phones as I exited. I queried if I should be doing anything, like contacting Edwin's family, and they stopped dead and told me that no one must know anything until they said so. It felt deeply wrong to not contact his family straight away, but knowing these two there's probably money on the line if I talk before they're ready.

After a few more minutes of frantic typing, they started conspiring together about when they could claim the old man's shares, and whether news of this was likely to cause a noticeable dip in the prices thereof. Yep, my suspicions were confirmed. Those absolute vultures stood there, loudly speculating about how this could financially inconvenience them in the short and long term.

This is absolutely vile behaviour. Seriously, a man might be dead and you're treating him like a cash-filled piñata that you can't wait to crack open.

NOTE TO SELF – Buy a Dictaphone. I don't think anyone would believe how ghoulish the boys can be if they couldn't hear the evidence for themselves. It's too much.

It turns out Edwin had suffered a heart attack, due to all the activated-charcoal drinks he's been chugging, which had caused his heart medication not to be absorbed properly. I get that he was chugging them to spite me, but I still feel bad about this. I don't take any glee in him suffering. I mean, I might have felt that way if it were Rick or Chad, but Edwin I still feel some degree of sympathy for. Basically he's been off his statins for nearly two months and his heart was a ticking time bomb.

### 31 MAY

Rick and Chad pulled Jeremy in for a meeting to check on the progress of the main game. This was a first in my experience. I'd never seen them give anyone less senior than HR the time of day. I noted that the temperature in the room had been set to bakingly hot and the usually bright room had very dim lighting. Instead, an Anglepoise lamp was sitting on the table, at the end opposite to Edwin's usual seat. Initially I wondered if we were having technical issues with the office's smart environmental controls.

Jeremy arrived, looking surprisingly bright-eyed, and was motioned to sit in front of the table lamp, as the boys loomed menacingly over him.

'Take a seat,' Chad barked.

'Okay. Hello? I can't really see you back there, the light is rather too bright, you see?' He chuckled and added, 'Because I can't... see that is. Ahem.'

Unmoved by Jeremy's attempt to break the tension, Chad continued, 'You've been taking lead on the project for some time now, how far along is development?'

'Well, I've been getting on with as much as I can on my own. I'd say – staying on the conservative side – maybe twenty per cent.'

'Disappointing.'

'Well, I-I-I mean, I've spent the last three weeks working on getting the jump physics right. There's placeholder—'

'Jump physics?'

'Well, yes, that's my specialisation. Jumping, object physics, things like that. If it's not just an animation and needs to feel realistic, not too floaty, not accidentally plummeting into the void below the map if you happen to jump at just the wrong angle near a wall, or something like—'

'Jeremy. Jez? Can I call you Jez? I'm gonna call you Jez. I've entrusted you with a momentous project. I expected you to use this as your opportunity to shine. Are you going to shine for us, Jez?'

'W-well, I-I'm trying – and really I would rather you call me Jeremy – but you have given me the task of completing hundreds of people's work all by myself... solo. I'm sure you don't really expect me to—'

'That all sounds like excuses, Jez. You think you can just slack off and we won't notice? If people aren't supposed to fall into a void, why did you bother putting one in in the first place? Sounds to me like you're wasting time and resources.'

'No, it's not... That's just—'

'I DON'T WANT TO HEAR IT. GET OUT!' screamed Chad into the terrified developer's face as he slammed his palms down on the desk between them.

There were a few moments of silence while Rick and Chad glared in his direction as he scrambled out of his seat and out of the room. The poor guy was visibly shaking and pouring with sweat.

Once the sound of the elevator doors closed, whisking him away, they broke out into hearty laughter at the whole drama. Congratulating each other on not cracking up while he was still in the room. After which they reset the lighting and temperature controls to normal. I work for monstrous people.

I could leave this place. Maybe I should. But if I do, there won't necessarily be anyone else left here to witness this happening, and do anything about it. Fidg deserves better than to have her suffering swept under the rug, and so does Jeremy.

When I headed downstairs later, I found Jeremy at his desk wearing one of those beer helmets, which he'd filled with Crimson Method Behemoth Sweat. He was typing like the very devil was ready to snatch him to Hell if he dared to stop for an instant, all while he screamed at his screen.

*Those monsters will pay for all this. I'll see to it myself.*

In some serendipitous timing, I received a delivery notification for the Dictaphone I ordered. Tick-tock forces of darkness. I have the first tool in my arsenal, and with it I shall defeat the bosses who terrorise this land.

## CHAPTER 6

# Wait and See

**6 JUNE**

With June rolling around again, it's time for X3. Luckily the team did manage to get a serviceable demo together in time. It's a little prone to crashing in places, but people generally understand that this sort of thing is still in development and 'not representative of the final build'. In the case of this vertical slice, it could not be less representative of the final build as it's about 300 times more complete.

I'm once again on the road with Rick and Chad. This time the dev team will be coming along with us. Although not literally with us; the Devil's nipples would have frostbite before the boys are seen in the same seating class of a plane with anyone who doesn't hold an office on or above the sixty-third floor.

It seemed an odd choice to have yet another week where only poor Jeremy is working on the game proper, but Rick expressed to me how absolutely vital it is that we fly them all out here for the expo. This is because they'll be filling out the front ten rows of the press conference and cheering every full stop and comma in the announcement speech. This used to be done by overly excited fans, but you can't practise cheering with fans in the room, as there's always the risk that one of them will leak details of the announcement.

The boys don't want a repeat of that year where they revealed details of the *Call of Shooty* spin-off about big-headed plastic figures to a room full of unimpressed Gamers™, who'd heard every last detail the day before the announcement, thanks to some overly excited fan who'd been in audience reaction practice sessions. No, the crowd response must be perfectly curated so that those further back will be caught up in the cheers of their peers and make all the right noises for the fans at home. A strategic hype wall to keep the fans singing in the company chorus line.

Meanwhile, the devs are just happy to be away from their desks again. They're probably pretty thrilled to have that impossible demo out of the way at last too. At this point they'll cheer for anything, even the miniature promotional cans of Crimson Method eXtreme Xnergy eXperience Fluid that are being handed out around the Expo floor.

The only people left back at the office who actually do any proper work were Clark, Candace, Jenette, Jeremy, and maybe Edwin – who pulled through from his heart attack, seemingly out of spite and to annoy Rick and Chad. The boys were already having me look into fitting an executive hot tub and smoothie bar in his office, once it was cleared out. The last thing I would need to see wandering round up there is those two in budgie smugglers *gag*.

Jeremy has finally stopped screaming at his screen, but he's also very twitchy and paranoid. He nearly jumped out of his skin the other day when I went to offer him a poppy-seed muffin. It's clear this job is doing some lasting damage to his mental health; he seems to sweat a frightening amount these days for someone who's only form of 'nourishment' intake is imbibing vast amounts of Meth beverages.

We arrived here on Friday, but the event doesn't start until tomorrow (Tuesday). Enough time to help the devs be fully recharged when our press conference rolls around.

Our booth is an enormous recreation of a real-world battlefield. I was proudly informed by Jean-Pierre – the extremely thin, long-limbed, pale, beret-wearing, pencil-moustachioed, (possibly fake) French-accented owner of the installation company – that every single bullet casing had been hand-gathered from a real-world war zone, the razor wire was authentic (though slightly blunted for the safety of the public) and even the barricades and checkpoint turnstiles were recovered after our own military forces departed from 'the country', though he failed to state exactly which country he was referring to. To Jean-Pierre, all this videogame stuff was beneath him; he was a visionary artist, and this was an exhibition of his very important work. I dread to think what he'll say when he's likely sifting Crimson Method Psynaptic Frenzy cans out of his authentic battlefield sand on Friday morning as his team's packing it up.

Once the installation was complete, late on Sunday afternoon, Rick held a meeting with the secondary installation team, made up predominantly of pyrotechnics and stunt coordination technicians who'd been hired for the event.

'It's great to have you here. Now, my original vision for this thing was to have people running across the sand, avoiding gunfire, huge explosions, because war is a lot of fun and focus groups have consistently shown that pointing a gun at something and pulling a trigger is mechanically satisfying.' The assembled techs shared worried looks as he continued, 'But Legal had some "reservations" about that, buncha pussies. So, I want us to go with the next best thing: landmines. That's got to be a thrill, right? Those kids are going to come running across this battlefield and you're gonna work your magic with gas ramps and pyros. All that movie stuff.'

There was some uneasy shuffling before their senior technician stepped up and started issuing orders to his team about how they would go about making it all happen.

On top of the explosive effects, he'd ordered a bunch of retail smoke machines from one of those Chinese 'we stock everything, even the kitchen sink, seriously, we can get you a kitchen sink for like twenty-five cents if you want, we don't even charge shipping' sites.

He had made at least one smart decision in that regard: there would be interns standing by these, just to make sure none of them started smoking in an unintended manner. That said, since the fire extinguishers they were to be equipped with had also come from said site, there's every chance one of those could catch fire too.

The plan seems to be to give the players a real adrenaline rush, so that the memory of how good our demo looks is seared into their brains for ever. Apparently Chad read about the technique in a book on psychology, but I've only ever seen him in the vicinity of one book: *The Skills of the Ultra Seducer*, which he always tries to hide under paperwork whenever anyone else is around.

I suppose, if players are so shocked and awed by the scenery, they may not think too critically about the extremely polished but very narrow section of game they're playing, as well as ignoring any possible bugs they may encounter in this utter sham of a demo.

I've spoken to a few of the now-refreshed developers, and they mostly seem really happy to be here at X3. For many years it was an industry-only event, spoken of excitedly in the gaming press and seen as kind of an impossible paradise for the public. It has been partly open to all for a few years now, but for most people it's prohibitively expensive, even if you can get tickets. As such, this trip is kind of a dream come true for a lot of them.

## Meeting minutes – 7 June

Drinks orders for the board:
One eighteen- and one twenty-shot latte (I just don't give a shit about this pointless caffeine pissing contest anymore).

Today is the day of our X3 press conference, so Rick and Chad ordered a last-minute meeting to talk things out before they start. Immediately following the conference, the show floor will open, allowing the general public to join many and various queues, for a chance to play a whole host of games due out any time from later this year, to some nebulous time in the following millennium.

As well as the public area, there will be private press showings of the game in a separate hotel across the road. We've ordered several crates of okay-at-best champagne as well as hiring a team to freshly barbecue some bulk-ordered burgers for them throughout the day. The hope is that a hot meal, plenty of free booze, and the sense of exclusivity of being invited to the private showing will help influence journalists' opinion of the game. Having seen how haggard some of those journos look already, I'm sure a free meal and a few drinks will probably earn at least some goodwill. Most of them look like they've been surviving on breadsticks and bar olives all week.

My job, once the show floor is open and I've avoided being trampled by the hungry gaming horde, is to keep an eye on the lines for our demo. Rick advised me that in previous years they have needed 'the occasional intervention', whatever that means.

The last point of business before wrapping up the meeting is getting me to finalise a press release they're planning. I was a bit confused as to why they wanted my input, as it just said: 'During this month, we want all players to know we at Supremacy Software appreciate them, no matter who they are, and that we stand by your right to be yourself' on a background of five horizontal stripes (red, gold, blue, white and black).

It took me a hot minute to realise that it's Pride month, and as seemingly the only out, queer person they interact with with any regularity, they wanted me to do a sensitivity read. This was the first time they've managed to avoid being completely tone deaf or using actual slurs, so I guess they are starting to learn. That said, they have neatly sidestepped actually mentioning LGBTQIA+ people at all.

I'll admit, the background threw me, I had to search around for a good while before I discovered it was a Chinese flag from about 1912. I have no idea how that fell onto their radar as Pride related, but that's a mystery for another day.

I did manage to get them to swap the background out for the Progress Pride flag, but they wouldn't budge on the wording. I guess my role is 'queer person internally who looked at it' and not 'person who actually had a voice in its content'.

While fairly vague, it is reasonably supportive, I'll give them a solid 4/10 for effort. An improvement on previous attempts. Could do better.

Once it was posted, it became clear the real reason they were finally acknowledging Pride month a week late was to deflect any online negativity that might come their way during X3. Suddenly, haters are clashing with allies on social media, serving the purposes of increasing engagement, promoting further tribalism among the fanbase, and deflecting any possible negativity regarding the conference itself. You can't criticise a corporation's products when they're mid taking a pro-LGBT stance seems to be the thinking.

One other thing I noticed at that point was that while most territories showed the version of the Pride month graphic I'd helped with, several of the feeds for our socials in more conservative countries either showed only the wording on a black background, or had not posted at all. They won't risk losing sales in Russia just for some half-hearted PR aimed at a community they really couldn't care less about.

While Pride done correctly is a riot and a protest, this is cotton candy corporate pandering with no teeth and no convictions.

NOTE TO SELF – If I am ever able to leave this job, if I get that bonus and it really does make a decent dent in my student loans, I need to post aggressively supportive pro-LGBTQIA+ messages to our social accounts in Dubai and all the others left out today on my way out the door.

Meeting done, I headed over to the theatre, just over the road from the convention centre. From the outside it was just another generic glass and steel building – though decked out with lots of promotional posters for *Call of Shooty* and a few other minor projects we are showing off today.

The walls were plain white, broken every 200 or so feet by huge, mounted speakers. From above the painfully bright lights were diffused through frosted plastic, which did nothing to make them less searingly painful to the eyes. At the front of the room stood a huge stage, backed by a projector screen bigger than any movie screen I'd ever seen. Here and there were staff moving around with clipboards or bundles of cables, and a few rows behind where I was to sit, a technician was checking a small screen attached to the tripod which held the 360° camera from which the at-home e-viewers would be able to experience the event in VR (for almost the price of a normal ticket, but without the horrendous hotel costs usually associated with these things).

It was then that it dawned on me that this was the first time that I'd been able to visit X3 in person. I've been shelling out to do the virtual event for years, but just like the devs, I didn't think I'd ever be able to afford to actually attend. Usually it's me sitting at my home desk, with my Voyage 2 headset on, floating weirdly just above the crowd, and playing that year's unofficial X3 drinking bingo game.

I tried to enjoy the moment, imagining what teenage me would have done to sit right there – with the option to have sat even closer. I had to quiet my inner cynic as best I could and try to just enjoy some of the hype and energy. Having absorbed as much corporate bullshit as I have this year, I deserved that one moment.

I made my way down to the staff seating area and found myself a nice spot a row back from the dev team who, after their first night of decent sleep in months, were bouncing off the walls with the kind of energy that comes from people who've been surviving on far less than four hours sleep for some considerable time.

Finally, they dimmed the lights and shifted the colour to something more reddish. A little ambience for the big event – though it took a few minutes for my poor eyes to recover from their recent photonic assault – and, moments later, journalists and excitable fans started to file in.

Once the room reached capacity, we were plunged into full darkness, and a gloriously distorted electric guitar started to chug out the opening of some pretty epic metal as a sizzle reel of previous Supremacy Software titles flashed by on the seventy-foot-high screen. As the music reached its peak, Rick and Chad entered from the wings, in full tactical gear, carrying (what I hope were) replica weapons to rapturous applause.

During the applause, a deep booming voice over the speakers welcomed those in attendance to the Supremacy Software X3 conference – Sponsored by Crimon Method. The orchestrated timing was impeccable from a marketing perspective, slipped in just quickly enough that the sponsors can probably clip the livestream so there's a few seconds of what appears to be massive applause for their brand. They get a celebration of their energy drinks, and Supremacy Software gets a cash injection that'll fund all of today's pomp and circumstance.

Once the crowd had finally settled somewhat, the pair opened up with a little bit of corporate self-congratulation: Thank you for being here, we do this for you, we're the most successful we've ever been, and we owe it all to you etc. It's all carefully crafted to blow smoke up the crowd so they'll go wild for whatever they see next. Have a little dopamine, our marketing department promises there's more where that came from.

As the crowd started to lean forward, eager for news, the pair set the stage for what was to come. More reveals than ever before, more world exclusives than ever before, and a tease for 'something explosive' that would be shown off before the day was done. Everyone knew it was going to be *Call of Shooty*, they've had teaser websites up for days, but they played the part, pretending it was a huge mystery that could be literally anything people might imagine. You can't just say it's going to be the game everyone knows it's going to be, that ruins the anticipation, you have to leave room for speculation it might not be, that it might be something less exciting, so when it is *Call of Shooty* everyone reacts with relief and excitement.

But, before that big reveal, they were going to be handing the stage to a number of other developers to present some of their own, smaller titles. Again, all part of the hype-building exercise;

ramp up the announcements so by the end people are at a fever pitch, ready to love *Call of Shooty* no matter what is shown of it, just because they've had to wait for it to show up.

As the stage lights finally faded, what followed was an hour and half of trailers from mostly subsidiary studios, owned by Supremacy Software but working independently, outside our main offices. Each shows off projects that they have reasonable editorial control over, but sure have a ton more microtransactions than their titles did before we acquired them.

The show opened on a CGI trailer for a sequel to *The Costs of Medressa*, a high-profile indie game from a few years back that really didn't need a sequel, as its tale of loss and grief ended in a very emotionally satisfying way. The trailer did nothing to explain what a sequel would be about, or why it would be needed, but that didn't stop three minutes of highly produced scene-setting shots, and rapturous applause from an audience ready for a sequel just because the first one was good. If it's critically acclaimed and financially successful, it has to become a series. No release date given, no further details, just 'we're making another one'.

One thing that quickly became obvious as the conference progressed was that Supremacy Software's definition of a 'World Premiere' is incredibly broad. It didn't need to mean the game was being announced for the first time, or even that the trailer is entirely new. So long as there was a few seconds of new footage shown, or some new feature mentioned for a moment, it's another world premiere. It's weaponised hype, and the crowd seemed to be eating it up.

Then there was a lengthy reveal of *Call of Shooty: Abroad*. A mobile release being developed by an external team from China, best known for games that are basically a series of vaguely themed, many-layered microtransactions strung together with advertisements and occasional morsels of gameplay – just to keep the money flowing in. No prizes for guessing why they were the ones chosen for that particular project. It's basically just three microtransactions in a trenchcoat.

The trailer showcased footage that looks not far off the scale and scope of the series' recent console releases. The opacity of the 'not representative of final gameplay' text on screen was set so low that you'd be hard-pressed to spot it without prior knowledge.

Then on to the latest offerings from Candace and Jenette. No surprises there, more deep lore dating sims wrapped around match-three mechanics. The main game being focused on is *Love on the Line*, a game that seems to be about two very beautiful people falling in love while working on an industrial cake-making line. It all seemed very wholesome, though there was a blink-and-you'll-miss-it scene of an extremely handsome man at what looked like a protest, which I still have no idea how it would fit into a game about high-volume baking and decorating.

I glanced over to Rick and Chad, clearly just off the side of the stage, looking bored and doing something on their phones, same went for much of the audience. Perhaps I'd just imagined it, but it seemed really out of place.

Next up was an announcement about the forthcoming *Call of Shooty* TV show which is in the early stages of filming. Only one name I recognised from the cast, but apparently no one memorable, because I already forgot who it was. Tacked on to that was a brief trailer for *Call of Shooty: Contemporary Wartime 2 Remastereder* (which will bring it to three releases for the same once-beloved game in the past fifteen years). Amazingly the audience still went wild for it, so I guess some folk haven't quite gotten bored with it yet.

As the conference went on, I couldn't help but notice the teleprompters, which hung from the ceiling a little behind me. While they're not uncommon to see at events like this, and gods know I'd need one to do a two-hour-long presentation, what was shown to be scripted, and to what degree, made me feel even more disillusioned with this industry.

'We're just so... we're just so proud to have been able to spend the last year... making the games you love. We just couldn't have done this without... You, the players!'

It was hard to see the words '*choked up emotional pause for emphasis*' appear on a screen, a few seconds before Chad gave a seemingly sincere performance to try and win over the crowd. The cynicism shouldn't have surprised me, but I wanted to think there was some magic left for me to find working here. Watching the X3 conferences used to be one of the highlights of my gaming year. Now I can't even enjoy the flashy spectacle of it all.

Then came the trailer for the Pride month DLC. Unlike the social media announcement, this was not something that was run by me first. Just as well, because there's no way I'm taking an ounce of responsibility for that gods-awful decision. One of the most prominently displayed guns literally had a straight Pride flag slapped on the side of it. Meanwhile, the entire bottom third of the screen was taken up with the prominent message 'not available in all regions'. I'm definitely re-marking that previous 4/10 for queer sensitivity which I gave them.

Finally the room grew quiet, and those of us who had experience of conferences like this braced for the 'one more thing' reveal. In a moment the screen burst forth with blinding white (my poor retinas) before fading to a fast flight over desert sands, and a generic metal track roared out of the speakers, causing seats to rumble. Smoke was blown into the crowd and the screen showed lightning-quick cuts of the game, highlighting every stolen feature they'd managed to wedge into the demo back to back, but never lingering on anything long enough to give a proper look. Just enough to whet appetites.

Towards the end of the trailer were a few minutes of extended gameplay footage, overdubbed with actors, dramatically coordinating their precision attack on the enemy. That trick has been done to death at this point; nobody believes these are real people using voice chat, because no one really talks like that – for a start, there wasn't anyone screaming about whose mother they'd had sex with when someone missed a shot, and the only female voice wasn't being creeped on or excessively berated by anyone.

With a final, huge explosion, the title hits the screen like flying debris and the release date is revealed as the dust settles from a destroyed building:

# 11 October

The audience around me erupted to deafening cheers and whoops, spurred on by the overly excited and well-rested devs in the front rows. It went on long enough that I ended up covering my ears, as I was starting to fear long-term damage from their enthusiasm. Imagine that, permanent tinnitus caused by Gamer™ excitement. I'd have to lie and say it was raving or something, otherwise I'd never live it down.

Finally the lights came up and there was an absolute stampede for the doors as fans rushed out to get in line to enter the convention centre when it opened. I stayed in my seat for a while before scurrying out via a staff-only exit. Luckily I was given an exhibitor pass, so I could just come and go as needed, without bothering with queues round the block in the baking LA heat.

As I wandered back across the street, it occurred to me that there's only four more months to get the game finished and out the door. Sure the devs cheer now, but goodness knows how they'll feel once we're back in the office and Jeremy's just ironing out the hitbox for damaged wooden crates and there's still 90 per cent of a game's assets to build and implement.

On the main expo floor there was almost a hush as exhibitors held their breath before the horde descended upon them. Here and there a few people were making final adjustments on their stands and professional cosplayers were seen readying their prop weapons or getting strapped into stilted boots/legs.

I was gripped by the reverent silence, but enjoying the space as I snatched those few minutes to look around the show hall, taking in the other booths. One that really caught my attention, tucked away in a corner, was a cool little platformer where your dialogue choices impact the size and shape of your character, as well as their abilities. I decided not to mention this one to the boys. My plan going forward is to be more selective about what I tell them regarding the small developers, especially indie studios. I refuse to be responsible for snatching their ideas just for them to appear months or even years before their own games actually emerge.

At last there was a noise behind me and I knew that the doors had finally been opened and the public unleashed like an invading force breaching the walls of a besieged medieval fortress. Their footfalls were thunderous as they tore towards the booths of the biggest AAA games. Clamouring to be the first to get their hands on *Zenneth Fables – Unending* under the watchful eyes of someone paid to stand around all day in highly detailed plastic armour glaring and posing threateningly for pictures.

Thankfully, I was still in the indie section when this happened, so things remained very manageable while I took my time enjoying such highlights as an as-yet-untitled game about a cheeky duck who wears a straw boater and terrorises a small English village full of middle-class, right-wing bigots. It was a very cheeky duck.

While there was initially a degree of separation between the chaos of the AAA crowd and the quiet of the Indie Village, I knew things were getting chaotic when that separation began to waver. Fans realising that they might not get to play a single game today if they joined one of the AAA lines started to flow, en masse, toward the quiet corner of independent creators. Hearing an audible gulp, I looked up to see one very anxious-looking developer who was making a sign of the cross and mouthing a silent prayer as the clamour of the crowd grew nearer. I took that as my cue to flee.

As I made my way back to our own stand, I was greeted with absolute chaos. Somehow the rope barriers had been demolished and there was now a thick mass of people winding around and around the booth, which eventually became an actual line, then went right out of the doors, down the corridor and, finally, out of the building entirely. The devs who'd been put in charge of marshalling the queue looked like they were about ready to break already as they struggled to wrangle an army of aggressively enthusiastic Gamers™.

Eventually, with the help of some of the event marshals, we managed to back them up enough that we could rebuild the planned queueing system and reinsert everyone in their original positions. This did, however, involve trying to get several hundred people to move backwards in order and naturally there were chancers who tried to use this opportunity to sneak in. That naturally led to fights breaking out, but if anything that just meant that people could be ejected from the event entirely.

Along the roped area were signs showing approximate waiting times from that point, but since that didn't account for the fact people were now lined up around the block outside, the last marker showing 'three hours' meant very little to those beyond.

Once things were reorganised, we managed to rescue most of the cardboard standees that had been arranged around the booth as well as the prepared goodie bags. They were all a little trampled, but if anything that added to the whole warzone aesthetic.

After helping to wrangle all that, I got a few of the team making up goodie bags and sent a couple more along the line to get people to complete their injury disclaimers, before reaching the simulated minefield itself.

Next I made my first report back to Rick and Chad, before heading off to take a look around the other AAA booths. Dawn Castle didn't take much looking for, as a bunch of kids armed with neon-coloured foam bullet guns were firing at each other while being chased by a large moving wall. Above them, strapped to a zipline that had been kitted out to look like a hang glider, another child dangled helplessly several feet above the crowd. Below, booth staff with long poles tried to manoeuvre them along the wire, giving the impression of some kind of horrifying child piñata.

Awed Comics' latest game in the Arachno-Lad franchise, the imaginatively titled *Arachno-Lad 2*, was offering guests the chance to climb a rock wall made to look like a skyscraper before being swung down and into the play area. Given how severely under-padded the area looked, it felt like a lawsuit just waiting to happen. Though I noticed that, like us, they were having people sign disclaimers before being allowed up.

*Rootin' Tootin' Cowpoke Shootin' Revenge* had gone to the effort of building a replica desert saloon, where journalists seemed to have exhaustedly congregated for a rest. It was a really good-looking stand, but the horse they had tied up outside the bar looked like it was struggling with so many people and so much noise (a very relatable horse). I'd put money on someone getting kicked before this event is over.

The booth for *Housegueist* was an escape-room puzzle, built as a miniature mansion complete with actors dressed as ghosts and zombies gliding or stumbling around and threatening injury should puzzles not be solved in time. The dismembered limbs scattered around were genuinely concerning in their realism.

Over at the *Penultimate Legacy XXVIII Remake* booth they were showing off a replica of the heroine's massive sword, with a competition to win a week-long, all-expenses-paid holiday to Iceland to the first person to actually lift it from its pedestal. Given that I watched them build the stand, and it's tied in with steel cable, I suspect that they won't have to fork out for that holiday any time this week.

When I got back to our own booth a couple of hours later, I found absolute pandemonium.

A large circle had formed some way down the line. Pushing my way through, I found the wettest brawl I'd ever witnessed. A young man cosplaying Brad Reckless (including a foam muscle suit under the iconic blue vest and jorts, topped off with stubble that looked to be drawn on in marker pen) was smashing an already snapped and crumbling replica chain gun around the head of a hooded figure (presumably some version of Mateo, hero of the *Doctrines of Death* series), who was punching feebly into his opponent's well-padded torso.

Surrounding them were a chanting and jeering crowd, taking bets on the outcome.

'Alright, break it up, you two, or you'll be banned from the demo,' I hollered above the din.

There was a collective groan of disappointment, but since no one seemed to want to risk missing out, they started to disband in search of other entertainment.

Mateo got up from his crouched position and poked forlornly at the now-limp wrist daggers he'd clearly tried and failed to gut his opponent with. It was a very impressive costume; he'd really nailed the design of the family crest seen in the first game.

With things seemingly settled for now, I marched to the front of the line to find any of the interns to help keep things in order.

'Tyler, Jacob, are you two assigned to anything at the moment?'

'We got told to be here, but they didn't actually give any instructions.'

'Great, allow me to instruct. In fact...' I fished around in my burgeoning bag of freely acquired merchandise and found a couple of grey plastic deputy badges I'd picked up on the *Rootin' Tootin' Cowpoke Shootin' Revenge* stand. 'There you go, you're deputies in charge of the line now. You keep order and stop them killing each other. If anyone is looking unwell, make sure they get some help.'

As soon as I'd pinned the badge to Tyler's chest, he fell into a wide-legged swagger and tipped an imaginary Stetson. 'Why sure thing, little lady.'

While they moseyed off in search of lawlessness, I rounded up a couple more interns to go in search of as many free food and drink samples as they could acquire, to be handed out to flagging denizens of the queue. Diving back into my bag of freebies, I offered up a few packs of Player Nuts (the brand-new bacon-flavoured, caffeinated peanut snack) and mini cans of Meth to the cause.

Hopefully that would stop those who had already queued for hours from starving or becoming dangerously dehydrated.

With that out of the way, I made my way across to the demo stations at the end of the assault course. Players who had made it through the gauntlet, while battered, bruised and in some cases slightly singed from pyros, seemed delighted with what they were experiencing. Especially as they were leaving with armfuls of promotional garbage of our own t-shirts, squirt guns, lanyards and posters.

It's a shame most of the things that they were excited about, like destructible environments and top-of-the-line graphics, aren't anywhere near implemented into the main build yet. Still, hopefully a lot of the actual code can just be imported and used again, saving the development team some time. I'd hate to see these poor, adrenaline-pumped, swag-laden teens completely destroyed by the final product, if it doesn't hold up. Today, at least, they were happy.

Once things were under control again, and I was fairly certain no one in our queue was going to die due to neglect on our part, I made my way inside the walls of the booth. It was a very narrow space, with a writhing mass of impressively tidy cables plugged into the high-power PCs which are actually running the demo (rather than the fake console shells which the public could see from their side).

Finding a safe and comfortable place to sit, I booted up my laptop to check on the press responses so far.

With the last X3 press conference concluded, and the show floor finally open to press and public, the very first game we rushed over to go hands-on with was this year's entry into the Call of Shooty series.

Returning to the series' modern-day roots, the trailer for the latest game caught our attention with its highly ambitious list of new features, *flashy visual upgrades, and strong level of technical polish.*

*While the demo on the show floor lacked a robust tutorial, throwing players somewhat roughly into the action to figure out the new systems on the fly, we have faith that these mechanics should flow together well once it has a formal introduction.*

*While the demo was limited to a very strict five-minute session – to ensure as many gamers as possible have a chance to give it a try – what we played promised to be an ambitious step up for Supremacy Software's big-budget flagship first-person shooter series. If this level of quality is consistent across the whole game, we feel certain that this title is going to claim a lot of game of the year awards. This brief hands-on demo got our hype meter all the way up to thirteen out of ten, so get ready to pre-order it yesterday.*

Overall, people were reporting very positively on their time with our demo. A few (very valid) concerns here and there are that the number of different gameplay mechanics are a little convoluted, but mostly people understand it's just a demo to show off the kinds of things players can expect in the full experience. Little do they know that this is currently the most complete experience and that the main game is a miserable little pile of unfinished assets and missing textures.

The other main takeaway which kept popping up was the classic: 'If the whole game looks this good, plays this well, and is this polished, it's going to be amazing'. Sure, this demo took the entire team two months to bang out and it's barely five minutes of sandbox content, with a handful of AI enemies thrown in and some top-notch visual effects. Since they're only planning to make the solo campaign six minutes long, the full game should be a cinch with the time we have left.

Just as I was picking my way over the bundles of cables and back out into the hall, Rick and Chad burst in and slammed the door behind them, making the already uncomfortable space about ten times more so.

'They're out there!' exclaimed a concerned-looking Rick.

'The players?'

'No, the goddam press.'

'From what I've been reading, they're really enjoying the demo, what's the problem?'

'What's the problem? I'll tell you the problem: they're asking for a statement about Roger,' replied a panicked-looking Chad as I tried not to show how entertained I was by their discomfort.

'Yeah, it's all "blah blah what do you say to allegations of abuse?", "blah blah blah protecting abusers and letting them keep positions of power".'

I covered my smirk with a well-placed cough behind my laptop as they continued.

'Where are they even getting this stuff? We need a full IT sweep. Get them to check every computer in on the development floor before we get back to the office. I want everybody's email checked for leaks.'

'Whoever broke their NDA needs to suffer. Well, get to it!' ordered Rick as he waved me away towards the door. 'And don't tell anyone we're in here. We need a secure area to discuss important... business.'

Describing it as a breach of non-disclosure agreement, rather than a malicious lie being spread, confirmed to me that they knew the claims to be true. Of course the truth wasn't what bothered them. No, they were angry that people on the outside were starting to learn the truth.

I squeezed out of the cramped cupboard – leaving the cowering execs to ponder their life choices – and made my way back down the line of hopeful gamers.

I may or may not have given a subtle nod in the direction of the executives' hiding place to Gareth Lane, who I spied peering across our display area, looking out for some sign of my employers.

'I understand, you couldn't possibly help me out, no hard feelings, I get that it's your job,' Lane responded in a comedically booming voice, making sure anyone in a ten-foot radius knew I had definitely tried to stand between him and that cupboard of anxious bastards. Got to love some plausible deniability.

The rest of the event passed in a blur of not exactly misdirecting journalists to where they might find Rick and Chad. Meanwhile, over at our curated warzone, those who had camped out in the queue had lit a fire on the display and were trying to cook one of the fake severed limbs, which they'd lifted from over at the *Housegueist* booth. Turned out they were just foam, albeit very well painted, and the fumes set off the fire alarms at some time during the early hours of the second day.

By the time I was up and about, it was being reported that several people who couldn't wait any longer had used the desert display as a human litter box. I stand corrected; what Jean-Pierre will be sifting out of there on Friday will be considerably worse than a few empty cans of Crimson Method Psynaptic Frenzy.

Come Thursday lunchtime, there were bruised, twitchy, dirty, smelly, starving, but highly dedicated gamers muttering to each other about how they'd struggle to survive 'once this damned war is over'. Hopefully they won't need too much therapy to recover from this extensive queueing experience and will adjust to life on the outside with relative ease.

## 13 JUNE

Back in the office, I got in early this morning and took the stairs (I'm trying to get at least a little cardio in). As I rounded the corner up onto the dev floor, I was shocked to see a huge plastic dome in the middle of the room. At first I wondered if it was some kind of corporate art thing, but on closer inspection I realised it was built out of monitors. During our absence, Jeremy had apparently added every other monitor in the entire department to his system, so he could keep everything he needed visible at all times. Apparently 'The Focus Dome' boosts productivity, although he claimed that losing his mouse pointer on one of over two hundred screens was a real danger.

Rick and Chad better not hear that, they'll have the whole team locked in the damn things. Regardless, Clark is taking it down with the help of a few of the interns. He told me it smelled like a rotting corpse in there and the carpet was developing mould from all the moisture which had run off of the lone programmer. Furthermore, they had to send Jeremy to get hosed off in the showers before he could have his debrief with Rick and Chad.

I nearly collided with Rick as he hurried to the boardroom.

'So, game's finished, right? We're all done?'

I tried not to laugh in his face. 'It's a very large project, and it's been left in the hands of a single person for an extended period.'

'You hear about one-man teams making games all the time. Why the hell isn't he done yet?'

'Well,' I began as gently as possible, 'those tend to be much smaller in scope than something like *Call of Shooty*.'

Rick looked completely stunned. 'No, we didn't waste our breath giving him the motivational talk last time for nothing. He needs to do better.'

Shortly after, Chad arrived and proceeded to set up his interrogation space. The air conditioning was set to high heat, and the blinding Anglepoise lamp was pointed straight at the slightly-too-short chair in which they would grill their subject.

By the time Jeremy knocked and entered, the temperature was sweltering. The temporary lead developer looked like he'd been jet-washed and bundled into fresh clothes. I wasn't quite sure if he was still damp from the hurried hose-down or if he was already nervous for the coming meeting.

Chad simply pointed at the assigned seat without a word and Jeremy lowered himself in. These usually sit outside of the HR area and really aren't designed for use at a desk. Consequently his chin was barely visible above the boardroom table and the boys loomed high above.

'We're of the understanding that your performance has been very disappointing in our absence, Jez. Do you think you can just sit on your ass all day because we're not here to watch over you?' Rick paused just long enough to imply he was finished.

'I—'

'What the hell have you been doing all this time?'

'Well, um, I wasn't keeping notes or anything, so I can't account for every specific minute from memory, but I tried to take your advice and work on parts of the project outside of my specialised wheelhouse.'

'Finally, some goddamn initiative.'

'I did try to work on some art assets, as you suggested, but that did mean having to teach myself how to use the 3D modelling software.'

'How hard can it be?'

'It's *very* hard. Most of our digital artists have over a decade of hands-on experience to get as good as they are.'

'Bullshit, it's all algorithms now. It makes itself.'

'It really doesn't. Do you know how many triangles it takes to make a realistic-looking gun?'

'What the hell have triangles got to do with it? It's a gun.'

'All the graphics are made of triangles. Very small triangles. So many triangles,' Jeremy whimpered as sweat poured from every pore.

They went endlessly back and forth, berating the poor man, telling him: 'it doesn't sound like you've done good metrics here' and 'that's not the Supremacy Software family way'. By the end he looked super upset; he may even have been crying, it was hard to tell with all the other liquid pouring off him like a broken water main. (I put out 'wet floor' signs around his chair and messaged Clark to bring a mop when he was done with The Dome.)

As with last time, they weren't actually mad at him, despite the words they said to Jeremy's face. They knew as well as anyone else that he wasn't going to miraculously finish the game in five days. They were just bouncing off each other, bad cop and other bad cop (because you know what all cops are). They made him fear for his job security in a childish game for their own entertainment.

When Jeremy was finally dismissed, Hannah met him outside the elevators and suggested he take a personal day to recover. She was very careful to ensure he understood that it would be unpaid, but mandatory. He wearily agreed as the doors closed behind him. As soon as the exhausted programmer was out of earshot, the boys broke out in hysterics at their antics. Ah yes, bullying your exhausted staff for fun. Good joke. Great.

I reached a hand into my pocket, and quietly switched off my Dictaphone. The operation was almost completely silent; so long as no one noticed the bulge in my dress, my plans could remain a secret.

Quest log update – Gather more evidence to destroy the enemy. Annihilate these absolute bastards.

But, carefully, so no one finds out it was me.

The last event of the day, for which I was summoned to observe, lords of the manor descending the stairs to the dev floor.

'Everyone, stand up from your desks and take a step back,' Rick bellowed.

'Hands where we can see them, if you know what's good for you,' added Chad, clearly still on his cop trip.

I wasn't sure how serious he was, but I did notice a few of the assembled staff raising their hands behind their heads.

They started yelling about 'betrayal in the family' and 'repercussions of breaching an NDA'. Behind them, most of the security team loomed menacingly, covering the main exit to this floor, while a group of IT workers I'm not familiar with went around and checked every single workstation.

Since they had arranged for a team to go through everyone's machines while we were away, this was mostly just a show of force. Luckily, *someone* got word around earlier today, so that if any of them did have anything incriminating, they had time to clear all traces before the sweep. I'm hoping that message got to everyone in time, because I dread to think just how far through court this company would drag someone in order to make an example.

## CHAPTER 7

# Heeren Today, Gone Tomorrow

**5 JULY**

After a long weekend, everyone's back in the office (though I'm not sure how many of the dev team actually went home on Friday). Thanks to the positive reception the demo got at X3, as well as a little recognition here and there, the developers have been spurred on to greater productivity. Hopefully some of the code is transferable, or at least can be more easily put together now they've seen what the core gameplay loop actually looks like in practice.

That said, the sudden arrival, in a number of team calendars, of an ominous 'major design meeting', scheduled in the next few days, naturally has a few people concerned as to what direction is going to be coming out of that. I've seen Rick and Chad's calendar, there's no reason this couldn't happen sooner, but I have a strong suspicion it's just another power play, as the pair deliberately hang the Sword of Damocles for a while to generate some fear in the working class.

This is just like when someone sends an email that just says 'We need to have a chat' without any further context. It doesn't matter if it's a routine catch-up or a huge, life-shattering revelation, dread and tension spiral out of control all the same.

Unsurprisingly, come 00:00:00 on 1st July, all the company's social media feeds removed any trace of a rainbow from our branding. Pride Month is over, time to pack the gay away until next year, when we're considered financially viable again. At least they didn't take the 'support' posts down, so that's some semblance of a backbone.

All the Pride skins have gone from the current loot box rotation, leaving a few to rage they missed their chance to get them. What's worse, they seemingly can't be applied to characters anymore either, meaning they just sit in people's inventories until they unlock again next year, at which point there will undoubtedly be a push to brand them inferior, and 'so last year' in the wake of whatever new releases they will definitely push out in an ill-thought-out hurry.

Other than that, reception to the Supremacy Software Pride season features was a mix of 'it's nothing but corporate pandering', to 'better than nothing, I suppose'. Of course the harshest critics are rightly pointing out that too much of the content boiled down to egregious stereotypes played out for cash. On top of that, the inclusion of straight Pride designs in an otherwise LGBTQIA+ Pride set rang alarm bells in certain circles. There was a vague apology for that, but the fact they included the line: 'It wouldn't be fair to exclude our straight players from our annual celebration of Pride' somewhat weakened any semblance of sincerity.

## Meeting minutes – 6 July
Drinks orders for the board:
Edwin – yellow power juice (Must. Not. Gloat.)
Rick and Chad – one twenty-two and one twenty-four-shot latte (suitably shuffled before I arrive)

For the time being, my plan to introduce plausible deniability into drink distribution is working well. Every meeting they ask for more shots, not knowing who truly has the greater amount of espresso. The fact that neither of them has actually finished the drink they requested in weeks seems irrelevant in this contemptible caffeine contest. By the end of the year I fully expect them to be staring daggers across the boardroom table from each other, lording it up over their gargantuan cups of undrinkable brown caffeine sludge, each convinced theirs is the superior empire of shit.

Meanwhile, the plants on this floor are all starting to die as the boys are clearly disposing of their unfinished beverages into the greenery. Neither of them would even begin to conceive of admitting their hubris, so for now I'm going to propose to Clark that we get some plastic plants on this floor.

The first order of business was the post X3 breakdown. While I didn't tell Rick and Chad about any of the interesting game mechanics I saw on show at X3, the pair seemingly did enough internet searching to find out about a few of the more mechanically interesting games at the event. That cool little indie game I saw flew under their radar, thankfully, I guess because it wasn't mentioned on the bigger gaming sites, but a few mid-tier developers had some interesting game concepts the executives had latched on to.

'That whole bullet time game looked great,' enthused Chad.

'Oh yeah, pure rule of cool. Feels powerful watching them explode while you duck and weave in slow motion.'

'Also, that split-screen thing, with cooperative progress, I like that for us too.'

'Totally, we gotta have that.'

I could tell they weren't just talking about things they'd appreciated: these were targets for theft. Mechanics they were looking to tack onto our already bloated and behind-schedule project.

'Those companies are so small, even if they try to make a fuss about us *taking inspiration* from them, we can bury them in legal red tape they can't afford to fight.'

'Nice.'

'There is still the matter of GCP; they're extremely litigious and are big enough to cause some financial disruption if they do take issue with our use of their patented mechanic. We don't have long enough to take it to court,' grumbled Edwin.

'That's not a problem. I get that time is an issue here, so I had Legal get a buyout underway,' Rick replied.

'I love a buyout – it's way quicker than reverse engineering,' added Chad with a broad grin.

'Exactly, they make it for us, and when they're done...' Rick waved to the door.

Their glee as they talked about the takeover was utterly wretched and sounded less like video-game executives discussing a new addition to the company and more like sixteenth-century colonists who had discovered a new, resource-rich land of peaceful people they could wring out for personal gain. Powerful white men strike again.

The door opened and a man I was not familiar with entered, with all the confidence of someone who owned the place, and strode to the seat next to my own. Reaching down, he snapped his fingers under my nose twice and barked, 'Coffee, black, no sugar, and make sure it's *hot*.' The way he tried to stare into my eyes as he did so gave the impression of a man who's read every 'assertiveness in business' book on the market, but never bothered learning to speak to an actual human being.

'What's keeping you?' he squawked, clicking his fingers again with each word 'Coffee. Black. No sugar. Hot.'

Turning to the others, he added, 'Is she simple or something?' causing a ripple of impolite laughter.

Everything about him was ringing alarm bells in my queer little head. From the crew-cut hair to the dark-coloured polo shirt worn under a suit jacket, to the fact he smelled like one of those guys who doesn't use soap 'because it washes away all the natural pheromones which women find irresistible' (though, in practice, most of us would be more likely to drop the contents of our stomachs than our underwear in his presence), told me that he was the kind of man who would try to convince me that his was the unwashed penis that could 'turn [me] straight'.

I shortly learned that this was Hugo Heeren, *current* CEO of Dutch developer Game CommandPost, who own the game and related mechanic the boys are after. Seems charming.

By the time I returned with his drink, they were all very deep in conversation.

'I would expect in the region twelve million for my personal buyout, of course,' said Hugo, lounging back in his chair. I noted that he'd swept my things onto the floor beside him and taken my seat.

'Come on, guy, let's be reasonable and call it eight,' Rick shot back.

'Ten, no less.'

'Sold! Ten for you, seventy for the company: we get what we want, you get a nice retirement package.'

'Then we have an agreement.'

They all stood and shook on the deal. From the way the muscles in the backs of their hands tensed, I could tell they were unable to hold back from a couple more dick-swinging attempts, trying to crush each other.

'Oh, at last,' announced Hugo, noticing I'd delivered his coffee.

As I went to stand up after picking up my notebook and pen, he held up a hand in a 'halt' gesture and took a sip of the searing beverage (I may have microwaved it after brewing, so it was reaching thermonuclear temperatures). I watched him momentarily wince before restoring his mask of superiority.

'Acceptable. You may proceed.'

Good luck with the tongue blisters, asshole.

He turned back to the boys and with a barely perceptible lisp continued, 'I think, as long as you let me know the date we're formalising the sale in advance, early enough that I can have my people buy up a good amount of stock before the price jumps, the merger will pretty quickly pay for itself.'

The executives laughed and nodded along as Hugo outlined his insider-trading plans, but by the time I'd managed to get my hand in my pocket to begin recording their crimes, they'd already moved on.

NOTE TO SELF – Just record meetings start to finish so as not to miss anything.

As for the sequel Game CommandPost had been working on? Scrapped. No point setting our new subsidiary against our own new release. The original is to be removed from shelves and digital storefronts, never to see the light of day again. It's to be a *Call of Shooty* 'original' mechanic from here on.

John (I'm pretty sure that one was John) from Legal popped in with contracts, and everything was signed and sealed – including the expected bonus for Hugo, of course – before I had fully processed what was happening.

A multi-million-dollar deal had taken place before my eyes and it was over quicker than a Hyper Grimaldi Sisters world record speedrun.

As (probably) John stood waiting for his pen back, he just

quietly stared at (through?) me in the most disconcerting manner. I have no idea what Legal's problem with me is, but it's really creepy.

So that's that. By the end of the month Game CommandPost will be dissolved, their staff will pack away their current project and be absorbed into the Supremacy Software family, on zero-hour, one-month rolling contracts. No benefits, no guarantee of an actual, functional job. Just 'we own you now, conform or leave' and probably 'never work in this industry again'.

The final surprising revelation was that because one journalist (just one) hadn't been entirely placated by low-tier sparkling wine and all-beef patties at the expo, they now want to bin the entire game so far and start again from scratch. All that work, tainted in an instant. Success turned to ashes in their minds because one person had been less than gushing in their praise of the demo.

*While* Call of Shooty *does show promising ambition, it's obvious that the project lacks clear direction. Rather than focusing on making any one aspect great, it tries to be too many things at once in a way which comes across as desperate.*

*While the series to date has largely been a serious and gritty war simulator at its core, this feels too much like a pastiche project, untethered from that focus. Seemingly without understanding why any of the gameplay features that it shares with its peers are desirable in their own settings, it blunders through the dark, grabbing at whatever it can reach to pull into its ungainly, stumbling mass.*

*I would like to be wrong, and while the demo was*

*entertaining enough, the build Supremacy Software*
*chose to show off fell a little short of the level*
*of cohesive design that I expect from a title with*
*the kind of AAA budget this series is known for.*
*Hopefully the team will be able to rein in some*
*of the feature-creep and polish us up a gem from*
*out of the dirt.*

It was right there: 'polish up a gem', but no, they wouldn't hear of it.

### LUNCH

Having given up on Ez being available for lunchtimes together, particularly with work on the game about to be scrapped and started over fresh, I sat and ate lunch alone in my little office.

Hannah came knocking to pass on a message that Jeremy would no longer be available for the development team to delegate work to while out of the office. When she mentioned that he'd be 'moving to a farm, out of state', I had a flashback of when my mom tried to soften the blow of my cat being run over. Luckily this wasn't immediately followed up by my brother thundering in to show me pictures of the accident on his phone. I've taken a note of Jeremy's email address and I'll send him a message to check in, once I'm home and on a more trustworthy internet connection.

### P.M.

I headed down to a meeting with the middle managers and senior developers to discuss the bad news. I was very anxious about having to face the poor developers only to load yet more straw upon the camel's back.

'Thank you for coming, everyone. I've been asked to relay a

few new ideas from the executive team regarding extra features they want included.'

I heard a small whimper from somewhere near the door and one of the senior devs mutter to their colleague, 'This is *Brad Reckless Eternal* all over again,' before being shushed by a nearby manager.

*BRE* was a complete fiasco; it had new features added every six months and was restarted from the ground up eight times over the course of its twenty-two-year development. Things got so bad that industry pundits started calling it *Brad Reckless Eternally* in Development. A friend of mine had pre-ordered it the day it was announced and by the time of release, the store where he'd done so had been bought out so many times, he had no idea where to try and claim his purchase from.

I went on to tell them about the decision to scrap all existing progress and restart, based on feedback to the demo.

'I think we can agree that not much progress has been made on the actual game, so to lose the assets and code from the vertical slice shouldn't cause too much disruption,' replied Hank, one of the managers. He nodded around at the rest of the team, seemingly hoping for a positive response, only to be met with grim silence.

I considered correcting him, and reiterating that *everything* had to be dropped, but given how much they already have going on, I felt that letting them cut that one small corner wouldn't hurt.

'One last thing before we wrap up. I can reveal that you will be getting some help. I can't say much at the moment, but we're looking at adding somewhere in the region of seventy-five extra coders and artists to the team in the coming month,' I concluded.

This, at least, did generate some positive buzz. A few correctly surmised a buyout, and began to theorise among themselves as to who Supremacy Software had swallowed up this time.

Hank thanked me for coming down and gave a single clap. When this didn't evolve into full applause from the team, he flashed me a fawning, greasy smile. It made me clench as I seemed to register on a primal level that he was attempting to brown-nose.

I started to wonder whether Hannah didn't have some requirement for a minimum level of smarm when hiring new managers.

He's clearly the ambitious type. Probably hoping that I'll put in a good word with the board if he sucks up hard enough. Joke's on him – they'd never listen to me, even if I wanted to recommend him for a promotion.

The last of the team filed out beside me and I hoped that the little slack I'd inadvertently attempted to cut them would be of help. The less time wasted on a needless restart, the better. They deserve more time with their loved ones. Besides, how would the executives even know? There's no way I'll be snitching on them.

# CHAPTER 8

# Potato Salad and Brownies

I AUGUST

Despite the senior dev and middle management agreement that they'd just rework the graphics and keep hold of the rest of their existing code for the game, it all mysteriously disappeared from the shared drive overnight. IT informed everyone who was raising tickets in a panic that the system was in fact running just fine and that the order came down from the executives to delete all existing progress.

Any descent was quickly quashed by Hannah, who dragged staff into one of the soundproof meeting rooms to let them know that when an order comes down from on high, it's to be followed and not sidestepped for their benefit. I felt terrible watching them be punished; I'd tried to save them a little unnecessary work, and now they were paying the price. The fight has really gone from a lot of these people. The best part of eight months at the hands of this company has broken their spirits.

At this point they're bordering on catatonic as they fight their way through an impossible mountain of work. Their fingers furiously type, their eyes stare unblinking at glowing screens. All of the jokes and banter has died off as no one has time anymore.

They hurry between their desks and the drinks machines and back in almost complete and eerie silence. I barely recognise the cheerful creatives that walked into the interview room at the beginning of the year.

I approached Ez, barely recognisable as the woman I befriended only a few short months ago.

'Hey, how's it going? You doing okay?'

She was gaunt and looked utterly exhausted. 'Absolutely, I'll have it done before I go. You can count on me.'

'Ez, it's me, are you okay?'

She finally turned and looked at me; her eyes seemed to be taking a while to focus further than her monitor. 'Oh, busy. Very busy. Can't stop.' She turned back and resumed her assault on the keyboard before her.

Just then I heard a throat being cleared in a way that somehow managed to sound accusatory. I turned to see Hannah, shooting an annoyed glare as she moved on with her patrol of the floor. I apologised quietly and left Ez to work in peace.

As I went I could see it was the same wherever I looked. All of these once lively souls were now hollow versions of their former selves. I couldn't even pick out the new starters from Game CommandPost. At first it was easy; they were the ones who still had some pep in their steps. Now they were just like everyone else.

I wondered if their old offices had been much different to our own or if this was just business as usual. Regardless, we've not seen a significant uptick in productivity, though things have stabilised again after the dip immediately following our team-building paintball expedition.

# Meeting minutes – 1 August

Drinks orders for the board:

Edwin – an ultraviolet power juice (This stuff is weird. It gives me sore eyes to look at and I can't visually process what I'm seeing once I pour it out of the bottle. Either way, I'm not raising concerns; I know how pointless that is at this stage.)

Rick and Chad – N/A

Today's meeting was an odd one. I was told that Rick and Chad would be joining us remotely, and half expected them to be appearing on the large wall monitor. However, after serving Edwin – who looked more dressed for a round of golf than a meeting – and taking my usual place, there was a sound like a knock at the door. When I answered it, I was met by the more tanned than usual faces of the boys, seen from an unpleasantly low angle and blown up to nearly twice their usual proportions across large tablet screens, mounted via poles to motorised robotic bases. People worry about the military applications of things like this, but I feel like these two are probably the most insidious things rolling around on them right now.

As they propelled past me, to their usual seating positions near Edwin, I briefly wondered if there had been any attempt for one to get a longer pole on which to be displayed on than the other.

Oh no, I've internalised their childishness. Help.

Apparently they were on a 'location scouting excursion' for next year's *Call of Shooty* sequel (there goes my hope for any innovation or originality for next year either). The tan lines from their hands-free headsets, the fruity cocktails they were drinking, and the very obvious beach bar in the background suggested that total immersion was a vitally important aspect of really getting a true sense of the location. Doing the hard jobs, as always.

Possibly inspired by their current locale, the boys have decided to announce a 'big summer event' for last year's *Call of Shooty*. More skins, more loot boxes, more work. Sure, the dev team probably doesn't have anything on right now. I imagine I'd have heard something around the office. Oh, wait...

Apparently there are concerns that keeping the multiplayer servers up and running is getting expensive. Gosh, how will a company this size, with the hoarded wealth of a small country, keep running servers for a game that never seems to stop charging people for new content. Honestly, they could keep it up and running from now until the next millennium and barely notice the financial hit.

'Right, new skins. I'm thinking we make all the guns look like they're crafted from, like, bamboo and leaves.'

'Pineapple grenades.'

'Board shorts, and how about they pay extra for toned abs.'

'Yes! Let's get some floaties in there. Re-skin the chainsaw as an inflatable shark.'

'What about the T-Rex? I'm thinking a bikini, I'm thinking surfing.'

'And wearing branded sunglasses, one hundred pairs of which will also be available to purchase from our merch site in a numbered case so you can own a piece of gaming history.'

Before I could wonder as to where these fonts of creativity got their ideas, a tanned, slender woman, in a bikini and sunglasses, could be seen walking by Chad holding a surfboard.

'Now, we got some real negative feedback for the rainbow loot boxes last month, and some of that wasn't even about the rainbows. A lot of pushback on the fact they could only get the items through randomised pulls which they had to pay for with real money.'

'Not a problem. How about we let them just buy items with the new Eonium Gems?'

Eonium Gems are the latest obfuscated currency to be added to our real money shop. Of course, you can't just buy them outright, that would be too easy and not nearly profitable enough. The Gems can only be bought with Red Sapphires, which have to be traded for Mega Credits, that can only be earned through burning Cyber Tokens, the basic level currency and the only one which you can buy with real money.

The story goes that some years back, an absolute math wizard – who we'd hired to develop the microtransaction system for that year's big football game – wrote a very technical algorithm which would calculate exactly how much everything should cost, at every level, so that it holds the most money in the economy without letting too much of it trickle down to where people can actually spend it. That person was immediately fired and given no credit for their creation. However, the finance team seems to worship them as some kind of dark god. There's even a slightly nightmarish oil painting up in their break room.

'We need a feature weapon for the event, the big deal that everyone is working towards.'

Chad's eyes flicked around desperately. 'Er, how about... a... Cocktail Cannon.'

'It fires tiny little strawberry daiquiris.' added Rick taking a sip from his glass.

'And if you get hit it makes the screen wobble around, until you sober up.'

'Now, I need you to stay with me here, I'm going to propose something that's kind of out there, but trust me okay?'

The others stared in rapt attention. 'What if we tell players that they can earn the Cocktail Cannon, just by playing the game?'

Edwin spluttered, 'You're throwing money away, boy.'

'You got to hear me out. We make it technically possible, but in practice, there's just no way. If you stop playing for even a minute during the event month, you're out of luck.'

'Go on,' implored Edwin, eyes still staring daggers at his junior.

'They need to go to the bathroom? Sorry, you missed out. They got to go to work? Oopsie, you didn't put in enough hours. They go to sleep? You snooze, you lose. Meanwhile, everyone who's paid for it is kicking their asses into the next century. And who's to stop us making sure that those who don't pay are forced into games with those who did. We turn up the FOMO so high, they'll be begging us for these things.'

'And if they still don't get on board, or look to be coming up short for the month, we email them reminders every day to give them that final push,' added Chad.

'Exactly.'

In practice the new gun will cost around $80, but the real money cost is so abstracted, few will take the time and effort to actually work it out before they start pumping all their money into Cyber Tokens. On top of that, there's no way to buy exact amounts of each currency, so small amounts are held at each level, keeping unspent money in our digital economy. Layers and layers of deliberately shadowy obfuscation.

Naturally, all the serious, competitive players are going to want the gun because of that drunk effect. When your enemy has a camera that is swaying uncontrollably, objects in view are leaving swirling vapour trails, and can't hold their gun straight, it's obviously a massive advantage to those who can sink $80 without thinking.

For everyone else, the game is going to be borderline unplayable. At least until they dial down all the effects at the beginning of next month and suddenly it's a worthless piece of digital garbage.

Moving on.

'We've had figures back from our focus groups and, apparently, there are a surprising number of women who play video games. Who knew?'

'You mean those cutesy mobile games though, right?'

'That's what I thought, but the numbers show that a lot of them have been playing the men's games too.'

'Huh?' Chad looked genuinely dumbfounded.

'So I'm thinking, since we hired the legally mandated minimum number of women this year, maybe we put some resources into a female playable character model.'

Three decades in, more than forty titles, and today they're finally ready to add someone who actually looks like me as a playable character to the game. My days of crafting the cutest twink the character creator will allow may finally be over. This is history in the making.

Rick continued, 'And if we do go ahead with this, those models are going to have to appeal to our core demographic too.'

Uh-oh.

'Of course, what's even the point if they're not fun to look at. Let's get them in customisable bikinis. Chicks love clothes and stuff.'

I felt my stomach drop like a stone.

'How about a new gameplay mode, you know, to introduce them.'

There was a moment's pause before they cried in unison, 'ALL-FEMALE BEACH VOLLEYBALL MODE.'

I felt the crushing weight of my momentarily lifted spirits as they fell on me like a boulder.

To announce the summer content Chad wants a fully rendered sequence of the jiggle squad volleyball players storming in from the ocean on the Beach Head mission map. In slow motion, naturally. Long shots of glistening women with guns, their breasts bouncing and glimmering up a sandy beach before one of them slaps a ball out of the air and it goes into actual gameplay.

Every level in the game is to have a dedicated sand court for use in the new mode. During normal mode gameplay players will be able to watch playbacks of actual recorded matches – a move that will certainly save on animation work.

In the volleyball mode itself, two teams of scantily clad women will jiggle around for five minutes at a time, with occasional slow-mo effects so the camera can zoom in on their cleavage if players pull off some kind of power move. You know, just in case anyone missed the breasts up to that point.

I don't know why I even allowed myself a moment to consider that, in a genre which has been entirely dominated by men since its inception, I'd entertained the notion that when women were finally to be included, that they'd be anything more than animated sex objects. Avatars of unnaturally large, wobbling breasts that would snap the spine of an actual human with such proportions, should they take part in any kind of sporting activity.

'We'll get the newbies from Game CommandPost on it, that should be more than enough to cover the DLC, that leaves the whole team to carry on with the main project.'

I'm not convinced, but what do I know, I'm 'just the PA.'

I'm not a prude, I like tits, big fan, but for all gods' sake, that was completely gratuitous.

After nearly twenty minutes of having to listen to them (even Edwin) going on about all the slowly wobbling boobs like they'd just discovered them for the first time and thought they might be the cure for cancer, they finally tore themselves away and moved on to urgent matters regarding the next game.

Extra staff to help get it finished? More development time? Improved staff morale that doesn't involve terrorising them for days at a time in the woods? Nope, pre-order junk. Of course, how will people be sucked into aggressive tribalism without cheaply produced rubbish that we push out in order to generate hype?

'Now, we have a whole bunch of plastic helmets leftover from two years ago. I've got a factory in China that can repaint the whole lot for pennies,' Rick began. 'Of course, we have a few authentic, military-grade helmets made up with the new logo, and ship them off to a small number of influencers, along with a small note saying that they're not the final product, just a preview.'

'Something for them to open on stream. That's some good marketing.'

'There's no way we're paying good money for metal helmets for the final product, but I've run it by Lega—' Rick let out a yelp of surprise as one of the legal team appeared by his side. I didn't hear him enter, but there he was, right on cue. He took a deep breath before continuing. 'Ah, yes, good. I was just saying that I emailed you guys about the helmets.'

The immaculately attired legal agent whispered into his ear.

'Oh, we can?'

More whispering and then...

'That's great.' Rick turned back to the table and watched as his stealthy adviser made his way back out of the door. I know because I watched him the whole way, just to check he didn't suddenly teleport.

'So, as long as we use lead-based paint, we can technically get away with referring to the plastic helmets as metal in our marketing materials. We just have to have a disclaimer on the back, saying that they're "detailed scale models designed for adult collectors" and not toys to be played with, or touched, or inhaled, then we're off the hook.'

Next into the box will be a set of branded dog tags. The job lot that arrived at the warehouse included a vast number of bent and damaged ones, because of the cheap materials used to make them, but they seem to think that may mean they can save money on getting them engraved as it will be much easier metal to work with. Plus Chad has suggested that they can describe broken ones as 'battle-damaged' because it's 'more authentic'.

The 'true soldier' edition of the game is also to include a highly realistic replica hand grenade. There are, however, no plans to include any safety markings to differentiate it from a real, live explosive. A fun afternoon for customs officials and anyone involved in random post office checks. Legal have been consulted on this too, and it seems we can respond to complaints of any item not arriving as an issue with the United States Postal Inspection Service, USPIS, and therefore not our problem.

Some versions will include a bullet-shaped USB stick with the CoS logo stuck on (because why pay for printing when stickers are so much cheaper). Another product from that wholesale company Rick seems to be in contact with. He tells us he's managed to get a few hundred 1TB sticks for around seven cents a piece. I dread to think what the real capacity is. That's assuming they don't come loaded with malware and keyloggers. Hopefully they won't be trying them on their own PCs or IT will have kittens.

The 'complete edition' will come with all that nonsense, plus a plastic disc box for the game, but not the game itself, just a code to download a bunch of desktop and phone wallpapers. Once again, Legal has confirmed that it's 'deceptive, but not an active lie', so that makes it fair game. Since this will be the third year in a row that they've done it, they see no reason to stop, as 'it's all extra revenue' and can be spun as not excluding those who purchased current generation gaming hardware SKU which lacks an optical media drive.

Rick tabled the idea of an 'ultimate true hero' tier which would include adoption papers for a war orphan. He suggested it should come with a certificate stating that a portion of your purchase has gone to help support a child in a war-torn nation, said with wording which was identical to a charity that's been doing a lot of online advertising lately. I can't say I was entirely surprised, but even so, in the context of *Call of Shooty*'s themes, it feels absolutely abhorrent.

'Uh, sir? Rick? I'm sorry to interrupt, it's just I feel like this has the potential to reflect quite poorly on us as a company.' All eyes were on me. No turning back. 'This could easily be seen as exploitation of people in horrible circumstances for financial gain. At the very least, it might be worth considering a donation of some of the profits to charity if you're going to bring real war orphans into this. Especially as you made the wise decision to distance the project from real world locations and peoples when you first pitched the idea.'

I braced for a stinging rebuke, or at least some dismissive and belittling rebuttal, but they just turned back around like nothing had happened.

Do I even exist? Did I die at some point and now I'm just haunting this boardroom? Is this my personal Hell?

'So, our final tier, Five Star General Edition. We go all in, no one's going to buy it, but it'll make great headlines. Gaming press will be tripping over themselves to talk about the most luxurious version of this game. For a cool thirty mil, they get a private island, a US military contract to host their own war, a solid-gold pistol with the logo on the slide, and a white tiger as a pet.'

I've learned one thing. If they don't even notice me giving an impassioned, and slightly butt-kissy plea to their faces, I probably don't need to worry about them hearing my hitting record on the device in my pocket.

Legal, on the other hand, I will need to exercise far more caution with. I can't help but wonder if their overall blandness doesn't act as some kind of invisibility shield. Something to keep in mind going forward.

The blue-sky work completed, it fell to me to inform the development managers of the new additions. Since I couldn't bear to stand face to face with another human being and tell them we need them to get to work on prehistory, wartime, extreme jiggle volleyball mode, to say nothing of the tropical DLC, I put it all in an email, which I bookended with a clarification that it was definitely not a joke.

Dreading having to answer more questions on the matter, I quickly swapped out the memory card on my Dictaphone for a fresh one and headed down to sixty-three, to see Maria, our community manager.

I found her right by the door, smiling to herself as she typed away at her computer.

'Can I help you?' she asked, tugging her earbuds out by the cord.

'I'm looking for the community manager.'

'And you have found her. How can I help?'

'The executives have decided on what tiers they want for the new game,' I said, handing over a copy of my notes.

'Oh my, they've really gone for it this year, eh?'

We joked about the top-level version of the game and the chaos which would ensue if someone actually tried to buy it. It felt good to laugh with someone. She's got a lot of very wholesome energy, which really helped to buoy my spirits after the grossness of the board meeting earlier and the general air of depression from the dev floor.

## 13 AUGUST

Rick and Chad finally returned to the office yesterday. Their tans are definitely nothing to do with a vacation, it was work and how could anyone possibly think otherwise. Both seemed hungover, possibly just a side effect of the very intense location scouting.

About mid-afternoon, a few hours after their return, they sent out an email blast to the whole company that they'd be hosting a company picnic in the quad, today (Saturday).

The first floor of our building has a pretty sizable 'garden', which is to say there's a few tables, some fancy pathing, and patches of artificial grass. The ceiling is designed to look like an azure sky, it's just a shame that the cloud pattern repeats six or seven times.

I guess the intention was to give an outdoors indoors feel, but really it's rather uncanny.

The boys announced that they'd be providing drinks and cooking barbecue, they just asked that everyone bring along a side dish or a dessert. I went with my Gram Gram's peri chicken wings because they're affordable, super-easy, and tasty as heck.

I arrived shortly after the scheduled start time, assuming that despite the alleged informality of the event, I'd be expected to fetch and carry for Rick and Chad.

The smell of propane-fired meat was heavy in the air and I dropped off my wings at the only table which wasn't creaking under the weight of a frankly obscene amount of beer, wine and spirits.

The boys were manning the grills and swigging bottled beer. On the opposite side of the quad, a large number of representatives from the legal team sat in silence, staring like owls at the room around them. Since I didn't like the look of either of my other options, I headed over to a group of about a dozen of the women from the dev team, who seemed a little uneasy.

'Hi. How's everyone doing?' I asked.

A few of them seemed scared out of their skin when I spoke.

'Did they send you over?' asked a dark-haired woman I was fairly certain joined from Game CommandPost, nodding in the direction of the execs.

'Oh no, I try not to spend too much time with them. Besides, they appear to be deep in focus committing crimes against meat products right now.'

She didn't say anything more, but I got the impression that I wasn't entirely welcome, being seen as one of 'those upstairs'.

I spent an hour or so organising the drinks table by size and turning all the labels so they could be read. Anything to distract from the bizarreness of the space, the constant staring from Legal, but being too scared to stray further from the slowly growing group of women developers.

It was about the time their numbers had swelled to around thirty, that something clicked.

'Excuse me, sorry. Has anyone heard from any of the guys? It's just I noticed that apart from the New York staring squad over there, and Rick and Chad, it's only us.'

'They weren't invited,' responded a lady in orange dungarees in a quivering voice. 'I sent a message to Craig on the animation team; he said he didn't know this was happening. Then, about twenty minutes ago, he messaged me back to say he was outside but Security wouldn't let him in.' That news sent a concerned murmur through the group.

'Food's ready, come and get it,' yelled Chad.

Not wanting to be rude, and feeling desperately hungry after weeks on a virtual starvation diet, I headed down the food table to see what was on offer. I was greeted with the smell of carbonised cattle and barbecue sauce.

Heaped on foil platters was a mound of blackened meat pucks. Several of which were giving off plumes of white smoke, their humiliation continuing even after they had been liberated from the grill.

I put my back to the pleased-looking arsonists – who were already loading the grill with fresh victims – and helped myself to a burger bun from an unopened bag, which I filled with ketchup to try and disguise the lack of burger. Shuffling back down the table, I tried one or two of the potato salads which I had seen being added to the collection since my arrival.

No one said anything, but even I could tell that everyone felt uncomfortable eating anything we hadn't either prepared ourselves or had watched be delivered by a trusted source.

I ate nervously and wondered if I couldn't just make my excuses as soon as I was finished with my plate.

As the boys incinerated their latest batch, the air became more acrid and I returned to my recently organised drinks, hoping for something non-alcoholic to clear my throat. A couple of the devs were also moving along the table, but neither met my eyes as they searched.

'Mixers, thank gods,' muttered someone a little further up, near to the vodka and rum.

'Have you checked if the rings are still attached?' enquired the woman next to me.

'Looks good,' came the reply as she tucked a catering-sized bottle of lemonade under one arm and passed a cola across to my neighbour and began to head back to the main group. Taking a look for myself, I discovered some orange drink to add to our safety haul and followed behind the rest of the foraging team.

As we passed out plastic cups of soda among the nervous crowd, I was relieved to see Candace and Jenette arrive with a large plate of brownies.

'Take a couple for later, sweetie,' Candace whispered conspiratorially.

'Something's wrong,' said Jenette, matter of factly.

'They only invited Legal and the female devs, which I suppose is how you two ended up here.'

'We get copied into all the developer emails; I added us to all the lists,' Jenette said, her eyes still sweeping the room.

'They're coming.'

I followed her gaze toward the grill and saw that the boys had abandoned their company aprons and were approaching the circle of developers.

'Good to see everybody having a good time.' Rick raised his beer to the crowd with a smile.

'We're just going to have a quick chat with a few of you. Nothing formal though, don't you worry about work today. This is just a family picnic,' chuckled Chad before making straight for one of the younger women and guiding her away to the edge of the 'garden.'

The remainder of the group closed ranks, all eyes outward, ever watchful for potential predators who stalked us.

'We should keep an eye on that young lady,' advised Candace. 'I'm not worried about the Legal creeps, but the seniors are a different story.'

I realised in that moment that I'd already lost sight of her, and the boys for that matter. Did they go inside? Or rather outside? My sense of language to describe this room was struggling somewhat.

Eventually she did return, along with a broadly smiling Chad.

'How about you next?' he asked a petite blonde. I was already sensing a pattern.

She looked pleadingly towards the group, but followed after her employer.

Rick returned just as they reached the wall, and it seemed they had split up to cover more ground. He sidled up with a smirk and picked out the next youngest and smallest woman he laid eyes on.

They could have unfurled crimson banners from every wall at that moment and it wouldn't have even begun to match the number of red flags we were getting from the men in charge.

'Candace, keep an eye on that door, you come with me, I know what to do.' Jenette took my arm and led me to the circle of anxious developers. 'Y'all got your cells? You get swapping numbers, then start messaging one another saying you're needed home or late for something. Let's get everyone out of here safely, okay?'

This plan was met with approving murmurs, and they set to work putting it into motion.

By the time Rick was making his third trip, everyone's phones were starting to buzz and each attendee began a show of goodbyes and apologies for having to leave so soon.

I returned to Candace to watch the tinted glass door through which the boys had been leading the youngest guests.

While a few more members of the team were taken aside before they could escape, numbers were thinning out significantly. Candace and Jenette resolved to stay back while I fled, reassuring me that they wouldn't leave until they'd seen everyone safely off.

'Thank you so much for saving us. I'll pop by next week.'

'Let someone know you're home safe, okay?' said Candace with a sympathetic look. 'And don't forget to take a brownie.'

I think everyone made it out okay, but it seemed like we shared something today. I can't prove that there was anything to be afraid of or not, but we all felt something was off.

I'm emotionally wiped out and about ready for bed. Tomorrow brings the promise of an excellent brownie and cartoons in my pjs.

## 14 AUGUST

It was a good and rich pecan brownie, very chocolatey, good and chewy. I am somehow disappointed that it did not contain any drugs. If I'd known, I'd have had a few while at the party. The chocolate might have helped with my overall level of anxiety.

## P.M.

I take it back: this brownie is amazing. I've been laughing my ass off for a solid hour. Going to try mixing all the cereal I have in a mixing bowl. Also, I wanna see if I can order gummies to the apartment. My rug feels amazing right now.

# CHAPTER 9

# Crowdsourcing

**5 SEPTEMBER**

With August out of the way, the temperature in the city is becoming cooler. I've been walking to work in the morning wearing lightweight summer clothes. Meanwhile, the air con in the office is always slightly too cold to be comfortable in anything less than a cardigan. I've been keeping spares in the back of one of my filing cabinets to change into.

Ordinarily, I'd be worried about the oncoming seasonal blues, but the office is kept not only at a steady temperature, but is also consistently lit, at least on the development floor. You can never tell the time of day or even the time of year. There are no clocks on the wall and all the computers are set to automatically hide the clock if your mouse isn't directly over it. Perhaps that's why so many of them fail to go home on time, if at all.

As we near launch day, executive meetings have significantly dropped off. I'm not sure why – it's not like they're involved in any of the actual work on the game. Still, there's very little to be done right now apart from letting the devs get on with their jobs. They're already putting in eighty-hour work weeks in some cases, so short of flogging them, there's no way to drive them any faster.

Yep, they're fully internalised now. I shouldn't even think that, though – it might be enough to spread the idea to Rick and Chad. At this point, I'm not convinced that they wouldn't just do it for the power trip.

Sadly, it's not that far-fetched. All too often, in the last few weeks, I've seen Hannah marching up and down the lines of desks, brandishing her field-hockey stick and banging on the backs of people's chairs if they slow down for even a few seconds. Who are people supposed to go to regarding the conditions here when even the head of HR is in on the appalling office culture? Anyone who does manage to complain gets dragged into one of the soundproof meeting rooms and chewed out, away from prying eyes.

There's now only about six weeks left until release, and today's meeting will include Harold, who is head of the dev team. The aim is to discuss where the project is at and what needs doing to ensure it remains on track for the agreed release date. Hopefully they won't have much to report as, at this point, even if they did agree to get more staff (they won't), they'd need to be trained up, and there just isn't time for that.

## Meeting minutes – 5 September

Drinks orders for the board:

Edwin – clear power juice (I'm pretty sure this is just water, and the company he orders these things from have made an absolute chump of him for ordering them)

Rick and Chad – thirty-seven-shot lattes (I'm done with the illusion they're different – I just label them so they can get the pathetic need to outdo each other out of the way as quickly as possible)

Soon after I was settled in with my notebook, Harold arrived to give his presentation to the board. He's a tall, very thin man, looking now very undernourished and desperately exhausted. He wore one of those t-shirts with the washed-out colouring and pre-faded print, designed to make it look like a vintage item. The parallel of something fairly new which appeared utterly worn out quietly entertained a back corner of my brain.

'So, the game is coming together at last. Many of the core features should be ready in time for release, but that's not to say that there isn't a lot still to be implemented,' he began shakily.

'Examples?' asked Chad.

'Well, since you insisted that the entire audio team work on live-recording our own reloading, gunfire and explosion samples, rather than the more traditional choice of purchasing sounds from a stock vendor, they've been unable to make any progress on the game's soundtrack.'

'I love those gun noises. I don't want to have to pay every time some kid pulls a trigger,' Rick demanded.

'It's just that that was months ago, and since then you've refused to sign off on anything, so they haven't been able to move on to anything else.'

'Yeah, because there's not enough cool gun noises yet.'

'We have literally days' worth of samples, sir.'

'Good, keep at it.'

I was surprised to hear Rick taking an actual interest in any of the little details of the project. He's usually all about the money and seemingly nothing else.

'I understand this is a sticking point for you, sir, but we still need time to insert that audio into the actual game.'

'Surely someone not working on the gun noises could do that. Do I have to think of everything for you people?'

'As I said, you've had everyone with any audio experience tied up on this project for some time now. Unless you want someone with zero experience to take over, I must insist that we're at least provided with someone to help with the soundtrack.'

It's become clear in recent months that one of the company's biggest issues is that the executive team has no understanding of how long anything should take or the types of skills required to complete a given task.

How long could twelve new character models, each with twenty costume and hair variations, take? An hour? Probably less than that, right?

The boys sat in silence for a moment before Chad raised an eyebrow and asked, 'Customer engagement?'

'Sure, it's about time we fire up the ole hype machine and get customers involved in the whole process of marketing.'

The plan, as I understand it, is that they're going to hold a competition on social media. Winners receive whatever cheap garbage they can slap the game's logo on. Tote bag, t-shirt, pen, mug, pin badge, a digital copy of the soundtrack they helped create and a 'blink and you'll miss it' thanks in the credits of the game itself (in miniscule font, moving so fast as to be almost, but not entirely, imperceptible).

All they have to do is put in all the hard work of composition, performance, recording, editing, mixing, and of course signing away their moral right to the production (whether they're picked as winners or not). That way, even if we don't use their submitted work for this project, we hold all the rights, for ever, to use as we see fit. Moreover, it will be added to our online content-checking system, so if that piece ever finds its way onto any of the major music- or video-streaming services, it will be immediately flagged for a copyright claim, and we can either take it down or leach all the advertising revenue from it.

They could easily hire a musician to make the music, but

no, they'd rather just exploit people. I'm pretty sure the thrill of exploitation is all that keeps them going at this point.

I'm to notify Legal, who apparently have a standard Ts & Cs document ready to go for this kind of thing, and then PR will be recycling the competition page from the last time we did exactly this.

I realise it's not actually illegal to use your more fanatical customers as a source of free labour, but when you consider the amount of money this company makes, it definitely raises moral questions.

One more thing to add to the dirty-laundry list when I break the lid on this company to the public.

While they were on the subject of marketing angles, they agreed that it was about time they had some of the interns work their way into gaming meme pages and start posting about the upcoming release.

There were a lot of outdated references to cats, fast food and heavy use of Impact font. I foolishly pointed out that most people are using short video formats these days, but they sneered and said that short videos died off years ago, and I needed to keep up with the times. Either they know something I don't, or they're thinking of an entirely different platform from the 2010s.

Faced with the usual disinterest in my suggestions, I didn't bother to mention that taking away the interns meant that there'd be a gaping hole in our makeshift QA team. There's no point in me trying to save this sinking ship.

For months now I've been trying to manage the constant, simmering rage I feel towards my employers. It gnaws at me every minute and sits on my chest with the density of a particularly muscular dog as I sleep.

The weight of pressure I feel as I fight to remain calm is

suffocating. I have to keep grinding for experience points until I'm powerful enough to draw my sword and slay them. Meanwhile, I push the feelings down to stop them overwhelming me. I have to remain numb to it for now, or all my efforts will go to waste.

Chad's next suggestion was also in the competition genre. This one would involve fans sharing their extreme excitement about the game using our chosen hashtag, and in return we would share their post, as well as follow them from our corporate social media accounts. Utterly meaningless to us, because no one checks our notifications, but perhaps a little cred to them, being followed by a faceless corporate entity.

Rick followed up with suggestions coming as fast as they were extreme. Name your baby Call of Shooty, win a t-shirt. Get the game's logo tattooed across your whole face, win a hat. Of course, these would only be available to the first person to do so. Imagine the disappointment of getting out of the labour ward to discover that yours was actually baby number six to be called Call of Shooty McGee, or whatever. Or worse, that you were going to be needing several grand for laser tattoo removal after losing out on a hat to someone whose 'artist' was willing to seriously blow out some lines to get them done in the chair ten minutes faster.

Lastly, Edwin (I was kinda shocked: this is the first I've been fully aware of him actually doing any work or having any responsibility beyond chair warmer) has been working with the CEO of Crimson Method Energy Drinks on a sponsorship of their newest product, Crimson Method Power Crystals. They're packets of pure caffeine and sugar crystals that you just pour in your mouth and chew. Finally rid of all that pesky water from their drinks, Power Crystals will offer the highest caffeine-to-volume ratio that is legally permitted by the FDA (thanks to some loophole regarding dried goods and labelling).

Apparently feedback from focus testers showed that it shreds the roof of your mouth and ruins your gums. However, the open wounds allow the stimulants to get into your bloodstream more quickly. I had questions, but I kept them to myself. Especially when I saw that the copy described it as offering gamers 'the highest CPS of any product available without prescription'. CPS here meaning caffeine per second and not clicks.

For customers, all they need to do is buy a bag and enter the code on our website (along with a huge number of personal details, which we will be permitted to sell as part of the terms and conditions of entry) and they get cool character skins added to their account. Not full sets, as the bags suggest of course, just bits here and there. Some pants, a shirt, a shoulder pad, a new right boot. Naturally, they will also offer these items for purchase in the in-game store, for some highly obfuscated amount. With many items being given secret rarity and therefore a higher cost in the store, Edwin is convinced that fear of missing out will drive all the sales both companies could possibly desire.

Finally gorged on their own self-importance, they scurried off to their own offices, the boys carrying their suspiciously full mugs of coffee.

### 9 SEPTEMBER

The dev team continue to spend their days running around like someone's got a fire lit a few inches behind their ass. Some free samples of Power Crystals made it to the dev team and they've been bouncing off the walls for a few days. Lots of wide eyes, lightly bloodied shirts and furiously moving fingers as they reach heights of productivity that no human being has ever attained before.

Right now, most of the jobs that need doing urgently to get the game ready for launch are way above my pay grade. Nobody really needs micromanaging, and there's not a lot we need to organise meetings around, and so I have been finding ways to fill my days ramping up work on my own personal project.

Ever since the Dictaphone arrived a while back, I have been making an effort to record as many conversations as I can. I hadn't really been doing much with them yet, but I have spent the past few weeks listening back to the recordings at triple speed in my office with headphones on, working out what I could or could not safely use without making my NDA-breaking status clear.

While I probably couldn't directly quote anything I knew was exclusive to closed-door meetings, I could probably paraphrase events I knew others were either present for, or had been big enough moments that word about them spread internally around the office without my input.

I also spent a decent amount of time on my personal phone looking up various gaming news sites, and individual writers at those outlets, trying to get a sense of who, if anyone, I could use to disseminate what I had learned so far.

A lot of journalists were instantly struck off my list of potentials, from those who had taken weak stances against abuse at other developers to those who had, in spite of their critical reporting of abuse, wasted no time in rushing to praise those companies' next big releases, dropping abuse stories as soon as they were no longer 'new news'. I knew I needed someone else to ensure what I had to say was taken seriously, but working out who that trustworthy person could be was proving difficult.

I suspect it was the lack of other tasks around the office, and my need to at least appear busy with non-espionage tasks, that led me to be one of the few people to even notice an all-persons email appearing in my inbox at around ten to five. The subject line just read 'Press Enquiry RE: Abuse Allegations.'

My office door was shut, but I tilted my monitor away from it, just in case anyone should walk in on me. It read:

*Hello,*

*My name is Gareth Lane, I'm a reporter for* World Gaming News (WGN). *Over the past few months, I've been investigating reports of abuse, mistreatment, and sexual harassment within Supremacy Software.*

*My investigation began around the time of Roger Meinder's reshuffle between roles, and the later departure from the company of a member of your development team (who will not be named at this time).*

*Since then, I have been following up on unsubstantiated, but repeated, rumours around the working culture at Supremacy Software from a number of current and former employees. As there have been a great number of specific details which have matched between accounts, I felt this required further investigation.*

*I am a strong believer that where there's smoke, there's fire, and as such, I would invite any Supremacy Software staff who have experienced workplace abuse or harassment – particularly from senior staff – to contact myself with information at this email address or via your encrypted messaging service of choice.*

*You can be absolutely assured of confidentiality, so I hope that some of you will feel safe enough to step forward and tell your story.*

*Sincerely,*

*Gareth Lane (he/him)*

*Lead Reporter – WGN – US*

Almost by the time I'd finished reading it and made a note of the email address, it vanished from my inbox. Seemed like IT caught wind of it and managed to clear it from every computer in the building. Probably before most people even noticed it was there.

Still, I read it. I saw it. I know it happened. This is exactly what I have spent the last few weeks looking for. Gareth Lane is, without a doubt, the right person for me to loop in on this.

Lane has a platform already, he's a writer for *WGN*, and I couldn't hope for a much better outlet to host this information if I want it seen by a mainstream audience. He has been persistent in following this story, without being aggressive toward me in our personal interactions over the months. He hasn't just given up on the story just because he saw some light pushback, and he seems to be prioritising anonymity for the sources he has so far spoken with about the story.

I've been hesitant to reach out to anyone myself, because knowing who to trust with confidential information when your job is on the line is difficult, but Lane reaching out has told me everything I need to know. If I am going to take the risk of talking to just one person, I feel like he's going to be the right one to talk to. I don't know whether I trust him in a broad sense – I will do some research before contacting him – but perhaps I can wield him as the sword I'll slay the beast with. He can certainly act as a useful weapon when the time comes to strike.

I need to work out exactly what my next move is, but, make no mistake, I'm taking this company down. They're going to pay for every dream they've crushed, every poor kid they've driven out of the industry, every person who's suffered at the whim of some douche who couldn't keep their hands to themselves.

# CHAPTER 10

# Spoopmas

I feel like I have enough evidence now to start the boss fight. With that in mind, and covering myself to the best of my ability with a VPN and burner email, I've written a message to Gareth Lane.

> *Dear Mr Lane*
>
> *I've been looking into your work and it seems that you have a reliable history of protecting your sources as well as telling hard truths to powerful companies within the gaming industry.*
>
> *If you would be willing to extend that kind of protection to myself, I would like to open a dialogue regarding your concerns related to staff treatment at Supremacy Software.*
>
> *I'm sure you will understand that due to non-disclosure and non-disparagement agreements, I am unable to freely discuss these matters. Breach of one or both of these agreements would be catastrophic on both personal and professional levels.*
>
> *Since our entire IT system was purged of any trace of your email asking people to come forward within minutes,*

*I cannot be sure how many others will have seen it, and I suspect fewer still might respond.*

*I am keen to speak to you, but I need strong reassurance that I can put my trust in you. Terrible things are happening here, Mr Lane, and I need to ensure justice for those who are suffering. That will require a platform. A platform which you have.*

*SwordBearer – a concerned member of the Supremacy Software staff.*

An hour passed, and I just couldn't leave my screen or do anything else. I don't know why I expected a response on a Sunday night, but having pushed the first pebble from the top of the mountain, the anticipation of an avalanche was all I could focus on.

Then, at last:

*Hello, and thank you for reaching out.*

*I would like to assure you that keeping my sources anonymous is my very highest priority. I have been involved in investigative journalism for nearly a decade and fully appreciate the risks involved in whistleblowing, especially where powerful corporations are concerned.*

*Without people such as yourselves, forcing those in power to make necessary changes in their workplace culture would not be possible.*

*I understand that a big part of being willing is seeing evidence that journalists such as myself have a proven record of having made it safe for others in the past, and I hope you have found that to be the case.*

*I would like to verify your identity, but I'd feel better*

*if we did so via an audio call, so that there's not an email*
*linking this burner email thread to your name.*

*If you can pick up a pay as you go sim card, and call*
*me on the number below, we can discuss who you are, and*
*then resume discussions in this email thread if that would*
*work for you?*

*Thank you for trusting me enough to reach out.*
*Gareth Lane.*

I threw a hoodie over my PJs and made my way to the TinySave for a sim card. I could feel my heart racing, my anxiety and paranoia causing me to scan every face in the crowd and check over my shoulder. This was it, this was really it.

At first I considered heading to the park to make the call, but you never know who might be lurking nearby. I eventually decided to head back to my apartment, empty out my closet and build a cocoon out of blankets to dampen the sound of my trembling voice.

'Gareth Lane speaking.'

I froze. Was I making a mistake? What if it was an elaborate sting by the company? Was this the moment I destroyed my life?

'Hello?' came his voice from the other end of the line.

I fought not to hyperventilate, but I was trapped in a very small closet in a snare of my own design and I could feel the claustrophobia setting in.

'Is this SwordBearer?' he enquired.

Something about hearing that name flicked a switch in my head. 'Y-yes.'

'I appreciate that this is scary; you've done a very brave thing by taking this step. Would you like a moment before we start to take a breath and settle yourself a little?'

I squeaked in the affirmative and after steadying my breathing for a few minutes I was ready to speak again. I appreciated that Lane just sat patiently on the line. He didn't tell me to hurry up or rush me in any way.

'What do you need from me to verify my identity?'

'If I could start with your name, please.'

I looked around the closet like I was expecting to see someone behind me in a trench coat, pretending to read a newspaper. 'Avery Paige.'

'Oh,' he exclaimed, 'well then, this should be much more simple to confirm.'

He asked me details of our first and last encounters, which was easy enough, as he cuts a very memorable figure.

'Excellent. Well, that's good enough for me. So, if you'd prefer to move back to email, that's no problem at all.'

I thanked him and ended the call.

*Hi Gareth*

*Thanks for that call. I am feeling a little more confident now that we've had a chance to chat without all of the cloak and dagger pretences.*

*I'm a bit worried about sharing anything that directly implicates me, where I am the only person who could possibly have sent you a particular piece of info, but there is plenty that I am willing and able to disclose as there are lots of people internally who would be reasonably aware of these incidents.*

*Below I have attached summarised accounts of events where individuals were pulled aside by management and aggressively questioned about impossible deadlines as a form of entertainment. At this stage, a majority of the development team are aware of the occurrences, so it would be nearly impossible to trace to me directly.*

*That said, thanks to my position, these are likely to be the most thorough and accurate accounts you could receive as I witnessed them personally.*

*I have also attached as much information as I could find about Roger Meinder, from second-hand accounts I have heard, as well as information on the timeline from complaint, to public rumours spreading, to his being shuffled to a new department, and where he ended up.*

*I've provided a full account of the Fidget situation, and how she was left to face public harassment without any support from the company. I have spoken with her myself before reaching out to you, and she's happy for me to provide you with any additional details.*

*Lastly, there is a statement on a team-building exercise which took place in May. Given my unique position at that event I would appreciate it if you could frame it from the point of view of those who were injured by the frozen paintballs, rather than from within the fort.*

*I'm going to keep collecting as much information as I can and will provide you with anything which doesn't self-incriminate. Perhaps there will be a time where it is safe to reveal everything else, but not yet.*

*SwordBearer*

### 3 OCTOBER

There's just over a week until the scheduled launch date for *Call of Shooty* and I do not believe it's possible to actually finish the game in that short amount of time. Sure, the dev team has made incredible progress, but nothing is working fully just yet.

Graphical elements flicker in the most unpleasantly seizure-inducing way (we found that out the hard way when we had to call a medic for one of the interns who was doing testing. Not one of the fancy medics we called for Edwin; I suspect poor Gary will be taking out a personal loan to cover that little ambulance ride), players often can't see each other, hit detection for bullets either doesn't work at all or else catapults players miles outside the map, and sometimes the gravity just inverts and half the players fall upwards at alarming speeds. That's to say nothing of the players whose faces don't load in properly and leave bodies wandering around with tongues lolling out of their necks and balancing teeth like some kind of cosmic horror.

The progress that has been made has come at a very high cost. The amount of crunch is absolutely appalling. All the developers in non-management roles were put on mandatory overtime. Well, not technically mandatory, but thanks to the posters that went up everywhere reminding the team that 'we're a family' and 'team players stick together', everyone seemed to get the hint that any who didn't keep doing the overtime should be considered 'other' and shunned.

That was shortly followed up by Hannah sending out an explicit email advising that those who still weren't on board were risking their end-of-year bonus, as well as their credit in the game – something that would stand as a glaring omission to a future employer. 'Oh, you worked on *Call of Shooty*, but I don't see your name here, were you not involved in actually finishing the game?' Nobody wants to have to explain their way around that industry nonsense.

For a day or so there were rumblings of a mass walk-out – something I was internally cheering for, but before anyone knew it, security goons were up here taking the organisers one by one to soundproof meeting rooms 'for a little chat'. Given the wheezing and crumpled way many left those rooms, I got the impression that Security was being far more extreme than Hannah had when she was having such 'chats'.

By the following week, all thought of rebellion had been aggressively quashed and everyone was back to their cowed and anxious selves. Slaving away at their desks, occasionally being 'playfully tapped' on the head with Hannah's hockey stick as a reminder that 'we're all under pressure right now'. While trying to get video footage of this would be too risky, I've been grabbing audio recordings in an attempt to verify my account of what I've seen happening, and to make sure my written summaries of events are as accurate as possible.

I've started to genuinely wonder if Rick and Chad actually would stoop to publicly assaulting the dev team (or at least having Security do it while they watched). At first it was just an out there thought that crossed my mind, now I'm not so sure. I saw what they were like on the paintball trip, I've seen how our head of HR acts; this company is not not above causing physical pain to assert dominance.

For the last few weeks, the team has been working twenty-two-hour days. They sleep at or under their desks – or what passes for their desks – for the rest of the time.

The Meth Crystal issue seems to be getting worse. Someone has been shipping in more and more promotional boxes of Crimson Method Power Crystals. Now almost every member of the development team bears the telltale mark of the bloodied chin and shirt. A few are starting to lose teeth from the excessive sugar. None of them eat properly, so they've all slowly become more gaunt and pale. Should history show that this is how the zombie apocalypse started, be assured, the game was not worth the outcome.

If this is what it takes to get these games out every year, I can quite understand how I joined the company at the beginning of the year and found that there were no developers at the company. Working for Supremacy Software is a dream job to a lot of young people. Most of those that we interviewed at the beginning of the year came in with these big, romantic ideas about the role they'd be playing, the brilliant gaming future they would be helping to shape. This company has done nothing but wrench and wring every single last drop of life from them, a complete sacrifice on the altar of the gaming franchise. They're being used to destruction and I wonder what will be left come release day.

And, the more I think about it, the more I realise I am the same. Reading back over my early diary entries when I started here, I was excited about the art we were going to create. At this point, most of what feels notable here day to day is the corruption at the heart of this financially driven business. I started with such ambitious dreams about what working here would be like, but the realities of the workplace have eclipsed anything that might have been my original goals for the year.

## Meeting minutes – 3 October

Drinks orders for the board:

Edwin – a single-shot latte (here comes a new challenger!)

The top-floor plant pots (which Clark has just given up on and installed little faucets in the bottom of, to drain off the unnecessary liquid) – forty-plus-shot lattes

Rick and Chad have uncovered my ruse to switch out their mugs and so have each presented me with their own, along with orders to 'just fill them up'. And so a new arms race has commenced; who can find the largest possible mug. Naturally, as I'm just a PA, each of them has charged me with finding a drinks receptacle. As soon as one is ordered, I have to move over and order a larger one for the other. Part of me is wondering if I could find a company willing to put a handle on a hot tub. How far would they go to keep this preposterous nonsense up?

The meeting starts with the kind of tone which they usually only fake to scare the crap out of lead developers. Gone is the laddish buoyancy of previous months. At last, someone has them rattled.

'We gotta talk about this Lane guy.'

'Yeah. I don't usually worry too much about these journalists, but this one is getting brazen. That email of his landed in every inbox in the building. That's a level of determination that makes me think he's not just going to go away if we ignore him.'

'IT caught him pretty quickly and managed to purge the system, but we have no idea when and how he might strike again.'

'He's been asking about things that happened this year. That limits the number of possible suspects to new hires.'

'He mentioned Roger by name, we should have Hannah look through any complaints against him and form a shortlist,' added Edwin forcefully.

'Good plan.' Chad nodded. 'The way I see it, what he's heard doesn't mean shit, but I want whoever breached our non-disclosure and non-disparagement clauses dragged through court, destroyed and silenced for good.'

I sat frozen in fear, trying not to let my poker face slip from a very deliberate and crafted air of confident disinterest. They can't know already. They mustn't.

'It's got to be one of the guys on the development team. Probably pulling a white knight act for some piece of ass. Those types are always trying to earn woke points with dyed-hair liberal chicks. Besides, females lack the emotional fortitude to break the rules. They lack the killer instinct.'

Chad grunted agreement.

Blatant sexism aside, I was a little reassured by their apparent conviction that a woman could never be the one to tell their secrets.

Edwin suggested the developers should have to secure their cell phones in their lockers before entering the work area, so they couldn't use them to take pictures of the working conditions or to send any emails while they're in the office. All this would be disguised as security around the game itself. He just wants the fans protected from spoilers. How noble.

Chad started formulating a response to the allegations, his anger having cooled to a dangerous, quiet rage which I struggled to hide my amusement of.

'First up, blanket denial of all accusations. Point the finger at a jealous ex-employee.'

'Or a corporate rival, trying to hurt our image ahead of our big game launch, for their own financial gain.'

'Oh, I like that. Then we hammer the point that all this came from an "anonymous source", very convenient.'

'How can anyone defend themself from some coward in the shadows, who refuses to prove their knowledge? We're the victims here.'

'Anonymity is for the cowardly and deceitful. I say we lean on that. We're the Supremacy Software family; people have trusted us for decades. What are you going to do? Take the word of some snake who's attacking not only us, but our loyal fans?'

'Exactly, make it sound like an attack on the fans, they'll have doxxed this guy by lunchtime. Problem solved.'

'Okay, but before we send a mob after him, how about we approach *WGN* directly?'

'What are you thinking?'

'Threaten is a strong word, but we could... *suggest* that if they were to publish the story, that not only would we be seeking damages for libel, but their days of receiving press invites, review codes and extremely lucrative advertising spots, might just come to an end.'

With that, they moved on to the next order of business, a Halloween event.

They're such arrogant assholes. Totally convinced that their plan would be sufficient to quash the charges levelled against them. Their complacency will be the fulcrum, and I shall use Lane as the lever to push them over, into the yawning abyss.

Back to the meeting. Halloween is my favourite holiday, and every year I look forward to the special events that are introduced. I suspect that what I'm about to hear, and the hardship that is bound to be caused by today's decisions to the development team, will mean I will never participate in another fright fest as long as I live.

Rick and Chad want light-up pumpkin helmets, glowing skull masks, a screaming banshee gun which launches enemies using concussive force (costing the requisite $80 in Eonium Gems or 44,640 minutes of solid play time within the month that the event is running), new grenades which launch a cloud of vampire bats that latch onto enemies and steal their health, scary eyes stickers to slap on the side of guns, night-time variants of all the maps, zombie dog sidekicks, a pumpkin ball for the volleyball mode, and, of course, the T-Rex will be a living skeleton for the whole month. There was also a suggestion of candy corn bullets, but, given how fast they move, it's not like anyone can actually see them, especially in the dark.

I could have told them that no self-respecting pro player would want a glowing target on their head, but we all know what that would achieve.

Somehow today's wave of 'creativity' left them less satisfied than usual and they ended up sitting in thoughtful silence for a while. I could have sworn that Edwin actually started quietly snoring. Seemingly hearing this, Chad blurted out a suggestion of a whole new player vs environment mode where they'd be forced to fight off waves of anthropomorphic, goth girl dinosaurs in heavy eyeliner and skimpy black lace dresses. Rick gazed at his colleague with a look of absolute pride.

Let's forgo any consideration of Chad's thought process in that moment and just state that a whole new game mode will be hugely time-consuming and we're already on the brink of a horror movie-esque end of the world event on the dev floor. I think trying to push them any harder may actually be fatal. Either they'll work themselves to death or else snap and string the execs up outside the front gates as a warning to others.

Perhaps they saw me fighting to hold a response in because Rick snarked at me that it wouldn't be a problem; they'd just up the forced overtime to twenty-three hours a day, with two thirty-minute breaks, 'wherever they can fit them in'. Somehow they think that bullying is all they need in order to implement all their plans by the end of the month.

### LUNCH

I retreated to my little office to swap out the SD card in my Dictaphone and stash the used one in the back of my purse, behind a store card.

It's far too early to feel truly safe, but right now Rick and Chad's complacency has me completely off their radar. Still, who's to say one of them won't experience a moment unclouded by complete misogyny and consider the possibility that women are also capable of industrial espionage.

That said, I have to be on my guard. If Lane reveals me, whether by deliberate action or accident, I'm going to be nuked from orbit by lawyers and probably locked up in a hole so deep I'll never see the sun again.

As I sat pondering what my next steps should be, Rick barged into the room and threw a large leather case on my desk.

'Bring that – we're going downstairs. When I give you the signal, open it and hand me what's inside.' He stormed out and off towards the elevators; his pace only briefly slowed as he had to squeeze past the copier, which took up most of the narrow corridor leading from my little office.

Smelling an opportunity, I hit record on my Dictaphone, picked up the case and followed him down the stairs and out onto the development floor.

'Everybody, on your feet!' he yelled to the entire floor. His ability to project so powerfully was seriously impressive.

'You know, we let you have it pretty easy here. We've got a nice little family environment. Everyone pitches in, we all pull together as a team.' He paused menacingly and eyed those developers closest to him. 'Now it seems that some of you have been taking advantage of that.

'We're supposed to be a family, the supreme in Supremacy, the cream of the crop, the absolute peak of the AAA games industry. Up until now, we've been very generous, giving you room to do things your own way, but now we're coming down to the wire, so I'm telling you, you'd better find the time between all the snacking, the chatting, the sleeping at your desks, and get some goddamn work done.' His use of the weighted pause was masterful.

'If you're one of those who isn't pulling with the team, if we find you away from or asleep at your desk for more than thirty minutes per day, well, that tells me that you are not contributing to the cause like your colleagues. That says you're harming my family.' A few of the developers shuffled uncomfortably.

'I'm sure that if someone hurt your family, you'd fight back, right? Well, I'm just like you. If someone hurts my family. I fight them back. That's just self-defence. If you hurt my family, I hurt you. It's that simple.'

It was then that he turned to me and snapped his fingers. I opened the case to find a long black cane with a leather loop at one end. Embossed along the side in rich silver letters were the words 'The Union Buster'.

I'd joked to myself about him flogging the developers not long ago. Was I about to witness that very thing?

He snatched it out of my hands and began swishing it around, sometimes mere inches from the faces of the quaking devs.

As it cut sharply through the air there came an intimidating 'thoom' sound.

'Overtime will be *mandatory* until release. I had hoped we could keep things informal, but you have shown you cannot get your fair share of work done without strict rules in place. Anyone not pulling their weight will not be getting their portion of the huge end-of-year bonus pool. Furthermore, their name will also be struck from the final credits.' He continued to march up and down the desks, swinging his weapon with such ferocity, I felt sure it would only be a matter of time before he miscalculated the distance and actually struck one of them.

'Your work will be done on time, alongside the seasonal content. If you fail, well, your names may just become public knowledge – some of you seem to love it when private company matters are discussed with the press, so I'm sure you'll approve.'

I tried not to let it show, but I felt a chill run through me at this. Every one of them has seen how Gamers™ can be towards individuals they feel have done wrong by their beloved franchises, and to threaten to weaponise that against the team was worse than if he'd actually started thrashing them one by one. Throwing that in with a mention of the leaks made my blood run cold.

Finally spent, he strode back to me, thrust the cane into the case and marched back upstairs. I closed the clasps and started to reach into my pocket to turn off the Dictaphone, as I turned to leave. Barely six inches behind me there stood three members of the legal team. I hadn't heard them approach, but, just as usual, their eyes burned into me. There was no emotion on their faces, no way to tell what they were thinking; they just stared, pupils like hungry voids sucking everything in, patiently waiting for... something. I reflexively apologised for nearly walking into them and tried to subtly remove my hand from my pocket, not daring to touch the Dictaphone in their presence. One did glance down at my pocket, but they made no other move and did not respond to my words. I'm not sure if it's paranoia, but I swear they're getting creepier.

### BACK HOME

I powered up my PC and randomised my VPN location a few times before finally connecting to my burner email. Somehow I'm already getting junk mail for 'male enhancement' pills and fortune tellers trying to get me to unlock my true potential through the medium of definitely real talismans available for a knock-down price of $75 + shipping.

Inbox cleared, I copied the recording of Rick's outburst from earlier. I trimmed out my own voice at the end and a little from the very beginning to make it sound like he'd already started screaming when someone hit 'record'. I sent it over to Mr Lane, along with an explanation of the events, which concluded: ...*right now, they seem to have completely discounted me as a possible whistleblower.*

*I can't say for sure how long that will last, but for now, I'm feeling comfortable enough to send you this.*

    *SwordBearer*

My spy work done for the day, I cooked up the other half of a pack of ramen I'd opened the previous evening and caught the end of a livestream from my favourite catgirl vtuber.

Not long after the stream finished, I had a reply from Lane:

*SwordBearer*

*I'm glad to hear that things seem pretty clear for you right now. The fact you're so far off their radar is very reassuring, and makes me confident that we can push forward fairly safely. Obviously only send me what you feel comfortable and safe sharing, but I am happy to take this as it goes.*

*That said, this recording is incredible, a lot of very damning quotes. I suspect this will be invaluable in bringing at least one person to justice, when the time comes.*

*Speaking of which, I think we will have the most impact if I aim to get the first article published as close as possible to the planned release date for the new game. As such, if you do have any more information you think is pertinent, and safe to share with me, feel free to send it over and I'll either get it into the initial exposé or a follow-up article, depending where it would fit best.*

*Stay safe, and don't feel you have to take big risks. This is already more than enough to cause significant reputational damage.*

*I really appreciate your help in all of this.*

*Gareth Lane.*

There's no way they can refute the evidence in my possession. I have the smoking gun, and it's firmly placed in Rick's sweaty palm. I got you, you bastards.

## 7 OCTOBER

With less than a week left until *Call of Shooty* is due to release, journalists have been beating down our door (in the most respectful manner), trying to get their hands on review copies. Right now, no such copies exist. Sure, thousands of discs have been printed and packed into various editions of the game, currently leaving warehouses in China on various boats. However, as far as I can tell, those discs contain nothing more than a few out-of-date assets, some junk code to pad out the space (disguised as encrypted game files), and a download link that will hopefully provide access by launch day. Officially, it will have a day-one patch. Unofficially, that day is looking to be at least a few weeks from now. Assuming they want the game to be actually playable.

Within seconds of my workstation booting up this morning, I had an email pop up marked 'urgent'. It seems that with less than four days to go, they've finally relented and agreed to move the game's release date. I was instructed to generate a press release advising that due to circumstances beyond our control, we needed just a little more time to work on the game. Our new date is to be 1 November, the first bit of sensible news I've heard regarding the project, but, honestly, I'm not convinced it will be enough.

Not only that, but I'm worried about how the Gamers™ are going to react to the delay. Maria has been charged with making daily countdown posts leading up to the eleventh. As well as interacting with any mention of the game online, to drive up engagement. It's not hard to see them taking their frustration out on the person who's been getting their hopes up. Multiply that one hundred fold when that person is a woman.

Sure enough, within twenty minutes I received a request from Hannah to produce another 'solemn.jpg'. I selected 'delay' and 'community', as well as entering the new release date.

*Dear Gamers,*

*We understand our fans are passionate about the properties we create, it's one of the things we love most about you.*

*We are terribly sorry to have to tell you that* Call of Shooty's *release is being delayed to 1 November. We would like to apologise for our community manager's posts leading up to our previously announced release date, which will have understandably led many of you to be very excited for our upcoming experience.*

*We know that this decision may lead to some disappointment, especially at this late stage, but please rest assured that our family is hard at work to provide you the finest product we can, because we care deeply about your happiness and enjoyment of the services we provide.*

*Supremacy Software*

Of course they've thrown her under the bus.

I made a copy of the file on a USB stick and delivered it to Maria's desk with a note of apology, and an invitation to meet for coffee if she wants to talk.

'Oh, it's you.' She sniffed, her eyes puffy and red. 'I'm so sorry for how I look.'

'You have nothing to apologise for. Can I get you anything? Do you need a tissue or some water?'

She heaved her mouth into a smile, but her eyes were welling up. 'No, no, you don't have to bother yourself. I'll be fine. They're just disappointed, you know? We can all get upset when we have disappointment.'

'You have my email, if there's anything you need or if you just want someone to talk to, I can respond right away or come down again.'

'Bless you, you're too kind. Right now I have a lot of people who want to talk, so I have to get back to them.' She blew her nose loudly and turned back to her monitor.

If the company won't support her, I'll do everything I can. They can't keep doing this to people.

# CHAPTER 11

# Cause for Celebration?

We're a day away from *Call of Shooty*'s revised release date and the game is still fundamentally broken. The enemy AI is either utterly lethal or suicidal, the coop AI is likely to be tried for war crimes, the user interface keeps changing size depending on which direction the player is looking, and the title screen occasionally sounds like an angry chicken aggressively demanding you 'destroy Bethany' (gods know who Bethany is or what they've done to enrage the chicken).

There are occasional rumours of an *entire* session which didn't have a game-breaking bug, but everyone is keeping that quiet, just in case that's seen as proof that we're ready for release.

Most of the game's assets are finished and there's almost no sign of the eye-meltingly-bright, neon chequerboard pattern which was being used as a temporary texture until the art team were done. All of the maps are completed, now it's just a matter of sending QA through to make sure there aren't any weird bugs caused by looking at the sun while jumping backwards and using a taunt animation, or whatever.

The game looks really good. Nothing like what people saw at X3, but good in its own way.

As the game still wasn't ready, Rick gave in and agreed to: 'Push it back two more weeks, but not a day later. I don't care if we have to send out code that turns every goddamn machine it comes into contact with into an expensive paperweight. We can't afford to miss out on Black Friday. That's our payday!'

I pumped out another auto-generated statement for the public. Thankfully this time they went with the angle 'we're polishing a near-perfect experience to perfection', instead of pointing the finger of blame at some innocent member of the 'family'.

I was so glad to hear about the delay, not just for the sake of the poor overworked dev team, but because things have hit a bit of a roadblock with Lane.

*SwordBearer*
*Sorry for the recent lack of communication, I've been butting heads with the senior editors over that audio recording. Even though it's clear to me the audio's real, we have to legally cover our asses when dealing with powerful people and allegations with potential legal ramifications.*

*Thanks to corroboration from a secondary source, they have finally agreed that there is enough evidence to give it legitimacy.*

*At this point, I'm fairly confident in saying that the recording will be the cornerstone of my whole piece.*

*I can't get into the specifics of what else is going to be in the report until it's ready, but you're certainly not alone in having concerns about the company.*

*Thank you once again for all your help and for putting your trust in me throughout the process. Please stay safe, this should all be over soon.*

*Gareth Lane*

Every email I get back from Gareth reassures me a little more that I made the right choice in trusting him. My chance to strike a real blow against this company is achingly close. I'll put such a dent in their sales figures they won't know what to do. An extra layer of failure they can consider on the way to prison for what they've done.

While progress on the game as release date looms has been impressive, all is not well down on the dev floor. I've taken to holding my breath as I pass, even going up in the elevator. It's not a slight against them personally, but you take that many people, force them to stay in one place for months on end without sleep, fresh clothes, or the vaguest hint of a shower (or even a wet wipe wash at their desk) and things start to get a little over ripe. Rick and Chad didn't notice for the longest time, as they tend to come up the executive elevator from the car park, straight into their offices. However, in the last week or so the reek of caffeine sweat and despair finally made its way up to the top floor and into the boardroom.

I did suggest getting the devs a couple of hours off in order to go home, scrape the lumps off and have at least a rinse, but they're concerned if any of the development team leaves the building, they may never return – frankly I wouldn't blame them if they did just make a break for it. As it stands, Clark is being ordered to spray them all down with fabric freshener and dry shampoo, as well as turning up the oxygen pump and the extractor system.

I'd initially thought that by 'oxygen pump' they just meant air conditioning, but no, it turns out that in order to keep the dev team in a good mood, they pump extra oxygen into the air on that floor. It's something Edwin once heard they do in casinos to keep people euphoric. A complete myth, but I can't be bothered to try and correct him anymore. Either way, I now know why I always felt so positive when I was down there.

I've got an appointment tomorrow morning for a company to come in and start fitting an airtight door system. They want to pass it off as a security measure, but the fact people will have to go through a sort of decontamination chamber to get out will probably tip someone off.

As launch day approaches – for the third time – I've been trying to feed as much last-minute information to Gareth Lane as possible.

*Hi*

*I'm not sure how much spare word count you have for the article, but I wanted to give you an update on the current state of things.*

*Right now, staff are being forced into total crunch. Many have not left the building in months, and without time for breaks or personal care, their health and hygiene is suffering.*

*There are bottles of urine under desks as many are too scared to take a bathroom break since they are chastised for doing so.*

*Due to increased security at this time, I've been unable to provide photographic evidence, but if I do find a way to do so safely, I shall send them your way (with appropriate content warnings).*

*SB*

I attached the latest batch of safe-to-use audio recordings. Part of me is desperate to just drive the blade home and send everything I have, but I must be patient. If I get found out and end up in court, I'm looking at costs equivalent to ten years' salary for breaching non-disclosure or non-disparagement agreement *per infraction.* Once the boys are sitting in court and I can be assured of full whistleblower protections, then I'll send it all crashing down on top of them.

> *SB*
> *Thank you for your latest update and the additional files. The larger the body of evidence we have, the better. If not for the initial article, then certainly for any follow-up we do. I'm sure the public will want more details and clarifications and all this information will answer a lot of that.*
> *I've agreed with my publisher to go live on 14 November as it should have the most impact, right before the big release.*
> *Keep safe.*
> *Gareth Lane*

## 14 NOVEMBER

I woke up early today, feeling an odd tension. Initially I just thought it was hunger as I've only been eating one meal a day for a while. Huge thanks to my landlord for increasing my rent as a holiday gift to himself.

He deserves it for all his hard... property ownership and complete lack of maintenance work on the building. I bet that really takes it out of him.

I comforted myself that it's nearly bonus season, so heating and nutrition is only a few short weeks away.

I could hear a rattling buzz by my door and peered out from underneath the covers to see my phone, which had fled my nightstand and was making a break for freedom, dragging its charging cord like a tail, after somehow pulling it out of the wall socket.

At first I thought I was still dreaming, but then I remembered: today's the day. I rolled out of bed, protected from the frigid air by the six layers of pyjamas I'd taken to wearing, and chased down the escapee.

'Back in your cell... cellphone.' I towered over its quivering form and snatched it up before it could fully slither under the door and out into the promised Land of Hall Way. 'There's no escape for you, my pretty.'

My notifications were a mess. Between the automatic alerts I set up a few months back to flag if there was any press relating to Supremacy Software and abuse, and several panicked emails from work requesting everyone at the office immediately, things were blowing up.

Sure enough, on the first page of *World Gaming News* (entertainingly flanked on either side by a huge animated ad for *Call of Shooty* and the words 'Last Chance To Pre-Order') was the headline:

*The Human Cost of Supremacy Software's Annual Release Cycle*

*When it comes to big-budget console gaming, there's no company today with as much instant name recognition as New York-based Supremacy Software. Their titles, regardless of actual quality, demand a level of recognition and attention by virtue of their flashy spectacle, commercial success and surprisingly consistent critical reception.*

*However, behind the flash, polish and visual sheen of the company's annual releases lies a depressing human cost. Over the past eight months, an investigative report of working conditions at Supremacy Software, conducted by WGN, has discovered a company whose success has been built on a foundation of young, fresh-faced developer talent, overworked to the point of collapse, after which they are cruelly discarded. At the top of the company, an executive class whose ruthless use of fear and threats of violence ensure total compliance. Multiple sources have confirmed the presence of an office culture which routinely protects those in management positions from seeing consequences for actions which have, at times, veered into illegal acts of abuse.*

Specifics about which individuals were involved in events were omitted, either to protect his sources or because they were unable or unwilling to corroborate. Either way, the overall picture was clear. Supremacy is a studio rife with abuse from top to bottom. Mistreatment of staff, unfair overtime practices, sexist language, as well as physical and sexual abuse.

There was a full transcript of Rick's outburst last month, including mention of the sounds of a swishing cane. The way he repeatedly name-dropped the company meant there was no way he could plausibly deny the events.

He's finished.

There were a number of witness accounts from the paintballing weekend. I'd not heard a full description of what happened when the legal team went on their night-time sortie up until then.

*They didn't even feed us or provide shelter for the night. So we all huddled together under the trees and tried to rest. Someone with better survival*

*skills than me built a fire and we all tried to get*
*some sleep. I don't know what time it happened, but*
*next thing I knew I was being repeatedly shot by*
*this looming figure that just stared down at me.*
*We all ran. I know some didn't find the rest of the*
*group again until daylight. Since then, I'm scared*
*to sleep. I have a panic attack if there's a loud*
*noise. I'm so tired, I keep seeing those staring*
*figures on the edge of my vision.*

I was horrified to read about someone referred to only as Ms R, who'd received unwanted sexual advances from one of the executives during that creepy barbecue. Since they talked about being singled out and taken off to another area, I figured it could only be one of our huddled group, but I couldn't be sure who, or which of the execs was responsible.

*He took me into a private room and was pushing me*
*to drink champagne. Since I hadn't seen it being*
*poured, there was no way I was touching that*
*stuff. When that didn't work, he started asking*
*if I wanted 'to climb the corporate ladder' or if*
*I'd be 'willing to accept a raise... in return for a*
*raise'. So a lot was implied rather than said, but*
*he made his meaning abundantly clear.*

Had Legal been there as an alibi? I saw a few of them making notes. Of course that would imply a deeply concerning level of premeditation.

Reading through, it became obvious that there had been far more folks involved in passing information than I'd ever considered. I guess IT hadn't shut down that email nearly as quickly as they'd hoped.

My mind flashed back to the barbecue and how suspicious the dark-haired woman had been towards me. She'd been acting like I was an agent of the executives, at worst, or another Hannah, at best. If that's how some of them see me, it's no surprise I wasn't their first choice to confide in about what was happening.

I'd assumed that Fidget and Ez would account for me to the others, but with such a huge team, I guess they can't know everyone.

*The more staff with whom I spoke, the more such stories came to light. Each witness corroborating the accounts of several others, each with a story more ghoulish than the last. Were it not for the mountains of evidence provided at great personal risk by those involved, any one of these narratives could be taken for exaggerated tales of cartoonish villainy. Instead I found the truth to be far more disturbing than fiction.*

*Those who reported issues to Supremacy's human resources department reported they were offered no support whatsoever. Those targeted by extreme public harassment, stemming from public perception of their role within the company, were advised that since abuse was coming from external sources they were 'matters relating to private individuals' and therefore none of the company's concern.*

*During this investigation I was able to uncover reports going back nearly six years concerning a manager by the name of Roger Meinder. This included court records relating to numerous cases of sexual assaults of young women, at which his wife at the time had been star witness for the prosecution.*

*However, despite numerous complaints of such assaults by Mr Meinder, which took place within Supremacy Software's New York offices, he was permitted to keep his lucrative pay package and position of power while being quietly moved to a different department.*

*The culture of abuse and covering for that abuse is deeply rooted within Supremacy Software, so the question must be asked: is it possible to rebuild and reform this company, or is the rot too deep for anything to be saved?*

*If this article has distressed you in its content, there are links below to a number of support services.*

*Furthermore, if you feel the human cost of annually released big franchise games is too high and that you can no longer support an abusive firm like Supremacy Software, there is still time to cancel your pre-order for* Call of Shooty, *which releases tomorrow.*

My pulse was racing as I read through the article. I felt the thrill of released tension, knowing that I'd finally struck a blow against evil. A feeling which was mixed with deep dread as I frantically searched for anything which might incriminate me directly. After two full readings, I was certain I was in the clear.

Time to stand over my defeated foe and claim victory. Their reign of evil has finally ended.

On my way upstairs from the lobby, I noticed a large number of the security team standing around by the newly installed airlock which led into the dev floor. Anyone arriving or re-entering the area had to undergo a full pat-down and a scan with a handheld metal detector before they were allowed through the checkpoint. I've seen less thorough inspections flying international.

That's the end of my secretive recordings of the goings-on down there.

## Meeting minutes – 14 November

Drinks orders for the board:
Single-shot lattes all round

No time for the usual bravado and pissing contests today. No need for me to brew half a plantation's worth of beans. Not today.

The boys sat slumped in their chairs looking dazed and tense. Conversely, Edwin's face bore the smallest hint of a smile as he reclined in stately manner upon the high-backed leather chair, which was pushed slightly back. He had one arm outstretched, fingers drumming lightly upon the table where glass met mahogany and one leg crossed over the other, causing his pant leg to ride up revealing those blue argyle socks which he reserves for 'high-level business meetings' (aka vanishing from the office as soon as is reasonable in favour of a round of golf at the club). He seemed to emanate a wistful sense of complete peace, which made a surprising change from his usual bitter scowls on this of all days.

I took my seat, which is usually about the time they burst into life, prompted by the smell of roasted beans. Today though, they just sat in silence for a good five minutes. Each seemingly in their own little world, the boys occasionally nodding or silently moving their lips, as if planning their first words with extreme hesitation.

Finally Chad inhaled deeply through his nose and he patted the table next to Edwin. 'Well, buddy, it's been a good run, huh?'

At this, Edwin's smile widened and his eyes seemed to finally focus on the room around him. 'It has been a long and profitable ride, but this moment comes to us all eventually,' he replied, with a slow nod.

My heart was in my mouth, what the heck were they talking about? What arcane rite were they in the midst of performing, in order to slither free of the consequences of their despicable actions?

'Still,' Edwin continued eventually, 'I don't mind helping you boys out. The old golden parachute should cushion the fall a bit, eh?'

They all chuckled before breaking into a jovial chat about the article.

They were rather proud of handsy Roger for 'living his truth.'

Chad admitted that he'd been 'joking around with a few of the hotties at the barbecue'. 'You know, see if they're ready to handle some high-value assets,' he said, turning to me with an exaggerated wink.

If I'd eaten that morning, there's no way he wouldn't be wearing the contents of my stomach. As it was, I had to hide my revulsion by sipping my coffee.

Of course they were making arrangements with HR to have every one of Chad's potential asset managers quietly dismissed, as well as a few of the men on the dev team they considered either too good-looking (therefore a general threat) or 'possible SJWs, looking to score by standing up for their women'.

'No need to say they're the ones responsible, but if we happen to follow up the firings with an announcement that "following an investigation into allegations, we've taken steps to remedy the matter", the public will connect the dots.'

I was instructed on the inputs needed for our public response, and, just like that, they were ready to move on.

So much for my ultimate victory. I guess I should have expected a multi-stage boss fight when the beast had three heads. Still, one down, two to go.

'Tomorrow's probably going to come with some pushback, right?'

'Oh yeah, we let them start pre-installation as soon as that article broke this morning. No way to cancel their pre-orders, because it's already been delivered.'

'Yeah, but we all know there's nothing on those discs and the download is full of junk to pack out download size.'

'True, and even once the day-one patch drops with the real game, they're going to notice it's missing about forty per cent of the stated features.'

The solution to possible pushback regarding missing features was to prepare a 'roadmap'. The game becomes less of a complete product, as advertised, and more like an advent calendar. Sure, you open it on day one and there's a little candy inside to keep you going, but we're pretty sure there will probably be more to come by the end of Q1 next year, maybe. Thanks for ~~paying~~ playing, suckers.

People who bought the game aren't even going to know it's incomplete until they've played through the tutorial mission (which is just long enough to put them past the reimbursement window). Even then, they'd have to click into specific modes from the menu to find out what is or isn't present.

As for the developers, release day doesn't mean a damned thing. It's not the end because, for now at least, the company is willing to continue with adding content and fixing minor bugs.

The meeting finally wrapped up and they all stood. The boys

took turns to shake Edwin's hand, pat him warmly on the shoulder, and thank him for all he's done at the company. Whatever that might have been.

At last, Edwin headed for the door, stopping only briefly to lean over me, flick my cup onto the carpet, and then, with a smirk, ask, 'Would you mind cleaning that up, young lady?' before laughing his way out of the room. The boys followed behind, each taking the opportunity to kick the cup away from me as I reached for it. Clearly they needed to exercise a little power over someone today.

Let them have their fun, it's clear they don't suspect that I'm the one who leaked most of the information to the press. They'll get what's coming to them.

Back in my little office I went ahead and generated the 'parachute' announcement image for Edwin, as requested.

It read:

To Our Loyal Fans and Supporters,
We understand the turmoil created by recent accusations against the company creating your favourite upcoming game.

We would like to assure you that we take these allegations very seriously, and will be consulting with Union & Buster's law firm in order to conduct a very fair and thorough internal investigation. These allegations do not align with our company values and we are deeply saddened that someone has felt the need to attack our family in this way.

We would like to assure you that we are taking swift action and will be making decisive changes here at the company.

I was initially confused. Edwin has done nothing in the last year, as far as I can tell, apart from sit in his office polishing his putter. Eww, not a euphemism, not a euphemism. Ick.

But of course, that's the point! Edwin is just a scapegoat. He's not being labelled with anything specific. He's not being named as responsible for any specific misdeed that took place at the company. He's just conveniently old enough that he can retire, be seen as the only potential bad apple, and leave the company with a clean slate in the eyes of the press. Meanwhile, he's off to spend his senior years playing golf, sailing his new yacht and enjoying his huge pension, along with a steady flow of dividend payments from his company shares.

I was just considering that all was not lost – since there was no way they could get away with it, what with that recording, which fully caught Rick red-handed – when I received an email from Legal advising me to make an addition to the message:

*With regards to the alleged audio recording being shared in news coverage, we intend to prove that this was a maliciously created fake designed to besmirch the good name of our company by a jealous former employee.*

Oh gods. Really? They're just going to pretend my smoking gun audio isn't real? Surely they can't just pretend it's fake? I got literal audio of it happening. Lane could release the audio to the public and it'd be clear it's not doctored, right? Surely nobody's going to believe someone would fake something like that. There is no way they can just say it's not real, and sidestep any consequences, can they?

I suddenly realised why they were so damned calm upstairs. They're literally just hoping they can pretend the evidence isn't real, and confidently stride right past the article at a brisk pace.

I felt light-headed and dizzy at the prospect my smoking gun wasn't being treated as the dangerous irrefutable evidence it so clearly was. I'm shaking with fear and frustration. Is this just the world we live in now? Corporations and politicians alike are going to just shout the word Deepfake at any evidence of their misdeeds and count on the masses not knowing enough to dispute their claims?

No, I can't get disheartened. There's plenty of solid evidence throughout the article, backed up by multiple sources, even outside of that recording. There's no way that's the end of it. I'm sure the press will look deeper into things and conclude that the company is lying to get out of trouble. No journalist worth their salt is going to just believe what the company says, not with all that dirt I've dished up.

Once outlets start looking deeper into the story, they'll see Edwin's departure is nothing more than a clear attempt to cover their tracks, and that Supremacy Software has no plans to change any part of the culture going forward. This isn't over.

### LUNCH

I sat on my phone, checking for any updates regarding the article. Still plenty of momentum going on, a few outlets finally got around to fleshing out their placeholder article pages. Some sites included updates which featured our response, but no further comment on the matter.

I was concerned that it was only doing the rounds in the gaming press. Nothing had strayed into the wider world of journalism, though surely it's only a matter of time. Mainstream media is always a little slower to pick up on things outside of shock politics and celebrity gossip.

**16 NOVEMBER**

*Call of Shooty* finally released and the last twenty-four hours have been *a lot*. Reviewers were finally given code for the game around two hours prior to launch. Not nearly long enough to get it downloaded, played, and to formulate opinions for a review. That didn't seem to stop several of them though. By 2 a.m. there were at least five reviews up for the game – every screenshot was a still, taken from the launch video we put out. Lots of very vague language and 10/10 scores. Not even the faintest mention of all the missing features. Clearly they were desperate to just get their reviews out before anyone else. Seemingly all that matters to them is getting all those click-throughs for ad revenue. By midmorning more accurate reviews were starting to surface, but even those were scoring in the high 90 per cent range.

Only a single review even mentioned the abuse allegations, and that was in such a throwaway line, buried near the end of the piece, that it may as well have been written by our own PR department.

According to the games press, *Call of Shooty* is 'great', 'a triumph of modern game design', 'an absolute must', 'game of the year', 'a marvel', 'the last game you'll ever need', and – perhaps most laughably – 'absolutely flawless'. The first wave of reviews seemed infinitely more interested in stoking the confirmation bias of an audience that doesn't want to think complex thoughts about the media they consume, and just wants to be excited for products.

Meanwhile, on social media, those who dared to air their, very reasonable, disappointment at the number of missing features, were being aggressively shouted down by the usual tribalistic mega fans who dubbed the naysayers 'loser scrubs' or 'fake gamers' for not getting with the choir to sing the game's praises. It seemed that all the crunch and abuse had resulted in a game that was close enough to what they were promised and so the bad news was to be brushed under the rug of hype and never spoken of again.

At that point, many had been shouting their love and desire for a new *Call of Shooty* from the rooftops for months on end. No doubt they'd have felt pretty silly if they now had to own up and admit that it wasn't actually all that good.

The wave of praise that overshadowed the article in its first day or so live was incredibly frustrating, but I can only hope people will get back to the news once the shiny new game excitement has had a moment to settle.

Of course, the issues didn't end at the game itself, the 'premium editions' of the game were causing all sorts of issues. Children were being rushed to hospital after playing with the lead-painted helmets, reports came in that the tote bags were causing severe allergic reactions in some customers, and the dog tags are turning people's skin blue. So far I've not been requested to generate any further solemn jpegs. I suspect they want to keep apologies to a minimum during the initial rush. Don't acknowledge the bad thing and maybe those yet to drop their cash on it won't hear about it and change their minds.

I'm hoping that once the reviews-for-clicks period is over things will settle down and people will get back to the real news, the appalling abuse that goes on behind the scenes here. Right now though, it feels like our abuse means nothing. The masses got their game and they don't seem to care *how* that came to be.

Indeed, I've seen a disturbing number claiming the abuse was a good thing and 'if that's what making the new shiny thing costs, then so be it.'

Of course, release day didn't change anything for the development team. They're still under massive crunch. Fixing bugs, holding the servers together with duct tape and prayers, and of course, finishing the actual game. For them release was just another day of pressure, stress, and choking on their own unwashed stench.

### 25 NOVEMBER

The day before Black Friday I was told just after lunch that I *will* work late. Apparently it's something of an annual tradition. The invite list includes Rick and Chad, a select few from upper management who are being groomed for the boardroom, and Chad's nephew whom he says just 'graduated' from business school. Chad actually did air quotes when he said graduated, so I assume money and power were more involved in making that happen than any actual aptitude for business.

That evening I laid out the boardroom as requested; the large monitor was cleaned and set to display a website for which I had needed to pass through six layers of increasingly strong authentication in order to access. However, when I finally reached the end of the process, the screen showed only what looked like a perfectly looping video of a red silk sheet billowing gently from some unseen fan. There was nothing to say what I was looking at, why this wafting fabric was so strictly exclusive, or what possible reason a room full of up-and-coming, twenty-something white men would be organising a party focusing on it. The internet is full of ten-hour-long videos of unobtrusive background scenery which isn't nearly so hard to access.

The table had to be fully laid out with buckets of popcorn, chips, dips, a frankly obscene number of incredibly expensive alcoholic beverages, along with a huge, heavy flight case that turned out to be full of casino-grade poker chips (not the kind they sell as casino-grade online, these were actually more fancy than the ones we used when my cousin took me to Atlantic City for the weekend a few years back).

Once everything was set up I had nothing to do but take a seat and wait. I must have passed out from exhaustion and hunger because I awoke with a jolt at around 3 a.m. Popcorn momentarily cascaded down around me, and standing far too close, with a look of mild disappointment was Hank, that manager from the senior dev meetings. His ass kissing must have done the job with someone, since he'd been invited to whatever this was.

Already on high alert, my heart was going like it wanted to explode out of my chest, and, fighting my natural instinct to just punch him in the throat, I demanded, 'What the hell are you doing?'

One corner of his mouth began to crawl upward and he replied, 'You made me look like a fool, letting me think that the board only wanted the vertical slice scrapped. It seemed reasonable to repay the sentiment, after all "turnabout is fair play", wouldn't you agree?'

I stood up, sending yet more popcorn tumbling from my hair, and stammered, 'I-I was thinking of the developers, who already had enough on their plate.'

He snorted, tossed a popped kernel up into the air and almost caught it in his mouth. It bounced off his lip and into a bowl of chips, causing him to immediately turn away and become deeply interested in the variety of drinks on offer.

If that had gone as planned, I'm sure he'd have been so pleased with himself. I on the other hand was struggling not to rub it in as

I was still seething at the audacity of him having touched me while I was unconscious.

Had I been working anywhere else for the last eleven months, I'd have immediately been contacting HR to report him for inappropriate behaviour. I know where I am though; the only person who will save me is me.

Cautiously excusing myself, I headed downstairs to grab a can of Meth in order to wake myself up enough to avoid any further somnolence. In my head, my mom loudly chastised me while floating every possible terrifying outcome of being the lone girl asleep at a house party.

Before heading back, I made my way to the bathroom in order to tidy myself up and pick any remaining pieces of popcorn from my hair with visibly shaking hands. I took a few deep breaths and gulped down the goopy red Energy Gel as fast as it would pour. As the caffeine started to hit me, I could feel my upset turning into burning rage. Self-blame became sheer indignation at Hank's utter audacity and I used that as an anchor to compose myself.

I know what Hank just did isn't the worst thing that has happened here this year, not by a long shot, but this is the first time I've actually been the one facing down this corporate entitled creepiness first hand. The fact that he felt that confident mere days after Lane's story broke worries me. I worry the article hasn't so much as temporarily slowed down the rates of abuse within these walls.

Returning to the boardroom, I found Hank still checking labels on the many and various bottles of booze. He glanced over as I entered and ordered a bourbon on the rocks like this was a fancy bar and I'd been keeping him waiting.

Breathing through my anger, I did as I was asked, pouring out an over-generous measure into a deceptively large glass, which I handed to him with as close to a smile as I could winch onto my face at that moment.

Shortly thereafter, the rest of the men started to file in. Of course they were all men, I wasn't even surprised. The drinks began to flow (luckily most were more than happy to pour their own), the chat became more casual, and I was careful to keep myself quiet and tucked in the corner by the door, in order to remain as undisturbed as possible. Despite the seemingly good humour in the room, Hank's actions had put me on extra-high alert and I did not feel at all safe surrounded by this lot, especially when they appeared to be letting their hair down for the night.

I did however take the opportunity to fill up on snacks since I didn't want to pass out again once the caffeine wore off. Without something more solid inside me, I feared that should one of them force a drink on me, I was likely to be immediately drunk, considering how little else was in my system.

About an hour later, after a brief musical interlude, the screen switched from the flowing red fabric to a number of small camera feeds, each showing long queues of people standing alongside concrete walls. In the centre, one feed was displayed much larger, although it didn't seem to be in any way distinct from any of the others. People, wrapped up against the night cold, standing in lines, many of whom were hemmed in with those temporary metal railings you sometimes see at parades. All of the screens appeared to be live CCTV feeds. For reasons that didn't immediately become clear, everyone in the room became quite excited at this, and before I knew it, they were pointing people out and placing bets.

It took some time, but I eventually worked out what we were looking at. This had to be people lining up, waiting for the opening of the stores for the Black Friday sale. Some of them looked to have been camping out there for days. Sure, if you camp out because you're homeless the police will take all your stuff and move you on, if you're there three days early for a discount TV, you're warmly welcomed.

Still, I was clueless as to what the betting was about or why grainy, monochrome footage of people camping out for discounts warranted a party.

Finally, at 6 a.m., it began. On each screen, the feed flicked from the queues outside to colour footage from the internal store cameras, and doors opened with a desperate stampede, as if a tidal wave of shoppers had burst the barricades and were flooding inside.

'Here we fucking go!' yelled Chad, throwing his hands in the air and sloshing most of his drink down his arm and across the floor.

Suddenly it was all horrifyingly clear. They'd been picking their champions for the ensuing melee. Placing bets like it was a cockfight and these shivering consumers were their prize birds.

At the front of the surge, a middle-aged woman in a bright-red hoodie lost her footing and was trampled by the swarm that followed.

'The fuck is wrong with you, you dumb bitch!' yelled one of the seniors from Finance, throwing a handful of poker chips on the floor in his anger.

The others broke into derisive laughter as they continued to cheer on their own champions.

'You just can't pick a winner like me, bud—' Hank's jeering was cut short as an athletic-looking young man in a college blazer took a tumble into a display of printer paper and was buried in the resulting cascade. '*Fuck!*'

The boys were particularly happy to see the utter carnage over re-stocks of *Call of Shooty* Premium Edition. I watched in horror as one shopper swung a display console into a young woman's head in order to pry away the last copy, which she'd just beaten him to in a foot race. Something which elicited an ecstatic cry from the audience before me.

On every feed it was absolute carnage. People fighting, screaming, trampling, and, in a few cases, biting in order to get the best deals they could. All the while the appalling men I was stuck there with, cheered and whooped and continued to exchange chips as the horror show played out, now in glorious high definition on the giant screen.

I felt utter contempt for each and every one of them. A feeling which did not abate when Chad raised a toast to his nephew – whose name he was too drunk to remember (it's Chet) – as the newest member of the board at Supremacy Software. Of course, why not throw some nepotism in the pot. Just what this stew of filth needs.

While most of the party were happy to get their own drinks – only calling for me if they were low on some style of snack or the ice buckets needed refilling – Hank seemed to take personal delight in treating me as bar staff. Occasionally demanding I mix up some elaborate cocktails. Since I couldn't think of any other quick and plausibly deniable revenge, I made each one *way* stronger than is reasonable and by 8 a.m. he was slumped in a corner, hugging a plastic potted plant. I took the opportunity to duck back to my little office and grab a permanent marker from my supply and just... casually leave it on the table next to Hank.

It took less than ten minutes before Rick was loudly calling for an audience to watch him draw a dick and balls on the unconscious man's cheek. Pictures of this masterpiece were quickly snapped and uploaded to every form of social media, as well as the management private messaging group. Not long thereafter, they were all taking turns to make their mark, and within the hour he looked like a heavily tattooed, drunk biker who had been forced into a suit for a bet.

What?

I didn't do anything. I'm just there to predict and facilitate the whims and desires of the executives.

The party went on for hours, show after show as each time zone hit 6 a.m. and local doors opened. By the time we hit Eastern, I felt numb and desperate. Deciding that I'd just deal with any repercussions that might arise, I slipped out of the door and headed down into the presumed safety of Candace and Jenette's office on the floor below. There I passed out against the door, hoping my weight would be enough to make a casual investigator assume it was locked.

I stirred some hours later and snuck out of the building, spotted only by Clark, who just gave a look of curiosity followed by a friendly wave.

I'm exhausted and emotionally wrung out, but I have the weekend to try and decompress. Right now, I just know that nothing has changed, and I fear that nothing is going to change.

# CHAPTER 12

# Taking Out the Trash

## 5 DECEMBER

All hell has broken loose, and I'm not just talking about the demons who run this company. First off, following the initial (and quite presumptuous) reviews from a few outlets, there was a string of critiques towards the end of last month which quite rightly scored *Call of Shooty* much lower than the execs would have liked. While they wanted nine or more from all parties, our final aggregate score was actually 8.7 out of 10 (although that's mainly because the majority of review sites seem to treat a score of seven as being the equivalent of absolute failure. I blame the school grading system for that particular skewed view).

Reviewers rightly pointed out that there were tons of graphical bugs, unstable servers, features missing or not as good as they had been in our vertical slice demo, and one or two even dared to question the sheer number of microtransactions and real money obfuscating virtual currencies.

To be fair, they have added two extra steps to the previous financial obfuscation as yet another way to lock small amounts of money into the economy. You now spend cash to purchase Cyber Tokens, which are burned to make Mega Credits, which are invested into Tech Points, which are traded to get Nanomachine Vials, which are crafted into Red Sapphires, which are used to buy Eonium Gems.

Whatever else, 8.7 was not enough for Rick, who declared 'it may as well have been literal shit that they put out' while throwing anything that wasn't nailed down across the boardroom. Because apparently he turns into a toddler who's been served dinosaur nuggets on the wrong coloured plate when he doesn't get his way.

Meanwhile online, some of our more fanatical Gamers™ were sending death threats to anyone in the press who dared speak ill of even the most glaring error or disgusting monetisation features. Many were not only willing to forgive the flaws, but were angrily defending them as giving the game 'additional character', and actually making the experience of playing more interesting. All said with a smug air of 'well, if you don't see why it's so good, it's because you're not as clever as I am'. Those people are wild. Still, I suppose it's a sign that all the marketing, tie-ins, and carefully massaged hype have done exactly what they're designed for. Supremacy Software has spent a lot of money in order to add a non-stick coating of tribalistic fanaticism. Probably more money than they ever spent on the games themselves.

Not only that, there was a campaign of abuse targeting anyone who had ever said they were hired here, who happened to be perceived as female (including a very confusing few days for Michelle, the burliest French-Canadian man I've ever met). At first it was a few nasty messages to their personal emails, but before long there was doxxing and death threats, and at last we were hearing about SWAT teams turning up at their homes in the dead of night due to false reports of gunfire or terrorist action anonymously sent to the cops.

For others, there were envelopes full of mysterious powder

with threatening notes attached arriving at their doors. The sad reality, those who were actually being personally targeted hadn't left the office to see their loved ones in months. They didn't directly experience the consequences, but their families did.

To these elite Gamers™ the only reason anyone would have spoken out about abuse must be to hurt their precious and vulnerable billion-dollar company out of spite (and the sole targeting of women would be because 'everyone knows girls hate video games', right?). I've heard Gamers™ say some awful shit about women online, but even by their usual standards, some of this was horrifying.

Of course, we have a solemn jpeg for that.

Within two weeks of the game's release, the dev floor was empty. Just as the team started to breathe a sigh of relief, following days of furious patching to cover the worst of the problems, every one of them was out the door. Several actually had to be cut out of their chairs, as a combination of sweat and grime had somehow fused them to the fabric to a concerning degree. To save money next year, Chad has proposed just filling the department with plastic deck furniture, which will be harder to adhere to.

Once their ID badges were logged back in with the security team and they were unceremoniously ejected from the building, many just stood around outside the office for hours. Unsure where to go, or even what day it was, they just milled around, blinking vacantly like hollow, rotten-toothed zombies. I'm not sure how long they would have remained out there if Security hadn't called the cops to come and move them on.

Thereafter, Clark spent several days working alongside an external team to strip down the makeshift hovels which had been formed around every desk, and then sanitise the whole area. A year ago I might have been at least surprised to see the sheer number of bottles of frothy, stale urine that were unearthed from within those empty can and pizza box dwellings. That's to say nothing of the numerous pairs of oozing, soiled underwear which had been stuffed into drawers, and bloody, sweat-stained shirts, whose owners could be identified by the body shape they held with impressive rigidity. Now it barely fazed me, and I hated that.

During the final days of the development team's employment, Legal were buzzing around like angry hornets. Members of the team were regularly being taken off for random security interviews, keyloggers were installed on every computer, and listening devices were clumsily concealed in all the bathrooms and among the office flora. (I first discovered this when I had to put out a small fire which started as a result of Chad pouring his unwanted coffee into one of the bugged plant pots.) Perhaps most concerningly of all, a cell phone jammer was activated somewhere in the building. Okay, there's no way I can prove that, but one afternoon my cell just stopped working. As soon as I was thirty yards from the front door on my way home that evening, it all came back to life, and it was like that until the second the last of the devs left the building on firing day. Sure, why not throw in some completely illegal signal jamming; that seems like a great idea for a morally good and reasonable company.

Of course, only those at the top of this appalling heap get to see any benefits for success or departure. Using the low aggregate scores for *Call of Shooty* as an excuse, not one of the team left with even the sniff of a bonus. Legal have prepared an official statement, just in case any family members of the former devs are savvy enough to come chasing for unpaid overtime or bonuses. They'll be told that while the game is the fastest-selling product we've ever released, it failed to meet its *quite significant* budget and was, in fact, a financial loss. This is technically true if you only count the profit made on physical copies of the game sold, but once you factor in digital copies and all those microtransactions, the game has made unfathomable profit, a fact that will be conveniently sidestepped.

That would explain how they manage to give themselves such obscene bonuses at the beginning of every year, and why they always need a new team of developers come January. So much amazing talent, sucked up, wrung out, and tossed away like garbage, probably never to work in the industry again following their treatment here.

While further firings were brushed off as simply routine house cleaning, Gareth Lane did his best to keep the story in people's minds.

*Supremacy Software Staff Laid Off Despite 8.7 Aggregate Review Score*

*Supremacy Software's Calculated Attempt to Undermine Leaked Abuse Audio*

*Female Developers at Supremacy Software Targeted with SWAT Raids*

*Supremacy Software's Tech War – Crushing A Rebellion With The Tools Of State Surveillance*

The PR department insisted that all matters had been dealt with 'as part of an internal investigation. Following the conclusion of this review, appropriate changes have been made within the company. These included a degree of internal restructuring which has now been finalised. We believe that these actions will prevent any future occurrence of similar events.'

Hands washed, the games press unquestioningly reported on our 'bold, decisive action to protect staff' rather than the fact that this was yet more abuse. Since then the story has been dying down, old news. Those online who had smelled blood and were momentarily caught up in a mob who insisted 'no peace until the abused receive justice!' had already become bored and moved on, or were being shouted down by fans who demand they 'shut up' or to 'stop going on about it'. Maybe the seven-minute attention span claim wasn't so far off.

People are already tired of hearing the negativity. No time for downers when there's a new game to be diving into. Fewer press outlets are picking up the new information and it feels more and more like shouting into the void. They're happy to report record sales, record player counts, early esports hype, DLC rumours, even speedrunners (who already have completion times for the campaign down to tens of seconds). Nobody wants to look into the ugly face of how all that came to be though.

I'd foolishly assumed the full recording of the whipping threats finding its way online would be more than enough to finish them off, but most accepted our PR statement that it was some kind of fake.

One account (created very recently with no picture) came forward to say they'd actually acted in the piece and confirmed it was part of a campaign by a shady group on the darkweb who wanted to blackmail the company. I find it difficult to believe that wasn't someone from our own legal team working through the damage control plan.

Despite my hope that it would just be a matter of time before the mainstream press caught up with the world of games journalism, not one mention of it filtered onto a major news network. I have alerts set up on my cell to let me know if any of them do mention Supremacy Software, but so far, not one iota of interest from outside the bubble of the gaming world.

Not in print, not online, not even on twenty-four-hour live-rolling news TV. Sadly, mass media still seems to perceive gaming as something frivolous, meant for kids, unworthy of being discussed by proper adults.

The closest we came to genuine press outrage was when some governor from deep in the Bible Belt declared he would be 'starting a campaign to have microtransactions banned within the state'. The article stated his nephew (thirteen) had managed to completely drain the family bank account while trying to obtain an extraordinarily rare gun skin from one of our randomised loot boxes. Even that garnered barely more than a headline outside of local news sources.

Once the boys had finished congratulating themselves for hunting a whale worth more than $30,000, I was told to issue a solemn jpeg stating the importance of parental oversight on children's use of gaming consoles. That was followed up by a *generous* donation (a small percentage of the child's bounty) towards said governor's re-election campaign. By the afternoon, the story had vanished.

I've kept in contact with Lane, but it sounds like things have been difficult since the execs started pressuring *WGN*.

SB
*I'm doing my best to keep momentum going, but the attention span of the average gamer seems to barely last beyond the time it takes to read the article. Even less if one of these AAA publishers drops a preview trailer for the next big thing.*

*I have to believe that if you asked a gamer to their face whether they think the people who make the games they spend hundreds of hours playing deserve fair treatment and pay, that they'd say yes.*

*However, put them behind a screen, get them in a group of their peers, and it feels like no cost is too high, as long as they get the thing they want.*

*There has been talk of boycotts over working conditions, but ever increasing sales figures imply that either isn't having an effect or it's all just veiled hypocrisy.*

*I'm going to be honest, this isn't what I hoped working in games journalism would be like. I got into this for the same reason as most, to turn my love of talking about the games I like into a viable career, but somewhere along the way more and more of my job became writing about these cases of abuse, because so few of my peers care to do so.*

*It's painful to keep breaking or reading about the latest scandal in the industry, only for it to be followed up the next day with a gushing review or the latest announcement from the same company.*

*Hell, sometimes it's not even a different article, just 'hey, Big Game Company assaulted their entire dev team, failed to pay them properly, and then fired anyone who complained. Oh, by the way, here's an affiliate link to pre-order the deluxe edition of the game they were working on.'*

*I just wanted to make a difference, but it's painful to see this happen again and again.*

*I'm sorry, I don't know why I'm unloading all this on you. Maybe I figured you can relate.*

*Anyway, I'm not giving up. I'm going to keep reporting on corruption in this industry, no matter how much it feels like it's all falling on deaf ears.*

*Gareth Lane*

I can definitely relate. I suppose he and I are not dissimilar, but right at that moment, I didn't know how to respond.

## Meeting minutes – 5 December

Drinks orders for the board:

Rick & Chad – forty-three-shot lattes

Chet (the nephew) – a white chocolate, hazelnut, caramel, double macchiato with mini marshmallows, red sprinkles and a shot of bourbon (real professional)

Chet is an odd one. He started a few weeks ago and I still don't know what he actually does here, apart from drinking on the job ('just to kickstart the morning/afternoon/meeting/lunch'). Chad mentioned that his brother just wanted him out of the house, so asked for a little nepotism hire. He's very clearly related, but looks like what would turn up if you ordered Chad from a discount online marketplace, but had the dudebro slider turned up to eleven.

The first order of business was post-release bonuses. Must. Avoid. Visibly. Seething.

I tried to contain myself with thoughts of my own bonus. I've been scraping by all year and barely paying off the interest on my loans, but I remained hopeful that this would help me take a vacation, maybe pay down some of my bills, and even head off to see my folks for the holidays. I need a break from the ongoing poverty that haunts me, and I need enough money so I can afford to get out and look for somewhere else to work. A little bit of a financial cushion would at least buy me some time to try and find an alternative place to work, without the looming threat of imminent eviction.

I know I shouldn't be focused on that. Bringing down the company was always the goal, but I'd love to have the heating on and something to eat real soon.

I wish every problem in front of me was a puzzle with a definitive and well-defined solution. I wish there was a pre-programmed good ending, and a strategy guide I could look at to make sure I got there, but it's time I accepted that this game doesn't have any elegant little solutions, and there's definitely no way to guarantee a good ending.

Rick proudly showed off some charts he's had back from Finance, cheerfully declaring 'numbers go way up'. Sales are up, company stock is skyrocketing, user engagement is on the rise, and recurrent-user spending is 'off the chart' (because he'd clearly printed it at the wrong orientation and the top of the chart was on another page, which he didn't seem to have). Not only that, but outgoings are way down this month (I wonder why) so that means it's time for a little incentive bonus for the three of them.

Three?!

The three of them?

Only two of them have been here all year and all they did was abuse the staff and waste fucking coffee. Of course that merits $250,000 each. Of course. I'm a fool for not realising it. How can I not see their value as vital members of the Supremacy Software family? Chet just sniggered and nodded to me, saying, 'It's alright working here, eh?' I want to slap his annoying face and scream at them that all they've done is stolen the salaries of everyone they just let go.

These weren't even the full bonuses, just 'a little treat for all our hard work'. They're saving the real bonuses for January when digital sales payments start reaching us from various storefronts.

Finally they moved on to actual company business. It seems that they need some people to keep working on patching the game, as well as developing some festive content for the holidays. Gosh, I wonder who could have helped with that. Maybe a team of people intimately familiar with the code, highly skilled and talented. Where would someone find such an unlikely group? It's a MYSTERY!

Chad floated the idea that they just hire in a small team, as freelancers, nothing firm because 'there's bound to be a few folks who could do with a few bucks before the holidays, right?'

Rick replied that they should bring back a few of the guys who'd just been let go, 'Get the gang back together for one last job, and all that.' I honestly hope that anyone that does return goes ahead with some kind of heist on this place; they fully deserve everything they get at this point.

'One more thing. I've been talking to Legal and we've come up with a final nail in the coffin of last month's little press flurry,' announced Chad.

'Sure, what have you got?'

'We launch a one-million-dollar fund, to support current and former employees, who were impacted by harassment within the company in the past year.'

There has to be an angle to this, I've been here too long to trust anything that sounds this good.

'Woah, woah, woah, we can't just give away money because of boys being boys.'

'Hey, this is me, don't worry, we don't have to spend a single cent. If someone comes forward to try and make a claim, we take a statement, line it up with that Lane guy's article and bam! We take them to the cleaners for breaching their non-disclosure.'

There it is.

'Oh that, that is fucking genius,' Rick marvelled.

Clearly realising there was no way of topping that act of genuine evil, they closed the meeting. The boys quickly departed to dispose of their drinks in the nearest available shrub before disappearing off for the rest of the afternoon. Chet, however, hung back. I initially didn't notice as I was finishing the last of my notes, but when I looked up, he was there, sitting on the corner of the table, near the door and looking at me in that way that always sets my blood pressure to extreme and my adrenaline pumping like there's no next Wednesday. I can only describe it as 'hungry' and usually seen from creeps on the subway or in nightclubs just before closing. I was suddenly very aware he was between me and the door as I tried not to let my anxiety show, just went about packing up my things and making like I was having a tidy up before leaving.

He eventually stopped eyeing me up like a steak he was going to smother in Lubajelly, fold in half, and shove between the couch cushions while his parents were out for the afternoon, and asked, 'So what do they keep you around for, little lady?'

Inside my head klaxons blared, red flags waved, and the red alert light flashed with the fire of a million suns. In response, I calmly gave him a rundown of my duties. As I did so I could feel my mouth drying like I'd eaten a whole batch of Candace's brownies, and my final sentence ground to a wispy croak.

Finding myself unhelpfully mute, I made my way around to the far side of the desk on the pretence of needing to check the big monitor was switched off properly.

Chet sat there, smiling and nodding, clearly not listening to a word I said, just watching my body. My head may as well have left, along with his uncle, to be disposed of in a plant pot for all he cared.

Seconds before I fell into a full-blown panic attack, Clark opened the door and wheeled his cleaning cart inside, creating a barrier between myself and Chet. He gave a cheery wave to me and a reverential 'good afternoon, sir' to the exec, at which point I fled as quickly as I could, without actually sprinting.

NOTE TO SELF – make Clark the best holiday card my craft skills and finances will allow.

I headed back to my little office, but was afraid to stay there very long, in case I was cornered again. On my desk was a white envelope with a window. My heart sank like a rock, fearing that I was about to be the next cost-saving measure that would contribute to January's bonus pot.

I breathed an audible sigh of relief when I opened it and discovered a confusingly jovial letter which went on and on about what a wonderful family we all are, how our hard work is appreciated, how it's been a tough year, but we've all pulled together to make another amazing product, and hoping we have a fantastic holiday season, however we celebrate. The second page was made up of a long breakdown of all the 'great company benefits'. This included salary, a minimal healthcare package, discounts on branded merchandise and our 'fine catalogue of world-class games', the free team-building event (torture paintball), the 'value' of that awful barbecue (nothing like carbonised meat pucks and unwanted sexual advances to show the lengths of their generosity) and, finally, the company's 'subsidisation' of the lunch room and vending machine prices.

Good gravy, how expensive would those damn meals be if the company wasn't allegedly contributing 15 per cent of the price? I had no idea that was even a thing. It already costs more than twice as much as my local TinySave to get a can of Meth out of those vending machines.

Finally, stapled to the bottom of the third page (a brief quarterly earnings report) was a cut-out coupon for $15 off at Ristorante Brodaglia with a cheery note to: 'Please enjoy this token of our appreciation, a bonus for all you do.'

Fucking, what?! That couldn't be it. There needed to be some serious green coming as well because I was about ready to burn this building to the ground with the executive team locked inside. I've spent this whole year trying my best to take these fuckers down, watching people get hurt, losing my passion for video games, and growing to resent what was meant to be a dream job. I at least thought that, for all my putting up with this bullshit and fighting the good fight from the inside, my refusal to walk away would at least result in some kind of tangible reward. I assumed I would at least be able to get a little step up out of the paycheque to paycheque routine if I just held on a little longer.

Gods, I fell for the exact same trick as the dev team. Stick around despite how terrible the company is. We promise it'll definitely be worthwhile if you just stay through to the end of the year. Oops, sorry, your reward for pushing through the swamp of shit is essentially non-existent.

I stormed out of my little office and immediately felt an odd chill in the air. I was initially wondering what was wrong with the air conditioning when I heard Chet shouting, 'Get away from me, you freaky nerds!' I turned towards the commotion and my eyes fell upon the weirdest sight: the entire legal team was crowded around our new executive's office. They had arranged themselves in neatly regimented, curved rows, all staring at the most recent board member as if he were the main event on the world's smallest amphitheatre.

I couldn't help but shudder; they're creepy at the best of times, but to have them all gathered together like that, every pair of eyes boring though you with their typical, unsettling intensity, is the stuff of nightmares. The one standing closest handed a tablet to him and while I couldn't see what he was actually looking at, I guessed from the swiping motion he was looking through a photo gallery. With each swipe his face grew more pale and he seemed almost to shrink. After a moment, their leader took back the tablet and whispered something in the ear of Mr Business School.

I had no idea what was going on, but when I got back from my 'don't think about food at lunchtime' walk, I found a second envelope had been placed on my desk. This time it contained a cheque for $150 and a short note saying: 'We would like to apologise for our earlier administrative error.' It certainly wasn't the bonus I'd been hoping for, but far more welcome than their previous attempt.

What I've managed to piece together since that incident is that Chet had suggested a cost-saving exercise to the boys. Rather than the usual financial bonus, which is awarded to the general staff each year, they should make a deal with one of the local food chains in order to get a bunch of discount vouchers. Thereby saving the company thousands, but still showing a token of their appreciation. Naturally, the boys jumped at the chance to skim yet more money from anyone who wasn't themselves, since the savings would undoubtedly end up in next month's bonus pot and, thereafter, their bank accounts.

However, Chet reckoned without the power of our deeply sinister legal team, who – on learning that they would not be getting their expected cash bonus – decided to show him the power of collectivised bargaining (and very likely blackmail). I have no idea what was said, what dirt they have on him, or what would have happened if he hadn't budged on the matter, but it's at least a little improvement, and I got to see Chet have a bad time, and right now a tiny win is the closest I have had to a victory in quite some time. I'm going to try and enjoy it as best I can, at least for a moment.

### 20 DECEMBER

I had time to get furious about the measly $150 cheque. Sure, it's better than a discount for less than the price of a medium pizza at a mid-tier Italian restaurant chain, but considering how much the execs milk out of this company and how little they pay anyone who actually does any real work, I don't think it was unreasonable to expect more. I sobbingly let my folks know that I won't be home for the holidays. They seemed worried about me, but understand that I can't get away right now.

I put my best art and glitter skills to the test and managed to make a really cute pop-up thank you/Happy Holidays card for Clark (all that time I spent making them as a kid is paying off at last). He checked that I was okay and offered me a personal alarm. He has a ton of them, as his social worker friend gets them in bulk for her clients.

I've spent the last few weeks hiding out in Candace and Jenette's office and working from my laptop since the incident in the boardroom. Although seemingly that's an unnecessary level of caution, because from what I can tell Chet hasn't actually been showing up for work much, if at all. I can't help but wonder if it's something to do with his run-in with the legal team, or if he's somehow even more workshy than Rick and Chad.

The mobile team's latest project is called 'Love in the Lodge' which they told me all about over tea one afternoon.

'It's a steamy romance tale, full of drama and intrigue, set in a remote mountain ski lodge.'

'They're lodged right in there,' Jenette added with a wiggle of her eyebrows.

'There's a full cast of eligible bachelors, bachelorettes and bachelorex.'

'Lots of cosy sweaters, cute scarves, warm mittens, longing looks, held gazes, warm smiles and romantic dates.'

Until I'd met these two, I'd never considered that a match-three game could be anything more than an addictive puzzler. They put so much deep lore and really well-rounded characters into every one. Plus their enthusiasm is so contagious, I could listen to them talk about their games for days.

'So, dearie, it's nearly the end of the year. Are you planning to head home to see your family?' asked Candace.

'I... had plans, but they sort of fell out of the sixty-fourth-floor window when I saw what passed for my bonus.'

'Well, every year, the two of us have a waifs and strays gathering for those of us with nowhere else to go. Nothing fancy, but Jenette will cook one of her famous curries, and then we just enjoy some music and time together. If you'd like to come, we've plenty of space, Clark's coming along again this year.'

'That sounds really cosy, thank you so much, I'd love to join you.'

## 24 DECEMBER

I arranged a video call with Fidget and Ez to catch up and wish them the best for the festive season. I was so glad to hear Fidg sounding more like her fierce and funny self, just like old times, back on the dev floor with pizza for lunch.

Ez has started a dark comedy webcomic that seems to be gaining a lot of popularity.

'So I have this tentacle monster called Gregory who keeps dragging people to the void dimension because he's trying to be spoopy, but they're into him and just want to bone.'

'I love him and I would die to protect this precious baby!' squealed Fidg at the picture Ez had shared.

'So, did either of you read the articles that broke about conditions at Supremacy Software?' I asked eventually.

'I...' Fidget began.

After a moment her camera switched off and I wondered if we'd lost her from the call.

'I couldn't read it. I'm glad it got out there, but... I just couldn't,' she continued in a trembling voice.

'I'm so sorry, I shouldn't have brought it up.'

'I read them. For a minute it felt good that it was all out there. It just sucks that not a damn thing came from it,' said Ez.

'Yeah, kinda pointless, I guess.' I trailed off. Feeling bad for upsetting Fidget and not a little despondent for my utter failure to bring change.

After a few moments in silence, Ez decided to shift the topic onto lighter matters by telling us about a one-page role-playing game she'd tried out the previous week. Something about unicorns on a quest to kick the anthropomorphic manifestation of winter in the nuts and bring the sun back.

Before long we were all laughing at her group's antics and Fidget even put her camera back on.

I'd missed those chats with two such wonderful nerds.

### 1 JANUARY

Candace and Jenette's place is amazing. It's like walking into some kind of fortune-teller's tent. A strong smell of sandalwood incense has infused every fibre of the small apartment over their years of tenancy. There's no traditional seating to be found, just giant beanbags, Turkish cushions and bolsters. Wispy scarves of intricate and colourful design hang over doors, walls and from the ceiling.

Here and there were murals, clearly handpainted directly onto the walls. In the kitchen a fire spirit played some kind of bifurcated flute, the living-room skirting board showed images of cosy little mouse homes which might lie behind them, and in the bathroom, a huge, and beautifully detailed trailing willow tree rose up from one corner of the bath and stretched its arms across the ceiling and down the opposite wall. Everywhere is softly lit through intricate lampshades that throw amazing splashes of colour around each room giving the air of a chillout tent at a dance music festival.

Every windowsill or flat surface beyond the kitchen was filled with a staggering array of polished stones and unusual oddments from their years spent travelling the world. Each item came with its own story for the curious. From walking holidays in Europe, to busking around Asia, to the three years they spent together travelling across Africa, to hikes through South America, to nearly dying in the sun after running out of gas on a trip to Australia, to getting kicked out of Canada for having started a fight with the RCMP. On and on, they'd been all over the place, and somehow ended up putting down roots among a musician and artist collective, who had banded together to buy the building years beforehand and were looking to fill a recently vacated apartment at short notice.

Clark arrived just in time for dinner last night, bringing with him a pet carrier and a friend I hadn't expected to meet. Mr Blue is a beautiful and very friendly blue-haired nebelung cat who has been with Clark for nearly fourteen years. He's a bit slower than once he was from all accounts, but after a while of carefully checking me out from a distance, and giving my shoes an investigative sniff by the door, he came over to sit on my lap, to see the new year in.

As promised, Jenette's garbanzo bean curry was amazing, and we rounded the meal off with some excellent pecan brownies which were served with homemade non-dairy vanilla ice cream of Candace's own recipe. Before long we sat in a circle chatting away like forever friends. Our hosts and I sat on beanbags, but Clark, who struggles with his knees, was provided with a fold-out camp chair, seemingly the only such piece of traditional furniture in the whole apartment.

Lulled by a full stomach, the warmth and charming company, I found myself feeling extremely safe and relaxed.

'This has been so lovely. Thank you so much for inviting me. Your home is beautiful.'

'Thank you, and you're most welcome, dearie.'

'I have so needed this moment of peace and safety. Gods, holding everything together has been a Sisyphean task.'

'Holding everything together?'

'It was me, I was the one who was leaking everything to the press. I was recording meetings, Rick's screaming session with the whole development floor, a bunch of stuff about that creepy ass barbecue, everything I could dig up on Roger, the executives and their constant demands for the impossible. And where did it get me? Fucking nowhere, because seemingly nothing is capable of sticking to those Teflon-coated pricks in charge.'

The words tumbled out of me like a flood and, confession finally made, I found myself sobbing uncontrollably. This was a year of unspoken frustration stripped from my soul and in that moment I felt so raw and vulnerable.

They let me cry it out with only Candace's comforting hand upon my shoulder; a much-needed, grounding connection to my surroundings.

Finally looking up at the others, I saw that a box of tissues had appeared by my feet and Mr Blue was peering up at me with concern.

'I'm sorry, this is supposed to be a party and I'm wrecking the vibe.'

'Don't you apologise, sweetie. We're all here for you and all very much on your team,' reassured Cancace.

'That sure was a powerful swing you took at the beast, but there was no way you could slay it alone,' added Clark.

'You've done good and important work, though. That's more than anyone can ask of any single person,' put in Jenette, 'but you don't roll a police riot van over on your own. You bring a group together.'

'You rock it back and forward,' continued Clark

'And when y'all have enough momentum, you roll it over, together,' concluded Candace with a mischievous grin.

I looked around blearily. 'Have you... practised that?'

'It's our, er, maxim, I suppose is the best word for it.' said Jenette. 'You take a moment, sweetheart, I'll pop the kettle on.'

Face dried, nose blown, tea received and kitty petted, Candace helped set me straight (well, still queer, but you know what I mean).

'Because of your warning, there may be far less people who show up for interviews next month. If stories like the ones you're sharing keep getting out, those with an ear to the industry will know what it's like there and, eventually, they'll just stop coming altogether. The progress may be slow, but if you keep rocking it back and forth, we might roll that company over yet,' she continued.

'We?' I asked, a little wobbly on my beanbag.

It was then they dropped the reveal. For the last decade, they've been churning out those endless match-three and hidden object mobile games that were more than they appeared. Beneath the veneer of wholesome romance and handsome sprite work, they've been filling them up with chapters and chapters of anti-capitalist literature.

Apparently, their audience is predominantly women who are very into the whole idea of anti-corporate sentiment. Their final act of the last game, *Labors of Love*, had centred around an arc where the only thing keeping our protagonist from kissing the handsome love interest was the terrible working conditions and financial hardships they were facing under capitalism. It wasn't even subtle; two of the tile types were literally executives and CEOs which you had to match up in order to make them disappear, leading to the abolition of the executive class, thereby moving the company towards a workers' cooperative structure.

Of course Rick and Chad don't notice nor care. To them the mobile team keep churning out these very affordable games that feature a single microtransaction to remove adverts (alternatively, there's good money to be made on just running small ads on every screen). Sure they're very wordy and full of soppy romance nonsense in which they have no interest, but as long as the money keeps rolling in and the old hippies can be easily forgotten in their little cupboard, the boys have never thought to question the actual content.

These cunning old girls were putting in the hard work and really rocking things in their own way. Amazing.

'If you let us help you, and we all keep finding more folks we can trust, one of these days, we'll have the momentum we need.' Jenette raised her mug and we clinked a toast to unified action.

'Heroes are for fairytales and video games. It's easy to sit around a campfire and spin a fantastic story of a lone hero and their great victory over a powerful foe. Some would call that inspiring but, I say, what's more inspiring is when normal, everyday folks unite to overcome their shared troubles,' she concluded with a sharp nod.

'The greatest trick those in power ever played was convincing commoners like us that we needed them to be strong and safe. A community has power, a community builds safety.'

I knew they were right.

I'm not used to asking for help. I've always felt isolated, even growing up in a sizable family, it always just felt safer to be the weird kid out of sight of everyone, doing my own thing, in my own way, where I wouldn't bother anyone else. Maybe I just never found the right people before, but now it seems I have.

We finished our tea and fell into a comfortable silence, just peacefully enjoying each other's company and that being enough. It was so comforting not to have to keep talking 'just because'. We just were.

The gentle music played, Mr Blue purred in my lap, and before I knew it I was drifting off to the most peaceful sleep of my adult life.

# Let's Rock

**2 JANUARY**

I'm still here. Ready to rock that van... with help.

It's weird to think, a year ago I was such a Supremacy Software fangirl, hyped just to be in the building. Living the dream, only to find it was nothing of the sort. What a difference a year makes.

I've been idly thumbing through the laminated job bible I was handed when I started here. It's like I'm re-reading a very dry novel with a twist ending. So carefully written to avoid anything incriminating, but once you know how the story of working here ends, the breadcrumbs are right there. The section on removing bodily fluids from the boardroom carpet alone should have had me more on guard.

To be honest, I'm surprised I haven't had to remove more fluids from the floor, given the sheer masturbatory glee with which they congratulate themselves for ruining lives in their endless pursuit of money.

# Meeting minutes – 3 January

Drinks orders for the board:

Rick – latte

Chad – latte

I've stopped paying attention to Rick and Chad's drinks orders. They both get a latte. I think they've both destroyed most of their own sense of taste this past year; they don't actually seem to notice a difference in how strong or not their coffees actually are. If it smells like coffee, they'll accept it. I could have saved myself hours – not to mention most of a coffee harvest – if I'd thought of this a few months back. I did have to laugh the first day I tried it. Rick smirked to Chad that, 'She's finally learned how to make a decent cup of coffee after a year.'

I swear, holding in the laugh that nearly shot out of me like a sonic bullet almost choked me. Of course it's my fault that your coffees have tasted like hot brown misery for the last eleven months. Of course. Silly me.

Since Edwin left, they just sit opposite each other at one end of the table, seemingly happy to be equals, as long as everyone else is beneath them. Meanwhile, Chet is still taking a paycheque, but is nowhere to be seen. There was some mention that he'd gone to visit family for a skiing trip over the holidays, but no sign of a return date. Good riddance: the further away from me he is, the better.

As it's January, we've now got figures for all of the last year. There was the usual cheering and high-fives as each revealed the latest graphs over from Finance. Unison cries of 'niiiice' and proud acknowledgements of 'numbers go up'. Of course they go up when you do nothing but exploit your fans and fail to properly pay your staff, you absolute parasites.

By the time they started to segue into what a good amount for a bonus would be for the coming year, I was beginning to zone out a bit.

I found myself thinking about Gareth Lane. He'd done so much to break the story, pushed so hard to make sure the public knew what monsters were running this place. In the end, though, it just took a phone call from the boys to the owners of *World Gaming News*. They threatened to permanently blacklist the site and all their subsidiaries, denying them all future preview event access, interviews and review codes. When that was met with even a pause to respond, they dropped the bomb that they would also remove all our advertising from them. Since it's a site without much separation between their editorial and ad departments, they immediately fell over themselves to sack Lane, pull all his coverage, and offer at least 97 per cent scores for our next three titles. Integrity at its best.

Consequently, Mr Lane is struggling to find work in the industry. It seems like word got around and no outlet is brave enough to touch him. He's set up his own site and I'm hoping that he can keep a crowdfunded career going forward. His followers have always appreciated his honesty and refusal to bow to the wider industry's opinion. I think if anyone can succeed alone, it's probably him. If anything, he's way more free now, with no one to answer to but himself. Although that's easy to say when I'm not the one hoping that the public will just keep supporting me based on integrity.

Of course, the Gamers™ have seen his dismissal as being the result of a lack of credibility and are using it as a bludgeon any time someone mentions all the awful things that have happened here. Hard to provide an acceptable citation when your original and most widely trusted source is gone, and all you're left with are the self-published articles on your own personal website.

One thing that journalist does still have going for him is that when Supremacy tried to get his site taken down via the hosting company, it not only failed – because there was no legitimate legal basis for doing so – but he managed to get his hands on a copy of the takedown notice. Hopefully, enough people will see that as evidence that we were trying to silence criticism. It may not be enough to convince xXStabbyCat42069Xx not to keep paying for microtransactions, but it could just get some of the more critical thinkers on side.

Candace and Jenette have knocked together a program for re-sharing Lane's articles via sockpuppet accounts into the comments under any news article or marketing piece about us. They managed to bash the whole thing out in an afternoon, while working on their latest project: Romance Springs (a team of attractive massage therapists are drawn together when they realise that their services are being sold at ten times what they're getting paid per hour. They unionise and take over the luxury hot spring spa, also there's lots of deeply longing looks and eventual kissing. Naturally, it's a match-three game, because there always has to be some fan service.)

I hope that the article reaches enough people and doesn't just look like a spam virus link.

I finally found it in me to reply to Gareth's last email. I let him know that I'm not going to give up either; I'm going to stay here. I may not have been able to take them down alone, but this time I have a better plan. I know not to act like I'm in this alone – I have a whole adventuring party and together we're going to stay on the inside and destroy these smug bastards. We're going to get some justice for those who've been hurt by the company's callous treatment. We're going to see them ruined... eventually.

I tuned back in to the meeting just as the bidding stage had come to a conclusion, and they 'settled' on $30 million each. Such hardship – how will they cope with such a pittance? Maybe they should trim down the legal department to cut some costs. Hehe, let's see Legal have a quiet chat with them. I imagine they're privy to a staggering amount of dirt on our dear executives.

'So, what should we work on this year?' asks Rick.

They sat back in their chairs and pretended to deeply consider their options. Each one stroking their chin with as furrowed a brow as the Botox will allow. Children aping deep thinkers they saw in a movie, but would probably have bullied if they met such a one in person. They mimic the consideration of weighing heavy options, but it's not like they were going to suddenly come out and declare their decision to try something new and interesting. There's no risk of a deep, story-rich, single-player experience. It will be the same mindless multiplayer, microtransaction delivery system we've had for the last three years, to the exclusion of every other possibility.

Chad got that twinkle in his eye, like he was about to say something he thought was hilarious and insightful, but it made me want to punch him right in his smug face. They both had a bit of an excited wriggle about them, bursting to come out and say the line, as if it's the funniest, most original thing in the world.

'Same thing as last year!' sniggered Chad at last before they both creased up into peals of laughter.

When they finally recovered enough breath, Rick looked across the desk at his colleague and declared – with something that looked and sounded remarkably like genuine admiration – 'You are a fucking genius.'

'I know.'

# ACKNOWLEDGEMENTS

**Jane Aerith Magnet**

Thank you to Laura for helping this easily distracted dyslexic finally write a book like I always dreamed (I love you, wife!); to Mini B, a kind and gentle soul and the last connection to blood relations I have; to The Sisters of Chaos (Lilla, Davina, and Emma) for years of love and shenanigans; to Liam, a friend dearer than any family; to Gareth and Tina for keeping me alive through some very difficult times; to Chris for being such a kind and dear friend; to Matt for supporting me through the worst of times and keeping me from further homelessness; to Snorri for pushing me forward and helping me feel worthy; to James Stephanie Sterling for fighting the real fight against this monstrous industry.

**Laura Kate Dale**

Thank you to every game developer working in the video-game industry, both present and former, who has spoken up about working conditions within game-development studios, as well as pushing for improved rights within the workplace. From those of you pushing for unionisation, despite union-busting tactics, to those silently spreading the word behind the scenes, I thank you for making me aware of just how many games were built on the backs of poor treatment of staff.

# A NOTE ON THE AUTHORS

**Jane Aerith Magnet** is a former stand-up comedian who now writes board-game reviews as a means to justify an obscene and growing collection. Through a series of bizarre events she's been a cleaner, an accountant, a fast-food worker, a sex worker, an in-patient and a highly depressed retail-store manager who made less than minimum wage, to name but a few roles. She currently co-hosts *Queer & Pleasant Strangers* with Laura and occasionally dreams of swimming in a pool full of glitter, slime and tentacles.

**Laura Kate Dale** has worked as a full-time video-game critic for the past seven years, writing for Polygon, IGN, Kotaku UK, Destructoid and a whole bunch of other outlets. Her previous published books include *Gender Euphoria*, an anthology of positive, real-world stories from trans writers, and an illustrated coffee-table book called *Things I Learned From Mario's Butt*, about the educational value of assessing video-game characters' buttocks.

Unbound is the world's first crowdfunding publisher, established in 2011.

We believe that wonderful things can happen when you clear a path for people who share a passion. That's why we've built a platform that brings together readers and authors to crowdfund books they believe in – and give fresh ideas that don't fit the traditional mould the chance they deserve.

This book is in your hands because readers made it possible. Everyone who pledged their support is listed below. Join them by visiting unbound.com and supporting a book today.

A Quite Bitter Being
Matthew Abbott
Nicholas Abigail
Arthur B Ablabab
@ActiveKritizen
Marc Adam
Joseph Adams
Paul Adams
Agnilor
Alicejack Airheart
Yousif AK
Alex
Rob Alexander (Moosc)
Essam Alghamdi

Layth Alnajjar
Luis Alonso
Marc Ambler
Ancom Cat Dad
Carson Anderson
Jennifer Anderson
Jesse Anderson
Larry Anderson
andykisaragi
Kirk Annett
Antaiseito
Travis Arbon
Cade Archer
Stacey Arkless

| | |
|---|---|
| Alice Armstrong | Nathan Booth |
| Zachary Armstrong | Lillia Borud |
| Heather Arnold | Tom Bowers |
| Sophie Asbery | Erin Bowles |
| Stuart Ashen | Victoria Boyce |
| Brent Augustine | Sophie Bradshaw |
| Lucy Axworthy | Michael Braunton |
| Charlie B | Michael Breen |
| Josephine Baird | Danni Brennand |
| Richard Bairwell | Sjut Brethauer |
| Jack Baker | David & Colleen Breutzmann |
| Paul Baker | Dorian Broski |
| Sean Balfour | Joshua Brown |
| Marko Banušić | Mark Brown |
| Barabones | Julia Brunenberg |
| Jono Barel | Bryce and Rebecca |
| Jason Barnes | Colin Bundervoet |
| Sabrina D. D. Barnett | Bunty |
| Harry Bastard | Patrick Burden |
| Philip Bateman | Violet Elizabeth Burgert |
| Christopher Bates | Stacey Burghardt |
| Patricia C. Baxter | Brian Burke |
| Nicholas "The Droog" Bennett | Gerald Burke |
| Jessi Benwhoski | Stewart Burne-Jones |
| Isac Bergendahl | Rylai Busbey |
| Jared Berman | Andy Busch |
| Antony Bishop | Scott Caldwell |
| Jamie Blagden | Sebrina Calkins |
| Alice Blunden | Justin Calvert |
| Shane Bodman | Michael Campbell |
| Josh Booth | Ryan Campeau |

Carter
Tanis Celeste
Chai (he/him)
Charlie Chalkley
Adam chaplin
Finlay Charlton
Daniel Child
Aylie ChoccoBanana ♪
Shaira Bambi Choudhury
Christ-Man
Stan Claassen
Tom Clabon
Bridgette Clark
Blake Clarke
Alex Clayton
Jonny Clementson
Wayne Cogan
Jack Coldridge
Theo Colley
Sam Cook
Jess Cooper-Smith
TJ Cordes
Ray Cornwall
Stelian Costin
Patrick Cothran
Andrew Cowie
Daniel Cox
Mike Craft
Ryne Craig
John Crawford
Harrison Cullen

Craig Cunningham
Joshua Cunningham
Amanda D'Andrea
Jennifer Daily
Jenny Dale
Mosi Dane'el
Andrew James Daniel
Nick Davey
Natalie Piper Dawson
DD and Robin/ SquishyHo and
    Damerekat
Denise De Fazio
Joseph De Maria
Adam Deemer
Amuletta Dela Oso
Jen Denison
Steph Denncy
Katherine Dennison
Benedict Derrick
Mike DeSanto
Emily DeShong
Leo Desrosiers
Sebastian Deußer
Ellis Devereux
David Samantha Devlin
Taylor Dierks
Samuel Dixon
Laura Dobie
Daniella Doyle
Havelock Duthie
Morpho Duval

Shaun Dyer
Rue Dynamite
Christopher Eals
Jeremy Echols
Mervyn Edwards
Mark Egan
Pim Ehrelind
Jacob Ela
ElderlyGoose
Kye Ellis
Leanne Ellul
Seras Engholm
Zion English
Emeline Engman
Erin
Hope Evey
Todd F
Harley Faggetter
Richard Faith
Andrew Farthing
Jess Fedje
Curtis Ferrin
Peter Finlayson
Steve Fiori
Valerie Fleet
Leon Fletcher
Michi Floßmann
Tom Forster
Víctor González Fraile
John Franklin
Julian Hoyle Freewoman

Friends United Church of
    Kindness
Elizabeth Frost
Fukata
Brendan Gage
Shea Gallagher
Josh Gamez
Daniel Gannaway
Sam Garamy
Demi Garcia
Kassandra Gardner
Angeles Garrido Gonzalez
Stephanie Gawroriski
Callum George
Johan Georgsson
Seth Gerrits
Oliver Ghingold
Justine Giddings
Freya Gilbert Lausen
Jonathan Gill
Jamie Gillespie
Seth Giovanetti (Gio)
Mikey Gledhill
Bri Glenn
Ylva Gløersen
Sasha Göbbels
Matt Goddard
Mark Goff
Tyler Golemo
Hernán González Calderón
Zachary Good

Keladry Goodell

Keegan Gordon

Rebecca Gorman

Natalie Goss

Joseph Govreau

David Graham

Anthony Granziol

Ryan "Gooie" Green

Michael Greenwald

Rori Greenwood

James Gregory-Monk

Victoria Grieve

Jim Grove

Dani Growcott

Katy Guest

Benjamin Guy

Anna H

Laska H

Rebecca Hadsell

Sean Hagen

Bengt Hagnelius

Thomas Hale

Michael Hall

Niki Hall

William Hall

Russell Hamm

Chad Hansen

Ben Harding

Will Harding

Michael Hardy

Rach Haves

David Hawkins

Kieron Haywood

Alan Hazlie

Niall Hedderley

Egan Henderson

Angelina Hewitt

Dave Hibbs

Kat Higgs

Jessica High-Parcell

Allister Hill

Kyle Hill

Andrew Hingston

Lewis Hiscutt

Zachary Hittesdorf

Ed Hoc

Selena Hogg

Amy Holloway

Holly

Chandler Holman

River Holmes

Jacob Hooey

Sam Hopper

Beech Horn

Jordan Howard

Andrew Howland

Matthew Hudson

Robert Hudson

Ieuan Hughes

Tim Hunt

Morrigan Hunter

Spencer Icasiano

Hunter Ifearnán  
Felix Ihle  
Aled Illtud  
Mattias Inghe  
Aileen Irons  
Jes Irwin  
Robbie Jack  
Fredrik Jambrén  
Daniel James  
Sean Jian  
Harley Johnson  
Sherenne Johnson  
William Johnston  
Andrew Jolliff  
Ewan Jones  
Michael Jones  
Anthony Jordan  
Jorrit  
Chris "Rhinne" Joyce  
Ju Man Jack  
JZBeasty  
Suphanath Kaewboonruang  
KaiKabuki  
Kalliopi.S  
Ohad Kanne  
Tomasz Karcz  
Lorne Kates  
Remko Katier  
Kazara  
Seán Kearney  
Keffield  

Sean Kelly  
Cat Kendall  
Dan Kieran  
Thomas Kim  
Emily King  
Aaron Kingsley  
John C. Kirk  
Jennifer Kirsch  
Rose Knight  
Vallerie Knight  
Sandra Kolar  
Aisha Krause  
Steven Kroeger  
Eric Kromenaker  
Rebecca Kronenfeld  
Rafael Kuhnen  
Chloé Kuypers  
Petri Neturi Lahti  
Teemu Laitinen  
Edward Landis  
Kyle Lane  
Echo Laviolette  
Phillip Law  
Andries Leegstra  
Nicholas Lemr  
Sandra Lenardova  
Leo the Bat Controller  
Kip Levine  
Ash Li  
Robert Liebig  
Wiktor Liew

Jonathan Light

Craig Linderoth

Thomas Lingard

Matt Llewellyn

Marcello A. Lo Presti

Tobias Logan

Nathan London

William Long

Nicolas· Longtin-Martel

Justine Lore

Lilyth Lorraine

Carla Love

Keefer Lowe

Patrick Lucas

Lumentus

Elliot Lyne

Lyra

Raph M

Rob MacAndrew

Sophie Macfarlane

Conor Mackey

Liam Macleod

Joshua Madamba

Erin Maguire

Catt** Makin

Aviv Manoach

Patrick Marcinek

Katherine Marsee

Jak Marshall

Kit Martin

Edward Martland

Mary

Stephen Mc Devitt

Laura McCandless

Simon McDonald

Paul McGregor

Mila McKay

Jack McKillop

David McLean

Peter McMinn

Jon McPartland

Michael Mead

Ellen Mellor

Mabel Mensink

Merlin

Arne Meyer

Donald Meyer

Violet Meyer

Edward Meyerding

Heather MH

Dolores Miao

Anthony Micallef

Andrew Middlemas

Daniel R.K. Middleton

MikeDraws

Lauren Miller

Ryan Miller

Val Miller

Jacob Mills

Jack Millson

Randall Mitchell

John Mitchinson

Fran Moldaschl
MonstressHA
Dee Montague
Sasha Moore
Ryan Moos
Daria Morgan Ó Gallchobhair
Steve Morrey
Alexandra Moylett
Muja
Kyle Mullen
Celeste Munda
Adam Murphy
Maja Nauta
Carlo Navato
Martin Nehmiz
Jacob Nelson
Brandon Nepute
Natalie Neumann
Louise Newberry
David Nickells
Thibaut Nicodème
Luna Nicolaus
Derek Nielsen
Michael Notkin
Ian Nowell
Sygin Nox
Rebecca Nyarlathotep
Tom O'Neill
Sean O'Reilly
Cian O'Sullivan
Jakub Offierski

Olive
Thomas Oliver
Par Olsson
Jerry Ozbun
Egor Palchyk
Krzysztof Paplinski
Oliver Pawsey
Alyx Payge
Thomas Pedersen
Fabrizio Pedrazzini
Robert Pennington
Samantha Perez
Lucy Perreault
Athena Peters
Andrew Petracca
Jared Petty
Eleanor Peyreton
Eleri Phillips
Ryan Phillips
Bran Phillips-Lewis
Lavender Phoenix
Dave Pitt
Justin Pollard
Stavros Polymenakos
James Popp
Charles Poulter
Primrose
Jon Punke
Peter Quain
Rob Quincey
Daniel Rafferty

Erin Rafferty
Ramón Ramírez
Lex Redgate
Justin Renchen
Alexander Rennerfelt
Mario Reyna
Nicolas Reynoso
Taylor Rhett
Andy Ribaudo
Davide Riccioli
Adam Rich
Benjamin Richards
Neal Rideout
Katherine Rieger
Aron Riktor
Chris Riley (Treela)
Pamela Ritchie
Matthew Rixson
A Robbo
Catherine Roberts
Robin Roberts
Gareth Rogan
Angel Romero
Philipp Rönsch
Jacki Rose
Chris Ross
Eelis Rouvinen
Roux <3
Sarah Rowson
Federico Ruau Asprela
Robin Rubin

Erunor Rugby
Tess Rugg
James Rule
Andrew Runge
Cole Rush
Ben Russell
Faye Russell
Hannah Rutherford
Tim S
Cassandra Sailen
Spencer Sale
Sean Salisbury
Felix Sanchez Klose
Christian Sanders
Daniel Sandler
Rachel Sandler
Nafi Sanou || TheSoooped
Nikki Sayer
Zoey Schaffstall
MJ "jello" Schoerbel
Nikolas Schröder
Samuel Schwager
Chris Schwartz-Brown
Colin Scott
Laura Foxgloves Scutt
Douglas Searle
Chris Sharpe
Kyle Sheldrake
D Shepsis
Kayode Shonibare-Lewis
Verity Shush

Brendan Shust
Mark Simonians
Gedi Skog
Michael Skov
TB Skyen
Tomáš Slapnička
David Small
SmitFish
Adrian Smith
Elizabeth Smith
Gregor Smith
Hannah Smith
James Smith
Julia Smith
Sam Smith
Marcus Soll
Derek Sollberger
Amelia Sparke
Cassie Spencer
Eric Spikol
Sarah Spruce
Lisa St.John
Paul Stalter-Pace
Sam Yvonne Standen
James Stanton
Dan Steadman
John Steinbach
Charlotte Stephan / Lady Zaziki
Richard Stephens
Craig Stewart
Jessica Stewart

Kess Still
Connor Stokes
Pedro Stuginski
Michael Sturtridge
Luke Summerhayes
Liam Sutton
Ron "MegaRon" Swarthout
Edward Sweet
T.H.O.R. from S.W.E.D.E.N.
Nulani t'Acraya
Tallulahhh !
Dylan Luna Tanner
Eliza Tantivy
Angelo Tata
Emily Taylor
Terryn & Manny
Maíra Testa
thatjonguy
Narmada Thayapran
TheOneWhoSucks
Aryn Thomas
Duna Thomas
Lee Thomas
John Thomason
Pads Thompson
Riaz Thompson
Josh Thornton
Ben Thrussell
Richard Tomlinson
Tony (he/him)
Phoenix Toothill

Charles Maria Tor
Rachael Toroja
Callie Ghoula Turner
Callum Turner
Joe Turner
Ryan Turner
Robb Twomey-Dunphy
AJ Tyagi
Stefanie Ulrich
Ryan Unruh
Jennifer Vail
Nicholas VanFossen
Jason Vaughn
Tori Vaz
Marion Vestheim
Riley Vincent
Leodore Vitamor
George Voinquel
Artemiy Vorobiev
V. Vuksanovic
Brendan Walker
Liz Walsh
Melissa Walter
Jason Walter (@stoicfnord)
Christopher Walton
Aaron Ward

Katie Watts
Martin Webber
Jack Weeland
Nick Weinberger
Ash Wetzel
Seth Whitby
Tim White
Timothy White
Nova Whitehouse
Tyler Whittaker
Lisa Whittingham
Mog Wilde
David Williams
Thomas Winski
Alex Wishart
Jacob Wisner
Michael Wohlfeld
Reven Wolfe
Abigail Wood
Abi Wright
Toshi Xyrho
Jeffery Yeary
Lynn Zehm
Omar Zeid
Stephanie Zia
Dominique Laura Zine